CW00494531

Maria Callas

Maria Callas studying the score of *La gioconda* during recording sessions at La Scala, September 1959

Maria Callas

A RECORD OBSESSION

JOHN PETTITT

THE ODDA PRESS
2000

First published in 2000
Reprinted with corrections 2001 by
The Odda Press
Home Farm House
Menston, Ilkley
West Yorkshire LS29 6BB

© John Pettitt 2000

All rights reserved. No part of this book may be reproduced, stored or introduced into a retrieval system, or transmitted in any form or by any means (electronic, mechanical, photocopying, recording or otherwise) without the prior permission of the author.

The right of John Pettitt to be identified as the author of this work has been asserted by him in accordance with the Copyright, Designs and Patents Act 1988.

ISBN 0-9539006-0-6

Designed, printed and bound by
SMITH SETTLE
Ilkley Road, Otley, West Yorkshire LS21 3JP

FOR

ROSEMARY

DOUGLAS CAROLINE ANDREW

"A beautiful voice is not enough" – Maria Callas

CONTENTS

ACKNOWLEDGEMENTS

Probably more books have been written about Maria Callas than any other performing artist. One of the best came out a year ago when the great singer's wonderful accompanist, Robert Sutherland, shed a lovely new light on one of her hitherto less spectacular achievements – the 1973–4 World Tour when she and di Stefano did what they could to recapture former glory. How I envied Robert having something new and worthwhile to say: surely every stone had long since been turned. But encouraged by Tennyson's immortal words as well as Maria's divine voice, I determined 'to strive, to seek, to find and not to yield'.

Thousands of words have been expended on Maria's incomparable recorded art – expended but never before, to my knowledge, compared. The unturned stone! I would like to thank my editor, Peter Dewes, for reminding me that there is life even beyond Callas; my foreign editor, Joao Malatian, for having faith in my prose; Frank Abe for his help with some photographic material; Malcolm Walker of EMI Classics and Peter Howe for clarification on certain aspects of Callas' career; Susan Hoyle and Bradford Central Library for reference facilities; my publisher, Smith Settle, for their forebearance and expertise; above all, my wife and family for their endless patience with my record obsession. In the wider context of work on Callas' career, I would like to thank the founders of the Maria Callas International Club, Jeanne Dworak (formerly Handzic) and Karl van Zoggel for entrusting the running of the Club to my care, to my friends Martin and Liz Cove for their unfailing hospitality after innumerable Club meetings, and to universities and other educational centres for indulging my passion.

Finally, I am grateful to Alain Lanceron, whom I first met at the 1997 Paris Gala to honour the great singer on the 20th anniversary of her death, for his eloquent tribute to our beloved Maria.

John Pettitt
29th September 2000

FOREWORD

Twenty-three complete recordings of twenty different operas and eleven recital discs make up the recorded legacy of Maria Callas for EMI, from the first *Lucia* of February 1953 to the second *Tosca* of December 1964 which is an average of two complete operas and one recital per year during the glory years. To these treasures must be added eight 'live' complete recordings which EMI acquired for distribution. These are performances not recorded by the company officially but representing some of Callas' major stage roles (particularly the two versions of *La traviata* from Lisbon and Milan), with the exception of the Berlin *Lucia* with Karajan, a magical, historic evening which EMI had to have in its catalogue even though it already had the two studio versions. There are also various items recorded live in concert and sundry unpublished recordings mostly made just before and after Callas retired from the stage, from 1964 to 1969 – in all enough to fill two CD double-albums. These recordings, all regularly re-issued, have hardly if ever been out of the catalogue, and the list is completed by numerous 'Best of ...' compilations, some of which have become institutions (*La Voix du Siècle* has sold more than half a million copies in France).

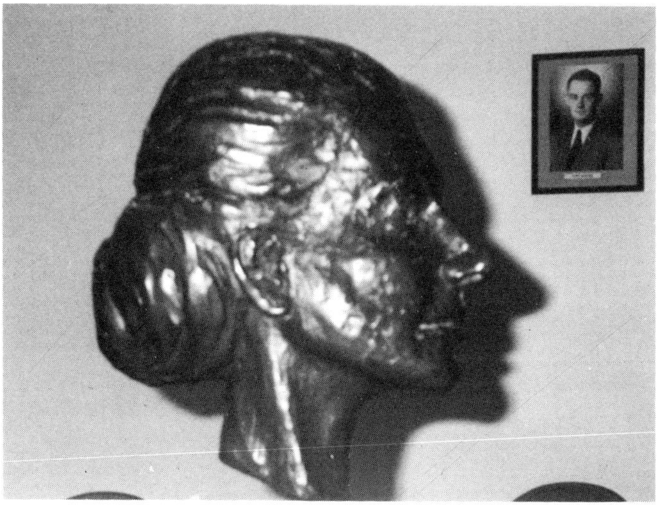

Austin Bennett's sculptured head of Maria Callas
in Alain Lanceron's Paris office

Hence the persistent question: why, 23 years after her death, and half a century after her international fame was sealed, does Maria Callas continue to cast such a spell over new generations who did not have the luck to see her on stage? Quite simply, because Callas' stage presence lives on in her recordings, and these recordings bring her to us for ever, not just alive but modern. For this magical, most unusual voice, so luminous and luscious, this magnetic, erotic, disturbing, disarming timbre, endowed with this power of making the notes say just that bit more than one usually hears, will forever stand the test of time. Would it be too much to say that the rarity of video footage, by definition dated (in black and white, with the costumes and decor of their time), makes it easier for each of us to recreate, imagine, fantasize about our own Maria Callas? She who, in the famous words of a critic of the time, 'has spoiled us for all the others', continues to haunt the opera houses and to reign in our hearts.

Alain Lanceron
Managing Director EMI Classics, France

PREFACE

Estragon: That's the idea. Let's abuse each other.
(They turn, move apart, turn again and face each other)

> Vladimir: Moron!
> Estragon: Vermin!
> Vladimir: Abortion!
> Estragon: Morpion!
> Vladimir: Sewer rat!
> Estragon: Curate!
> Vladimir: Cretin!
> Estragon (with finality): Crritic!
> Vladimir: Oh! (He wilts, vanquished, and turns away)
>
> Samuel Beckett: *Waiting for Godot*

'A critic is a creator of values' – F. R. Leavis. Many of Callas' recordings were greeted with the same kind of scepticism as her performances on stage. Critics and audiences alike were puzzled by a singer who couldn't seem to make up her mind whether she was Tosca or Lucia. It was some time before she proved she was both, and better than most. She had, as it were, to educate the public and that included critics, those professional arbiters of standards and taste, often the scourge of great artists like Samuel Beckett, Robert Burns, George Eliot, Laurence Sterne, William Wordsworth and, not least, Lord Byron:

> As soon
> Seek roses in December – ice in June;
> Hope constancy in wind, or corn in chaff:
> Believe a woman or an epitaph,
> Or any other thing that's false, before
> You trust in critics who themselves are sore.

Matthew Arnold was more sanguine in that for him criticism constituted 'a disinterested endeavour to learn and propagate the best that is known and thought in the world.' In Maria Callas, we do indeed have the best, a singer and musician of genius whose vocal and dramatic gifts brought an intense feeling to the lighter operatic roles (Lucia) and a rare refinement to the heavier roles (Tosca). It was a lesson which was not easily taught, nor indeed learned. All that was known for certain was that she was different, a safe critical response, found often enough in these pages. As time passed, however, during the course of no fewer than three complete reissues of her entire recorded legacy, hasty judgments by an entrenched critical establishment were revised and counter-revised as Callas acquired a kind of immortality.

Maria Callas was a phenomenon. Her performances at La Scala, Milan were the talk of the century and her private life was the talk of the town. Still, it is her recorded legacy that keeps her to the forefront of everyone's attention and that is the emphasis of this book. For every one opera lover who was fortunate enough to hear her in the theatre, a hundred at least will know her only from her records. Her great career, by a most remarkable coincidence, developed alongside the LP; indeed, the one fed the other and the legendary EMI Scala series of the 'Fifties is one of the great achievements of the gramophone. Now, half a century on and into the next millennium, new generations continue to marvel at her career, unique both in terms of its influence and artistry. Her stature has never been greater.

It would be foolish to separate Callas' stage and studio careers since they were almost entirely and uniquely complementary. Her prodigious musical gifts were totally at the disposal of the theatre and whether seen or heard her commitment was such that ultimately she is judged by her musical insights. In other words, great actress as she was, she was a greater singer. And that, in turn, points to the supreme importance of her recordings because as she herself said, 'It's all in the music.' And it is to those incomparable recordings of that very music that this book is dedicated; to Callas' singing, which has given a lifetime of obsessive joy to a host of admirers everywhere.

A PERSONAL PROLOGUE

Bliss was it in that dawn to be alive,
But to be young was very heaven!

William Wordsworth: *The Prelude*

My lifelong obsession with Maria Callas began in 1956 whilst I was serving Her Majesty, Queen Elizabeth II, in khaki; not the ideal setting for an operatic love affair perhaps but that is how it was. A family friend on a business trip to America brought back with him in brown paper sleeves some pre-release LPs of a new recording of *Rigoletto*, an opera I was not familiar with at the time but knew it to be one of Verdi's three great middle period works. But equally I knew it could not be as good as *Il trovatore*, the opera which had entranced me a couple of years previously with its gypsy camps and the scene which followed where I actually remembered a loving phrase from the lecherous Count's aria, 'Il balen', well enough to hum next morning. I had to have it and was bitterly disappointed to find no recording in the catalogues kindly provided by long-suffering assistants at Dale Forty's in New Street, Birmingham. There was a complete recording of *La traviata* I seem to remember but that was not what I wanted. No, it had to be Trov, not Trav. They already knew my tastes because previously I had bought sides 11 and 12 of an HMV *Pagliacci* on 78 in order to have that wonderful chorus at the beginning of Act 2 . Carl Rosa's *Tannhauser* had impressed me previously at the magnificent soon-to-be demolished Theatre Royal and also *La Boheme*, especially when the lights turned blue for 'Your tiny hand is frozen'. But neither quite sufficiently to add an operatic 78 to my growing collection of orchestral records.

This had begun on August 8th, 1952 with a plum label 78 of *Fingal's Cave* by Barbirolli and the Hallé; who else, after seeing these magnificent artists in action in Edinburgh's Usher Hall. The blonde tympanist, Joyce Aldous, perched high over the organ console, is my very first memory of a concert and I was enormously pleased to resurrect that acquaintanceship after three eventful years. And that in itself was completely by chance, because, in order to get me to bed at a civilised hour, my father set me up with a pair of earphones connected to the downstairs wireless. Most of my friends, of course, had crystal-sets but I was happy enough for it meant sharing the terror of Kim Peacock and Marjorie Westbury as Paul Temple and his wife Steve at the shrill whistle of the Coronation Scot. I think secretly I preferred their rivals Philip O'Dell and his girlfriend Angel, and even more that Sunday night serial at 8.30 on the Home Service. Grizelda Hervey was so wonderful as Irene, the lady in grey, in *The Forsyte Saga*, Belle Crystal virtually matchless as Lizzie Eustace, shamelessly making up to her cousin Frank.

Waking one morning, I remembered a marvellous tune which the orchestra had played the night before during the Winter Proms. Tracing it somehow to the second subject of the slow movement of Tchaikovsky's Fifth Symphony, I can now assume that sleep had long since taken over before the splendour of the Finale. Spotting a performance of the work at Birmingham Town Hall, I duly sat behind the orchestra at its next appearance and was kept waiting for forty-five endless minutes by an overture and Denis Matthews playing Beethoven's Third Piano Concerto. Then the work of works: not the unwanted 4th or 6th symphonies but the 5th which the programme had already suggested was often the favourite of all. It started gloomily and lasted too long. Would the second movement never come? After some shuffling and coughing here it was, that second subject even more sensational than I remembered it, especially the repeat which rose to unbelievable heights. Subsiding, we picked ourselves up with a waltz and ploughed into the finale. George Weldon, who earlier had raced to the rostrum with a pronounced limp, was dancing and weaving his way through the heady rhythms, scorching strings vying with jabbing woodwind: a triumph.

Yes, I decided, the Hornby-Dublo train set would have to go: trade it in for a portable record player. All those months of waiting to buy 12 inches of electric track were over; the *Duchess of Atholl* discarded in favour of a £35 Pye portable radiogram which had a compatible needle and three speeds, for what reasons I neither knew nor cared. I was far too eager to devour my new record of Mendelssohn's mellow music, quite unknown to me and probably the only Barbirolli/Hallé record in the shop. But it was enough. That is until holidaying in Charmouth and coming across a pile of records in a second-hand shop – all ten sides of the 'New World' on black label Columbia and a curious box of three in an illustrated cover, *The Tales of Hoffmann* conducted by Sir Thomas Beecham. No, I didn't want him; he was no friend of Barbirolli. I'd had enough of him over the lunch table at school. So I settled for the Dvorak. The next Gramophone however (September 1952) included information which put the Beecham recording into some kind of context. They were LPs which had to be played at 33 and now HMV and Columbia were catching up two years after Decca had taken the plunge. So I bought the Tchaikovsky B flat minor (Solomon) and the *Eroica* (Toscanini) for £1 12s 6d and £1 17s 0d respectively. The compatible needle was now in full use though how it coped with the delicate grooves at 33 after the rough and tumble at 78 I cannot imagine. Nor did it until weighted down with a variety of copper coins.

But of much greater concern to me at the time was the continuing absence of a recording of *Il trovatore*. Decca had been issuing LPs for at least three years (it was now 1954) and their catalogue included *Carmen*, *La boheme*, *Madama Butterfly*, *Aida* and *Pagliacci*. Columbia also kicked off with *Carmen* (so much for inter-company co-operation) and HMV with yet another *Carmen* (obviously the world's most popular opera), *Tosca*, the *Barber* and *Boheme*, in addition (final irony!) to *Rigoletto* and *Traviata*. I was in despair when suddenly across the Atlantic rescue was in sight. The March Gramophone did indeed confirm the arrival of an RCA *Trovatore* and I would now be able to hear that wonderful phrase once again from the baritone aria in act two. The precious LP was sought and bought; only acts one and two of the complete set because in those days discs were available separately. Immediately, Leonard Warren's warm, velvety baritone was to have first place in my affections, so much lovelier I thought in the immediate years ahead than Tito Gobbi's drier tones, until the Italian maestro at a stroke scotched that impression the moment he stepped onto the stage of Manchester's Opera House in *Don Carlos* nearly a decade later.

And what of Warren's colleagues whose phrases I had not remembered? I had to wait until Acts 3 and 4 joined the earlier disc before I could really appreciate the soprano's magnificent voice. Zinka Milanov soon became a favourite in our house; her recital of Verdi and verismo arias (*Forza* in particular) was my father's Christmas present that year. By Rupert Christiansen's reckoning in his book *Prima Donna* that allegiance to one singer or another (*vis à vis* Callas and Tebaldi) rather depended on whom you heard first, this account of a record obsession should be about Milanov, great prima donna of the Met. Miss Gwendoline Fairfax, for example, was sure that her first impressions of people were never wrong. But that is to forget our friend's trip to America over Christmas 1955 and the records of the new Columbia *Rigoletto* he brought back in the New Year. Now that I was sated with my beloved *Trovatore*, it was easier to listen to another great middle Verdi masterpiece.

Nothing, however, could have prepared me for what I felt when we reached the finale of Act 2. "Si, vendetta" swayed and surged towards the magnificent climax, capped by the most glorious note (E flat in alt) that I had ever heard in my life. Who was this marvel? Maria Meneghini Callas was a huge, exciting name to match that huge, exciting voice. The tension was maintained too with the tenor's glamorous 'La donna e mobile' – Giuseppe di Stefano, glamorous name too. And to follow immediately the incomparable quartet, incomparably sung. Was I in danger of allowing *Trovatore* to be displaced by its near rival? *Traviata* was still waiting in the wings, probably to my untutored ears because of its unavailability with either Milanov or Callas. One thing however was certain now. Anything with either singer was fair game which meant that soon my beloved Milanov would be left far behind for she had but two recordings to Maria's mighty eleven. Clearly, I had a lot of catching up to do.

Chapter One

1953

I PURITANI TOSCA LUCIA

I PURITANI

Callas' career on record had begun at the age of 29 in 1953 [the 1952 Gioconda on Cetra is considered on page 91] with a curiously rare work as if she was determined to put her special stamp on events from the start. Renata Tebaldi had launched her recording career nearly two years before with staple Puccini and Verdi – surefire successes of surefire works. Bellini was very different; fifty years ago when the Callas revolution was about to commence anyone who had heard of him thought him rather second-rate. Callas, like the genius she was and always ahead of her time, knew better and *I Puritani* which launched her voice on an unsuspecting public had already special significance for her. Taught by a celebrated coloratura soprano Elvira de Hidalgo she had learnt the Mad Scene, an audition performance of which immediately led to her first Norma at the Comunale in Florence on November 28th, 1948. Six weeks later she became the talk of the operatic world when she sang the complete role at a week's notice to cover for an ailing Margherita Carosio, finishing off her run of Brunnhildes in Wagner's mighty *Die Walkure* on the very same day of the *Puritani* dress rehearsal. Because we now know that Maria was determined, as she said, to do everything, this feat encouraged by Serafin was perhaps not so extraordinary, for it was rather typical of the diverse achievements that lay ahead. But it set the mould which eschewed any likelihood of the sort of safe recording career pursued by other sopranos.

Moreover, the Mad Scene had a direct link with the complete recording because it was included in her first RAI broadcast recital (1949) which in turn led to an Italian commercial recording on the Cetra label. When this was issued in the UK by Parlophone, thanks to the enterprise of Sir George Martin, Lord Harewood, founder and editor of **Opera** was bowled over by it. To borrow from Marlowe, this was the piece that launched a thousand discs: "The most exciting soprano singing to have come out of Italy on records since the war. The voice itself is magnificent, there is a certainty and rare command of style about the singing and real and affecting pathos in the treatment of the whole scene. Callas' legato in the slow section of the aria seems to open a whole realm of musical possibilities to her and the mighty E flat with which she ends the cabaletta reminds one of her extraordinary range and power."[1] Jack Freestone of **Gramophone** was almost as impressed: "She sings 'Qui la voce' with pathos and with good tonal variety. But the opening of the cabaletta is taken much more slowly than usual and the requisite brightness of timbre is lacking. The descending scales are well managed and the penultimate E in alt is a full note of good quality. Signora Meneghini Callas is an artist of such obvious gifts that I have possibly been more critical than usual though I feel that with a little more recording experience she will give us some exceptionally fine discs."[2] Well, indeed she did and if it hadn't taken La Scala four years to open its doors to her and make her 'recordably acceptable', Mr Freestone and the rest of us wouldn't have had so long to wait. Not that this would have unduly worried the grudging Desmond Shawe-Taylor who, "used to the fragile pathos of Madame Carosio", was "disconcerted by the rich tone and large scale of Callas' performance. Yet she was far from inexpressive and her very musical handling of the cabaletta (often treated as a mere excuse for fireworks) should convince any listener that here is a potentially great singer."[3] Fortunately that potential was very handsomely borne out – even if she did commence her recordings six years later than she was allowed to by the operatic mafia in Milan at a time when her voice was in pristine condition – thanks to Walter Legge at EMI. Hearing a BBC broadcast of the original Cetra recording, he at once embarked on a campaign to capture Callas for his company. This he finally achieved in July 1952, just in time to catch the beginning of the LP era.

LPC 50175

(The two other Cetra tracks were the 'Casta diva' from *Norma* – see next chapter – and the Liebestod from *Tristan*, which, sung in Italian, remained unheard in the UK until February 1959 when Andrew Porter in **Gramophone** described it as "a beautiful example of sustained interpretation, with a long line running through the whole piece, each phrase finding part fulfilment in the next until the climax is reached – and not merely a series of self-contained sequences. Sometimes people claim that Callas' voice changed essentially with her shape.

I cannot hear this. The art has become more refined, the phrasing often more intricate, but the essential timbre is unaltered. And eight years ago, which is about when these recordings were made, Callas was the same incandescent and spell-binding artist that she is now".)[4]

Given then that there was so much *Puritani* blood in Callas' veins, it is perhaps less surprising than appeared at the time that the opera constituted her debut in the exciting new Scala series on Columbia. The recording released in November 1953 certainly caused a sensation similar to her achievement on the Fenice stage nearly five years before. To begin with, it was the first time that Bellini's final opera had ever been recorded complete which alone set it apart from the already familiar fare on LP which had come before – *Carmen, Boheme, Butterfly, Tosca, Rigoletto*, the *Barber, Aida*. Callas' own special distinction would certainly be applied to these but not quite yet, and it was in the little-known bel canto opera that Maria made her bow on the international EMI label. Alec Robertson of **Gramophone** was enthusiastic without being ecstatic: "Madame Callas sings exquisitely in the Prayer with the chorus off-stage at the start of the opera but it is a little time before she settles down to her part in the duet with her uncle. Or perhaps it would be more true to say that it takes some time before the engineers get a satisfactory balance on her voice. There are some ugly sounds in this duet and the first authentic thrill comes at her cry 'Ah padre mio' before its last section She dominates the big ensembles magnificently and sings the Polacca in great style, shooting out a high E with thrilling effect. I enjoyed her most in the appealing pathos of 'Qui la voce' (though she is a little uneven here) and the few phrases that introduce it which are quite exquisite. The many florid passages do not, of course, daunt his great Norma but I feel they are more effective sung by a voice of a lighter calibre."[5] This was to haunt Callas for some time to come. Critics and audiences could not understand what Callas was about. Coloratura roles like Elvira had always (within living memory) been sung by light sopranos and as far as they were concerned always should be. She herself acknowledged that her 'heavy' voice in a 'light' role took some getting used to. Harold Rosenthal, though, in **Opera** was less unhappy about this. His objection took another form: "The Mad Scene is not quite as convincing as it should be, partly because she sings it with a concert ending. I am very surprised that Serafin sanctioned this." But elsewhere he is impressed: "Callas is heard to excellent advantage especially in the quasi-recitative passages to which she alone of present-day singers can give such expression. In the first part of the Act 1 finale, her voice is at its most beautiful while in the last act she is never less than first-rate."[6]

The first EMI Scala recording – *I puritani* [March 1953]. Maria Callas awaits her cue at the Basilica of Santa Euphemia.

It was left to our friends across the Atlantic in **Musical America** to embrace her unequivocally: "If the half-forgotten or at least neglected operas of an era of prodigious vocalism are to be revived on records, it is essential that they should be sung as much as possible in the style and spirit of their time. The phenomenal Maria Meneghini Callas has the technical virtuosity and the musical intelligence needed for this task of stylistic re-creation. Her singing is exciting both in its surety and in its felicities of phrasing and dramatic colouring. The voice itself is not memorably beautiful in natural quality but she sings so well that it seems warmer and rich in timbre when she wishes it to sound that way. Miss Callas belongs to the lofty company of Ponselle and Milanov."[7] – the ultimate compliment, I would have thought at the time, given my passion for the Yugoslavian singer's Leonora. However, lest we forget ourselves, Desmond Shawe-Taylor found the complete set confirmed the doubts he expressed about the 78 disc issued 18 months before. Granting her many virtues he finds " 'her main fault was a tendency to scoop upward intervals and to press on the high notes and beyond the limits of sensuously beautiful tone.' These faults so far from having been eliminated are still more pronounced in the complete *I Puritani*. For example the rises of a sixth – from B flat to G – which occur frequently in the Andante of the Mad Scene, are almost all heavily scooped and the terminal G is often unpleasantly shrill. It seems as though such roles as Tosca, Gioconda and Leonora in *Il trovatore*, all of which Madame Callas continues to sing in a very forceful style, are too heavy for a soprano who aspires to the pathos and delicacy of Elvira's music such as the gaiety and lightness required by the Polacca in Act 1." So, here we have further reluctance to accept a 'heavy' voice in 'light' music though he is careful to add that "by the ordinary standards of today she is dazzling and she fills with eloquence and significance countless phrases of arias or recitative which commonly go for nothing"[8] Dyneley Hussey of **Musical Times** was equally equivocal: "The soprano gives us some beautiful singing but one is always conscious of an over-careful articulation of the vocal tone which never flows freely and spontaneously."[9]

Fifteen years later, John Steane reiterated these doubts even referring to "hard, unsteady high notes and a voice which cannot produce the sheer beauty of sound which is a requirement quite as essential to the score as any interpretative qualities. Bellini's heroine should have that kind of limpid beauty of voice that will make her tones a celestial presence in the off-stage Prayer in which she is first heard and later she should have a sweetness and a light, maidenly quality for the Polacca 'Son vergin vezzosa'". Against this, he adds, he finds it "utterly impossible to think of phrases such as 'O rendetemi', 'Qui la voce', and the scales of 'Vien, diletto' in tones other than Callas'. In many other places, the greatness is also unmistakable." Even so, he concludes the recording "would not come high in my list of priorities among all the Callas re-issues that have been appearing since her death".[10] One might well wonder to what heights these rise.

Meanwhile, a further ten years on, to commemorate the 10th anniversary of her death, digitally re-mastered issues marked a big advance in the quality of recorded sound and Alan Blyth, who reviewed the LPs, was ecstatic: "The uniquely elegiac plangent quality of her Bellini singing is amply confirmed. I can hardly think of any music in all her recorded repertory I would rather hear her interpret than 'Qui la voce', 'Oh vieni al tempio', or 'Son vergin vezzosa'. They seem to adumbrate the very best of her art: the limpid tone (here in her prime, warm and sensuous), her moving, meaningful way with coloratura, pointed diction. That last attribute, allied to the vulnerable feelings Callas could always bring to her voice, are heard to marvellous effect in the recitative, most of all in the passage where Elvira is restored to her senses when her beloved at Arturo returns to her side."[11] He also finds the supporting cast, reviled for 35 years: bold, ardent and appealing (di Stefano); incisive, vibrant and near ideal (Panerai); cantabile truly Bellinian (Rossi-Lemeni); masterly (Serafin); and regrets only the huge cuts which were standard at the time. Maybe in the face of this very positive broadside John Steane when he reviewed the CD version had tempered his views. He refused to choose between Sutherland (glorious high notes, singing with feeling, phrasing broadly, fioriture of unequalled brilliance) or Caballé (often exquisite, especially in quieter music, but losing quality in loud high passages and not much sparkle in the cabaletta 'Vien, diletto') or Callas (who constantly amazes. The thrill of the first sound of her voice at the start of the great solo scene, the sadness which underlies the gaiety of the Polacca, the affection of her verse in the final duet all have the stamp of greatness.) By 1997, he had capitulated altogether, referring to the warmth and sheer beauty of Callas' singing in 1953 which twenty years previously he had said she was unable to produce. One expects critics to disagree with one another but hardly to contradict their own words!

But it wasn't until 1958, five years after the recording was first released, that I myself was similarly affected. It was a defining moment because, as a new, keen member of the Oxford University Opera Club, I decided to risk all and put on a performance of the work at one of the regular Wednesday meetings. Only then did I discover that not a single copy of the vocal score was to be found. So we turned to my first love, *Il trovatore* which was duly performed in a Church hall in Woodstock Road. The first rehearsal of the chorus was a disaster. I could not understand why they wouldn't come in. Fortunately, we had a distinguished bass at Keble, John Davies, and he took me to one side later that day and revealed one of life's little secrets: always give the upbeat. And that was that. Some months later, a large heavy package arrived at the college containing a dozen copies of *I Puritani* from a London publisher who had previously been unable to oblige. So, notwithstanding that Schools (the final degree examinations) were only a couple of months away, we met up again for three weeks of rehearsals for a performance in the newly refurbished Holywell Music Room (where Haydn once conducted). Christian Hunter, a much admired local soprano of the day, sang, in particular, a marvellous Mad Scene, and maybe it was because Patrick Costeloe in the heat of the moment outdid di Stefano and hit a top F (as written) that it was 'better than Callas'. I couldn't possibly comment. What I can say is that Robert Lloyd told me thirty years later at the Royal Opera House, Covent Garden, as I adjusted his Boris Godunov coronation robe, that Sir Giorgio was his first operatic role. Thus from tiny acorns, mighty oaks do indeed grow.

* * *

TOSCA

The second Callas recording to be released on the market could not have been more different. Almost as if to demonstrate she could do anything, Puccini's old warhorse *Tosca* reached the shops for Christmas. But in the 1950s, you were either an Elvira or a Tosca, certainly not both according to the critical establishment. Of course, Callas knew better and showed them up to be rather foolish. Alec Robertson having observed that she was a very good, if not yet perfect singer of bel canto, decided she was no Tosca and said so in no uncertain manner. In his **Gramophone** review, the greatest singing-actress of the century was found to be wanting in dramatic force, showing "little of Tebaldi's vocal acting which made one's blood run cold at the moment she stabbed Scarpia , and her 'Vissi d'arte' does not compare well with Tebaldi's beauty of tone and perfection of control. At the same time, she gives us some lovely singing in the first act and has her moments of drama in the other two ... but it is not somehow the great performance I expected. It is more than possible that Madame Callas' Tosca is more effective on the stage than on discs but whatever the reason her performance recorded does not equal to that of Tebaldi."[12] The Italian diva's Tosca was first in the LP field which, as Rupert Christiansen has already suggested, [but not too convincingly] counts for a lot. Exactly a year before, Robertson had found Tebaldi's Tosca "Magnificent. She never becomes a virago in Act 1 but tempers her jealousy with tenderness and sensuous charm. In Act 2 she rises to really great heights and I shall long remember her contemptuous 'Quanto?' as she asked Scarpia's price and her spine-chilling 'Guardami! Son Tosca o Scarpia ... Muori damnato! Muori!' as she stabs him. Earlier in the scene, she sings 'Vissi d'arte' with true emotion, lovely tone and, thank goodness, with no histrionic sobs at the close. In the last act another memorable moment is a thrilling top C as she describes to Cavaradossi how she stabbed Scarpia."[13] The very next month he dismisses Maria Caniglia's Tosca as strident, over emphatic, rhythmically slack, histrionic and ugly in turn, and it sank without trace. Much the same fate seemed to await Callas' performance according to Dyneley Hussey of **Musical Times**: "Unhappily Maria Callas makes Tosca sound too much of a shrew and her singing is often unrhythmical, though she makes some of the dramatic points well enough."[14]

Victor de Sabata conducts a *Tosca* session with Tito Gobbi and other members of the cast, under Callas' watchful eye. [La Scala, August 1953]

Fortunately Harold Rosenthal in **Opera** saw the situation, nearly 50 years ago now, in much clearer perspective. Although complete operas had only been issued for two years on LP, he had, with consummate perspicacity, no hesitation in ranking the new EMI *Tosca* with Callas alongside Christoff's *Boris* and the Decca *Parsifal*, as "one of the finest recordings of a complete opera ever made," even if he did rank Callas third to de Sabata and Gobbi: "Callas is a different sort of Tosca than those to which we are accustomed. It is highly dramatic, smouldering with passion, not as smoothly sung as Tebaldi's but authoritative to the highest degree ... and what other Tosca can invest the one word 'Cosi' in Act 3 when she echoes Mario's word, as she wants him not to laugh as the firing squad appears, with as much meaning as Callas? While the beautiful and sensual tones with which invests the section of the duet beginning with the words ' Non la sospiris' are unforgettable."[15] Rosenthal was not being polite or euphemistic when he called Callas' Tosca different; he was being accurate. Just as she brought drama and passion to a 'light' Elvira (and soon Lucia), she brought welcome musicality and taste to a 'heavy' Tosca, hitherto renowned for its beefy, not not to say, hammy nature. Even Desmond Shawe-Taylor, dubious over her Elvira, found Callas a "superb Tosca", though he had to parrot Robertson and Rosenthal on 'Muori! Muori!'[16]. I have to admit that in choosing to buy *Tosca* with Callas, I had di Stefano as much in mind as the diva and I remember, initially, being slightly disappointed that Callas' tears at the Act 1 exit on Gobbi's arm were not as distinct as Tebaldi's. I might even have chosen Milanov's Tosca, as I did her Aida. After all, had I not taken a 36hr pass from the Prince Consort's barracks in Aldershot in 1956 to catch her in the role at Covent Garden opposite Tagliavini? But, in any case, it was not yet available, coming, like her *Forza* and *Gioconda*, disappointingly late in her career.

Exactly twenty years later, at its first re-release Harold Rosenthal wrote: "I have always recommended the famous 1953 EMI *Tosca*, when reviewing every other recording, as being one of the great performances in the history of the gramophone and I believe this is a generally accepted point of view. Victor de Sabata disliked recording and one can only again regret that he was never persuaded to record more operas during his great days at La Scala in the post-war period. His dramatic and fiery reading of what can sound a hackneyed score is a revelation and so are Callas' Tosca and Gobbi's Scarpia–their scenes together, especially in Act 2, have never been the equalled."[17] Alan Blyth in **Gramophone** takes exactly the same view and gives Callas pride of place: "One marvels anew at the immense variety of vocal colouring and accent

Callas brings to the title role. In her later performance (1964), she may have added even more vocal subtleties to her interpretation but by then her voice was no longer in a strong enough state to fulfil the dramatic demands of the second act which she does superbly here. Countless phrases capture the imagination and remain in the mind for ever. And the whole reading strikes true, no posturing prima donna this, but a living, jealous, remorseful, romantic woman."[18]

Twelve years after that it was Edward Greenfield's turn in **Gramophone** to eulogise: "Wonderful as Gobbi's and di Stefano's performances are and superbly dramatic as de Sabata's conducting is, it is the performance of the unique Callas in the title role that provides the greatest marvel. And here more than ever one registers the facial changes implied in each phrase, with occasional hints of a chuckle (usually ironic) more apparent than I had remembered."[19] Now, fifty years on, as the new millenium dawns, we have what Michael Tanner describes as "the greatest *Tosca* recording ever made", when John Steane found Callas giving a "portrayal in which a vehemence and delicacy are wonderfully well mixed. The 'Vissi d'arte' maybe its centrepiece but it is the fine detail of everything around it that insures its lasting value."[21]

In the **Gramophone Classical Good CD Guide 2000 [G.C.G.CD G. 2000]**, its standing and lasting value, in the face of 20 rivals, is indeed confirmed as one of four recommended versions (Caballe/Davis, Leontyne Price/Karajan, and the Jane Eaglen recording in English). Edward Greenfield writes: "Walter Legge used quite often to question the necessity of stereo. Now more strikingly than ever on the CD of this great classic performance of the gramophone, one of his own masterpieces as a creative recording producer, it is easy to see what he meant. With off-stage effects, for example – so important in Puccini – precisely placed, there is a sense of presence normally reserved for two-channel reproduction. In the long duet between Tosca and Cavaradossi in Act III you can even detect a difference of placing between the two singers, Callas set at a slight distance, though whether or not to offset a microphone problem with so biting a voice one can only guess. The immediacy is astonishing, and the great moment of the execution with trombones rasping and the fusillade reproduced at a true fortissimo has never been represented on record with greater impact. What is especially delightful is that where on most previous CD transfer of mono originals the results have emphasised the single-channel flatness, often with sound lacking in body, this is full and weighty. The slightly jangling brightness on some percussion instruments gives some hint of the age of the recording, but with mono of this vintage it is amazing what bloom there is even on the violins, and when it comes to the voices, there one simply forgets the years, and drinks in the glory of one of the really great recorded opera performances as never before."[22]

After initial doubts, therefore, which would surely make their perpetrators blush, this *Tosca* remains supreme and Callas' re-recording of the work in 1964 would seem unnecessary. Originally made as the soundtrack for a planned film, later aborted, it never won the approval of Callas' other stereo remakes – *Lucia, Gioconda* and *Norma*. Edmund Tracey in **Opera** in 1965 wrote: "If we compare Callas and Gobbi with their old Columbia selves, it is clear that they lack the necessary expressive range. Of course, there are marvellous things. Callas' entry in Act 1, her colouring of such phrases as 'Oh! innanzi la Madonna', 'Non so nulla' (when Scarpia is questioning her about Angelotti), 'Muori damnato!' (after she has dealt the fatal blow) – such moments give one a thrill of delight that only she among living sopranos can communicate: the sense of total involvement in the drama and of having burrowed deep down into the very heart of the character. Except right at the end, 'Vissi d'arte' isn't at all bad; and almost everywhere there are flashes of intelligence and style. But the voice is often thin and ugly: strident and uncontrolled at the top of its compass and sometimes unwieldy and exhausted, as if the singer lacked the energy to fill out the notes with their full share of tone."[23] Philip Hope-Wallace in **Gramophone**, whose pages contain many of his doubts about Callas' achievements, was even less happy: "She retains her extraordinary power of investing some small phrases with an intensity of dramatic and musical meaning that not merely makes you hear it as if for the first time but lodges it week-long in your head. But it is useless to pretend that she can really let fly any more and there are places in Tosca where you can't get away with it without letting fly: those cries for help in Act 2, the climax of the racconto in Act 3. And the battle for security is on far too much of the time. The climax of 'Vissi d'arte' is achieved but what a disappointing poor, plummy sound."[24] When the set appeared on CD in 1989 Alan Blyth supported the general tenor of these censorious remarks but added: "Callas' interpretation remains very special even with reduced vocal means for the subtle inflections she brings to everything: some passages are even more pointedly enunciated than in the 1953 version. On the other hand by 1964, she was tending to distort some vowels particularly in her lower register where she was inclined to produce a curiously hollow sound. In spite of the reservations, as a portrait of the jealous, impulsive, ardent Tosca, the portrayal is as rounded is one could wish to hear. But 'round' is certainly not the adjective to apply to her singing at forte when you need, as PH-W graphically put it in another Callas context, to fasten

At the Salle Wagram in Paris [December 1964], with Carlo Bergonzi and Tito Gobbi, Callas records her second Tosca

your seat belts."[25] For Noel Goodwin in **Opera**, Callas' efforts oscillated between being "tellingly inflective to disturbingly squally."[26]

Callas, with reference to her distaste for Puccini at the time of her New York Metropolitan debut in the role, said that Tosca occupied the very last place in her scale of preferences. Her two recordings, however, tell a rather different story. And, after all, her career both began (August 27th, 1942 in Athens) and ended (5th July, 1965 at Covent Garden) as the tempestuous diva. But strictly speaking, in neither instance was the choice really hers: initially at 18, lungeing at any role to get herself established and finally at 41, accommodating her declining vocal powers to survive. But it is a role as indelibly associated with her as Norma, singing it thirty-three times altogether in six cities in Italy and South America, in New York, Paris and London but never at La Scala, her artistic home, except between August 10th and 21st, 1953 under Victor de Sabata, with Giuseppe di Stefano and Tito Gobbi, to record it for posterity.

* * *

LUCIA

With the third recording of the 1953 annis mirabilis to burst upon the operatic scene, Callas' reputation was complete. *Lucia di Lammermoor* was in fact the first of the three to be recorded but EMI understandably wanted the prestigious Scala imprimateur to make an international impression. For the Donizetti was the recording of a triumph at the 1953 Maggio Musicale in Florence where Callas had just completed four performances under Serafin. Di Stefano had replaced Lauri-Volpi for two and Tito Gobbi was brought in to establish for the first time what was to be EMI's illustrious team in the years to come. It may be incomprehensible now 50 years on, but this arrangement did not, in fact, please everyone. Desmond Shawe-Taylor lashed out in January 1958 in his **Gramophone** Quarterly Review: "There is a certain undeniable monotony in the casting of current operatic issues. This monotony can be explained by the shortage of front rank singers for the leading Italian roles; still the sequence of Columbia recordings emanating from La Scala makes a depressingly mass-produced effect when we find every soprano part allotted to Maria Callas, almost every tenor part to Giuseppe di Stefano, and Gobbi or Panerai as the inevitable baritones."[27] But surely, as Keats said, 'a thing of beauty is a joy for ever' and our gratitude to EMI for Callas' many recordings grows as each year passes and, as the very latest compilation states (October 2000), she is the jewel in the EMI classical catalogue. For Lucia, even the old doubters capitulated. Alec Robertson, after snipes at her Elvira and Tosca, was so excited by her Lucia that he had to "take a turn in the garden to cool down. Lucia's first solo 'Regnava nel silencio' is sung with a lovely legato by Maria Callas who has already (one need hardly say) established Lucia in the recitative as a person of character. She ends the aria with a beautifully executed cadenza displaying those wonderful rich high notes of hers, but preceded by some rather bumpily recorded trills – the only place one can say this of them. 'Quando rapito', with its exquisitely done decorations and finely moulded sequences, complete one's utter enjoyment of what is clearly going to be a great performance of the part." After praising her duets with di Stefano and Gobbi, he finds that the excellent performance of the sextet almost ranks it with the quartet from *Rigoletto* and the *Meistersinger* quintet. Finally, "Callas fills the Mad Scene with the deepest pathos and it has an impulsive, excitable note in it that conveys the derangement of the poor girl's mind. In the cadenza before 'Spargi d'amaro', Callas' superb vocalisation knocks the flute out and we hear him only as a little timid tootle in the background. Here is certainly some of the finest singing of our time. and there is one moment in the repeat of Spargi d'amaro' when the voice is recorded with all the actuality of three dimensional sound."[28] Harold Rosenthal in **Opera** agrees wholeheartedly and after recalling a multitude of other light sopranos in the role, continues: "Callas can do wonderful things in the upper register but her voice as we know has far more weight to it than the usual type of Lucia; indeed this Lucia is a dramatic soprano who can also sing coloratura music with the best of them. I was greatly surprised to find Callas' Lucia dismissed in a couple of sentences by Desmond Shawe-Taylor in the Observer recently, because he feels that her voice has become too dark and heavy and so misses the simplicity of the character. Could Pagliughi, Carosio, dal Monte et al even begin to invest their Lucias with the tragic overtones that Callas is capable of? Did such an intelligence ever colour the interpretations of Patti and Melba? – I doubt it. No, with Callas Lucia becomes a tragic heroine of the kind generally associated with the great classic operas. Her vocalism is not 100 per cent perfect but what gifts this artist possesses."[29] He is joined by Dyneley Hussey in **Musical Times**:"Maria Callas' performance in the title role gives Columbia's

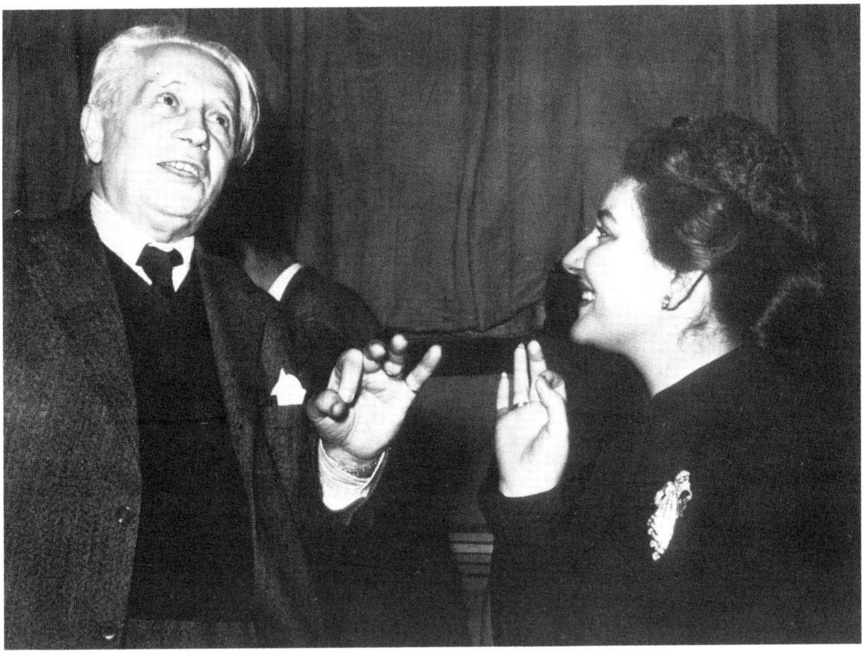

Callas recording her first EMI complete opera - *Lucia di Lammermoor* – in 1953 with her mentor Tullio Serafin

latest contribution to the operatic repertory special distinction. Without the brilliant technique of a Tetrazzini, Madame Callas endues Lucy Ashton with genuine pathos and a surprising degree of dramatic power. It is a pity that the exigencies of space necessitated a cut in the Mad Scene which ruins its admirable dramatic construction and turns it into a long soprano solo."[30]

This recording was made only seven months after her debut in the role in Mexico City, again with di Stefano at her side but with no Serafin in the pit. As the years passed and performances mounted up, 45 altogether, in Florence, Genoa, Catania, Rome, La Scala, Venice, Bergamo, Chicago, Berlin, Naples, Vienna, New York, Dallas, a re-recording in stereo was made to capture her ever-refined interpretation of the role. Serafin again was in charge, sanctioning similar cuts in the score, and on this occasion it had the benefit of the warm Kingsway Hall acoustic and the Philharmonia. A different supporting cast was assembled. Writing in **Gramophone**, Andrew Porter was very impressed: "In every way Madame Callas has refined her interpretation of the role and made it more exquisite, more fascinating musically and dramatically more subtle – in a word, more beautiful. I do not think that this means the line has been overloaded with emotional colourings or self-consciously artistic 'effects'. Sometimes she has achieved her result by simplification. For example, in 'Verrano a te' she no longer presses but spins a tender thread of legato: the duet is melting with Tagliavini at his most dulcet; the final verse in octaves is ravishing. The sound of the voice is very different from seven years ago. There is less weight behind it; it is more supple, more delicate. The timbre is not so dark, more tender and the less resinated. I grant at once that there is more confidence, more forthrightness in the earlier performance and that in the cabaletta 'Quando rapita' the high D and especially the high C of the final decorations are awkward and may touch a nerve of pain in the listener. But on the whole the singing represents Callas at technically her best."[31] Harold Rosenthal, too, in **Opera** likes what he hears: "Callas is a perfectionist and those who have seen her at work either rehearsing an opera or recording will tell of the infinite care she takes over the smallest detail, how she will go back over a single phrase time and time again until she appears to be satisfied with the final result. A role like Lucia repays that kind of treatment and once again we are amazed as page after page of the old score comes to life as never before and phrase after phrase in the recitative passages assumes a new meaning. In the recitative preceding Lucia's first aria, Callas manages to establish this character as a flesh and blood creature. In the letter duet with Enrico she is incomparable and once again the phrase 'Ah! il core mi balzo' tugs at our own heart-strings. In her performance of the Mad Scene, her utterance of the phrase 'Alfin son tua' has already become a model for all other Lucias and the mad scene itself is not the occasion of the traditional prima donna display of pyrotechnics, but part of the logical conclusion of the mental derangement that began when Enrico showed her the forged letter. This Lucia is no moon-struck girl but a deranged woman."[32] However unlike Andrew Porter he declines to choose between the two sets, old and new, and thereafter, at every re-release, the battle began again and it became even more fraught when in 1991 EMI decided to issue yet another Callas *Lucia* performance, this time live from Berlin in 1955, again with di Stefano but conducted by Herbert von Karajan.

Rodney Milnes when he wrote in **Opera** about the original 1953 reissue 20 years later, nearly came to blows: "For all the diva's mesmerising mastery, one recoils in horror at the indignities heaped on a great composer, sanctioned both by good singers and a fine conductor. The text is quite literally butchered, irrelevant and unmusical high notes are being inserted and held, and the singers, apart from Callas, seem not to have the faintest idea of how Donizetti should be sung – indeed, one of his many masterpieces ends up sounding like a piece of really blatant early Verdi. I found it quite insufferable. But Callas is Callas and despite the multiple 'betises', this is an object lesson in how to build a character out of notes and syllables."[33] Milnes, of course, was writing in the wake of Sutherland/Bonynge performances which tended to include every last note and syllable of the score. Completeness was very much in fashion whether it was dramatically convincing or not, as Charles Osborne made abundantly clear in Chicago in 1974 in his notorious public spat with Callas over cuts and high notes. Alan Blyth in **Gramophone** was much more composed and he, like Andrew Porter (perhaps for some of the reasons which so exercised Milnes above), preferred the stereo remake and hoped to welcome it alongside the older recording which, as he said, was "the starting point of the reassessment of Donizetti as more than a vehicle for light sopranos, for much of the Callas magic is already to be heard on this performance. The duet with Enrico immediately places her interpretation above any other, even Sutherland's, in heart-rending pathos and throughout the mad scene there are touches that no other singer can equal let alone surpass, unless it be the Callas of seven years later. By that stage she had eliminated some of the gulps and over emphases that had the Record Guide complaining of her lugubrious sound. On the other hand as that old bible put it she is always a wonderfully interesting artist discovering significance in the simplest phrases of the arioso and recitative."[34]

In London's Kingsway Hall, Callas records her second Lucia with [left to right] Leonardo del Ferro, Piero Cappuccilli, and Ferrucio Tagliavini [March 1959]

When the later set did come out again two and-a-half years later, Milnes renewed the attack "haranguing the swingeing and nonsensical cuts, high notes and cadenzas, as unidiomatic as they are unwritten, all adding up to a musically illiterate farrago." However, he prefers the later Callas "in marginally freer voice than six years previously, all the more vulnerable and touching a Lucy. It goes without saying that her characterisation is uniquely vivid, yet always from within the notes, never imposed from outside. Many phrases, sung with such penetration and understanding, leave their imprint indelibly on the mind: 'E la vita fuggitiva di speranze nutriro' in the Fountain duet is just one. The only problem is the handful of ugly and flapping high notes which she should not be singing anyway."[35] Alan Blyth again in **Gramophone** supports Milnes' reference: "Callas' more mature interpretation makes this the definitive *Lucia* rather than a Lucia for anyone contemplating purchase of the work and invests it with the benefit of her feeling for the text and her often exquisite vocalisation. For example, the passage of the mad scene from 'Sparsa di rose': the sense is conveyed here of poor Lucy re-living or trying to experience the happiness denied her when sane. The poignancy of these moments particularly at 'L'inno suona di nozze' is perfectly conveyed by the vocal expression. Then the pathos of 'Alfin son tua' even more of its second verse 'Del ciel clemente' is heart-stopping. These have the ring of dramatic truth to them – also the evidence of hard thought and work. Elsewhere, the coloratura is more delicate than before, also rather more careful. The high notes are more or less curdled."[36]

When this performance came out on CD, Alan Blyth maintained this view and, notwithstanding its well rehearsed flaws and stiff competition from a very complete Sutherland recording, regarded it as still the best. Paradoxically, the 1953 recording now had to wait its turn for two and-a-half years when **Gramophone** invited John Steane to air his views on the long running saga. Astonishingly, he found Callas artistically much the same in both, her singing "touched by genius in both: but it is a genius which has freer access through the relatively firm and indeed often beautiful instrument that her voice could be at the time of this, the first of her great series of EMI opera recordings."[37] Maybe he was persuaded by his preference for di Stefano and Gobbi and while I would be loathe to surrender the virility of that tenor along with the baritone's artistry, I think the prevailing critical preference over the years for the richer and more refined second recording is entirely justified. This is convincingly confirmed by its top recommendation (also with Studer) in the **G.C.G.CD G.2000** in preference to interpretations by Deutekom, Pons, Sutherland, Peters, Caballe, Gruberova, and Corradi. "Callas was certainly more fallible here than in her first Lucia, but the subtleties of interpretation are much greater; she is the very epitome of Scott's gentle, yet ardently intense heroine, and the special way she inflects words and notes lifts every passage in which she is concerned out of the ordinary gamut of soprano singing. In that sense she is unique, and this is certainly one of the first offerings to give to an innocent ear or a doubter to help convince them of Callas' greatness. The earlier part of the Mad Scene provides the most convincing evidence of all, and the coloratura is finer than it was in 1953, if not always so secure at the top. Tagliavini, after a rocky start, offers a secure, pleasing involved Edgardo and Cappuccilli, then in his early prime, is a forceful but not insensitive Enrico. Serafin is a far more thoughtful, expressive Donizettian than his rivals on other sets, confirming this as the most persuasive account of the opera ever recorded."[38]

Callas was a perfectionist always seeking to enhance her art and she would not have been disappointed that the recording which brought her first year of record releases to such a glorious conclusion should have been superseded.

News of the stereo remake helped to create a kind of *Lucia* mania in the late Fifties culminating in Sutherland's overnight stardom in Zeffirelli's production at Covent Garden in January 1959. Three months later this production reached the Apollo (then the New) Theatre, Oxford where for 12s 6d (0.62p) a performance I found myself on stage as Second Soldier with June Bronhill (a famous Merry Widow, making her delightful debut as Lucia) and Kenneth Neate (Edgardo). The sextet would have gone sadly wrong had my colleague and I not been there to bar the tenor's entrance. Some years earlier I had first remembered Maria's Lucia in costume with di Stefano, complete with high heeled boots, on the cover of the Columbia issue. But coming out the very same month as my long awaited LP of *Il trovatore*, it made no impression on me whatsoever. Milanov, Bjorling, Barbieri, and above all Leonard Warren were the only names that mattered on that smart red and gold label. I read that, in Philip Hope-Wallace's words, "Warren is an imposing Count, generous and self-indulgent sounding rather than villainous but he copes with the difficult 'Il balen' well and is at all times agreeable if never once truly distinguished." And Milanov? "A genuine voice for Leonora, once or twice so ravishingly good that her failings irritate the more. In 'D'amor sull'ali rosee' she offers us real poetry besides the proper trills; a soaring, veiled legato floated out in a wave which recalls only Spani, delights as few Leonoras have delighted in recent years. But it is sad to hear from the same singer barnyard crowings in 'Di tale amor' and in the Miserere even, and she sounds as if she found her gallop duet with the baritone in the last act altogether too much, as who would say, "Count, let's sit this one out!" – a duet where Callas was needle sharp and on the dot."[39] Callas? Who's she, I wondered. As for Milanov's failings, it was the soaring, veiled legato that mattered, rather more then than it does today, I have to admit.

33CX1131-2

By the end of 1953 Callas had swiftly become the brightest star in the operatic firmament. For four years after her memorable Italian debut at Verona as Gioconda in 1947 she had given brilliant but largely unrecognised performances in Italy and South America, as Isolde, Turandot, the two Leonoras,

Aida, Norma, Brunnhilde, Elvira, Kundry, Abigaille, Tosca, Fiorilla and Violetta to growing acclaim. But it was only when Francesco Siciliani, the enterprising director of the Florence Communale, engaged her to sing at the prestigious Maggio Musicale that she was invited to sign a contract for La Scala. Her sensational triumph as Elena in Verdi's *I Vespri Siciliani* finally forced Antonio Ghiringhelli, the Scala director to set aside his prejudices against the ungainly Greek girl from America. So much so that she was given the honour of opening the next two seasons during which she sang no fewer than six roles. The ugly duckling had suddenly become the beautiful swan. The recording career reflected this perverse state of affairs. In the four years prior to La Scala she had recorded only three 78s, a mere 20 minutes of music. In the two years following, she recorded four complete operas, a total of eight hours, establishing a pattern for the next four intensive years when between two and five complete operas would be recorded, sometimes reflecting what Callas was doing on the stage, sometimes not. For example, she recorded four roles for EMI which she never performed in the opera house. Conversely some of her greatest roles – Lady Macbeth, Anna Bolena, Violetta and Imogene (in Il *Pirata*) – were scandalously ignored causing EMI later to fall back on live performances, in inevitably inferior sound which has generally remained so relatively poor that some of these classic interpretations cannot be seriously recommended alongside her rivals recorded in the studio. Even as I write, BBC Radio 3 **Building a Library** condemned her superb Lady Macbeth to collectors of Callas only. History is so full of what might-have-been and should-have-been that maybe we should just rejoice in what treasures we have. However, the sin of omission was something Shakespeare himself took very seriously, so we can hardly wonder that it continues to haunt us.

Chapter Two

1953–54

CAVALLERIA RUSTICANA NORMA PUCCINI ARIAS

CAVALLERIA RUSTICANA

Although *Cavalleria rusticana* was recorded before *Tosca*, it was released nearly a year later. Unlike the great Puccini recording which was the first to take place in La Scala under Walter Legge's direction, Mascagni's work was recorded at the Basilica di Santa Eufemia, as was *I Puritani* which was produced by Dino Oliveri who was also in charge of *Lucia* in Florence. The producer of *Cavalleria rusticana* itself, however, is not known which may have something to do with its delayed release and also the occasional roughness in the sound. It was issued on a three-sided LP set which had everyone wondering whether the fourth could not have been used for a recital in the Decca fashion. But as it cost less, honours were perhaps even. It was not expected to have the same impact as *Tosca* seven months before but nevertheless, to resurrect Rosenthal's word, it was 'different' and in the best sense of the word. Philip Hope-Wallace, who in 1954 had taken over from Alec Robertson as the **Gramophone** regular opera critic, wrote: "What I think instantly strikes you is that in the rather conventional opening passage of Santuzza's distress you seem to be hearing the music sung for the first time. Callas is an exceptional artist in this creative artistry if in nothing else. Elena Nicolai (Decca) makes it sound very ordinary; Milanov (HMV) sings it most touchingly, with a couple of really beautiful high notes. Whether Callas' interpretation strikes you as 'beautiful' or not, it is arresting; in page after page of this durable favourite, the music comes at you characterised, experienced and weighted with an artistry wholly out of the ordinary. Against this you must reckon that quite a number of the notes, in an uneven scale, are overloaded, ill-placed or pinched, with an unpredictable or hooty quality. To ignore these may be easier for some people than others but to deny them in the wish to canonise a superlative artist and raise her above all criticism seems to me impossible. Enough that she makes the solo 'Voi lo sapete' deeply affecting, and the quarrel hair-raising, and with the superb amplitude of Maestro Serafin's conception, she makes the Easter hymn sound as one had forgotten it could sound."[1]

How interesting that as long ago as 1954 and so early in her recording career there is talk of canonising this great singer even if the critic himself finds the idea 'impossible'. Two years earlier in 1952 in Mexico City she was publicly dubbed on the facade of the Palacio de las Bellas Artes as 'Prima Donna Assoluta del Siglo' half a century in advance! No one should complain, as Rupert Christiansen did in his 1987 'Polemic' in *Opera*, if, as the millennium closes, she is now La Divina Assoluta. Harold Rosenthal rated the issue as 'certainly the best of the three available'. He states that Callas to the best of his knowledge had not sung Santuzza on stage but after the success of this performance surely would. In fact, he was wrong on both counts: Santuzza was her first role at the age of 15 at the Olympia Theatre in Athens when a student, and her last ever performance in the role was five years later in the same city, but as a professional, aged 20. He goes on: "The short scene with Alfio before the Intermezzo where she tells him of Lola and Turiddu's behaviour is one of the most exciting things I have heard on records and her singing of the hackneyed Easter Hymn and 'Voi lo sapete' sound spontaneous. It is easier to ignore the vocal unevenness in a verismo work than in Bellini and so the purists will probably find this Santuzza acceptable."[2] – hardly the sort of comment, though, to anticipate the recording's recommendation 45 years later, as is now the case!

At its first re-release in February 1974, Richard Osborne regarded Callas' singing and acting as the principal glory of the set and Serafin's sober and circumspect conducting as the principal disappointment. The pupil, then, outshining the teacher. He went on: "It is a measure of Callas' stature that unaided she can transform the Easter Hymn from a dirge into a chorus of thanksgiving – her thrice-repeated cry 'O Signore' alone is almost worth the price of the records. Callas' account of 'Voi lo sapete' I find here less complete and less moving than the one she recently gave us in the Festival Hall (at the second recital; the first (televised) performance was vocally too rough)." I wonder how many other observers, at first glance, find Maria's 1973/4 world tour performances superior to those of the golden age of the Fifties. It sounds preposterous. But, in fact, it isn't because her art was so assured, so complete that it is heightened as the vocal powers are diminished. I feel the same about her Tokyo 'O mio babbino caro'. I note with particular interest that Richard Osborne then recalls my first love, Milanov, who "on record has great simplicity matched with a richer quality of pathos. But how wonderful Callas is in the duet itself! Bjorling and Milanov are glorious here too and even more cathartic in the big climaxes with a vitriolic 'Bada!' from Milanov; but Callas is the richer, more commanding characterisation. The simple rise to the E flat of 'Turiddu, ascolta' alone catches in microcosm the half-threatening, half-pleading mood which Callas so vividly and hauntingly exploits in the scene. Callas' other strength is that she is not only a great singer herself but frequently the cause of greatness in others. The little scene with Lola drips unctuousness and spite, and Panerai is goaded into producing a wonderfully dark furioso quality in the big act two confrontation between Santuzza and Alfio."[3] Alan Blyth in **Opera** echoes much of this and finds Callas an "impassioned Santuzza, quite unforgettable in the Easter Hymn."[4] He returned to the scene 13 years later only this time for **Gramophone**. Again he is impressed, for "Callas lives the characters more vividly than anyone. The sadness and anguish she brings to Santuzza'a unhappy plight are at their most compelling at 'io piango' in 'Voi lo sapete' and at 'Turiddu mi tolsi' in her encounter with Alfio, strongly sung by Panerai, where the pain in Santuzza's heart is expressed in almost unbearable terms."[5] **Opera** is represented by Richard Fairman who finds "the Callas *Cavalleria rusticana* (and *I pagliacci*) easily the best choice among recordings, now on CD, of the opera(s) currently available. Callas' Santuzza is wholly compelling, utterly instinctive in its feeling for the drama and sung with her darkest and most weighty tone as though bearing an enormous burden of suffering."[6] Forty-five years on, di Stefano, wholly believable as the caddish Turiddu, particularly in the great duet, is better appreciated; as Michael Tanner said at the time of the 20th Anniversary issue, "Callas and di Stefano make a superb pair, as they always did and Serafin's uninhibited conducting thrills throughout."[7] J. B. Steane, for his part, wonders if the "set is finally dispensable until he listens again to the very first phrases of Callas' hapless Santuzza, each of them with its specific flavour, the very essence of her art."[8]

That it is not dispensable is clear from its joint recommendation with Karajan's recording in the **G.C.G.CD G.2000**: "The sound is much more confined than on the Karajan set, though rather more immediate. Serafin conducts swifter-moving performances yet ones quite as notable as Karajan's for pointing up relevant details. Both interpretations carry with them a real sense of the theatre and are quite free from the studio routine. It is difficult to choose between the two sets. Callas or Karajan enthusiasts will have no difficulty making their choice. Others may be guided by quality of sound. With either you will be ensured hours of memorable listening."[9]

★ ★ ★

NORMA

Cavalleria rusticana, for all its allure, was but the October *hors d'oeuvre* to the main November dish – *Norma*. Callas made her Covent Garden debut in the role in November 1952 and her Cetra 78 of 'Casta diva ... Ah,bello' was her very first recording, and none too successful according to both **Gramophone** and **Opera**: Lord Harewood, who had previously heard her on stage as Gioconda and Elena, found her "as yet by no means the equal of Ponselle either from the point of view of voice or of style; but there is some notable singing here, some slurring and attack from below to a large extent offset by the amazing articulation of high figuration (even better than Ponselle's) and by an astounding chromatic scale at the end of the second verse."[10] Alec Robertson, who for his part had never even heard of Callas, agreed with the editor of **Opera** *vis à vis* Ponselle (and Muzio): "She has a voice rich in tone that seems well fitted to the part of the High Priestess and begins with a reasonably good legato – essential to the aria – but her rushed approach to the high B's, sung at once fortissimo and not, as directed, increased to that, sounds as if she had lost her nerve, closed her eyes (so to speak) and hurled herself at the fence. Not quite what one would expect of a lady of Norma's stature! The chromatic scales in the cabaletta are fairly smoothly sung, but the whole thing is too explosive. I have no doubt that Maria Callas will do a great deal better than this in the future."[11]

And of course she did. Between her debut in Florence on 30th November 1948, still at only 24 years of age, and her last sadly curtailed performance at the Paris Opera on 29th May 1965, Callas gave a grand total of eighty-eight performances of the famous role, identifying her, in all probability, as the greatest Norma of all time. She sang it in seventeen opera houses, including La Scala, the New York Met, Paris, the Buenos Aires Colón; and at Covent Garden only months before the complete recording reached the shops for Christmas 1954. Philip Hope-Wallace of **Gramophone** for one had been immensely looking forward to it. But sadly, he found it badly flawed, both as to the quality of the recording and supporting cast – a blustery Rossi-Lemeni, Filippeschi 'a dancing bearing to Callas' Margot Fonteyn', and even Stignani in the duets merely sounded 'like a pupil to Callas' master violinist.' And what of the master violinist herself? "Where it is a question of musicianship and dramatic interpretation and coloration of the voice she is quite magnificent; her phrasing has an etched quality, she is at once a great dramatic artist and great singer in the way that Frida Leider was. The musicianship of her 'Casta

Discussing a point during Callas' eagerly-awaited recording of *Norma* with Nicola Rossi-Lemeni, Rina Cavallari and Mario Filippeschi [La Scala, April 1954]

diva' leaves most of the versions I know as non-starters, the glissando passages in the cabaletta 'Deh bello a me ritorna' shortly afterwards are breathtaking. Norma's anguish when she finds out that she is betrayed, the reproachful dignity and biting scorn of her scenes with the wretched Pollione and her hieratic magnanimity in dealing with her rival – all these are truly wonderful. She also truly makes you hear the music for the first time. However, this tremendous assumption is full of flaws. Artist though she be, she is not a technically satisfying singer. Her scale is lamentably uneven. Some marvellously attack high note on which she is wishing to exercise a diminuendo turns into a squally, fluctuating hoot as her voice 'goes back in her throat.' Her tone is often forced or 'boxed in'. The result for those who care about singing (as distinct from those merely interested in a dramatic interpretation) is a constant anxiety and strain."[12]

Harold Rosenthal in **Opera** confined his criticisms to peripheral matters and was more generous: "Callas here repeats her wonderfully human and dramatic interpretation of the druid priestess and while some passages are better sung than we remember them in the theatre – 'Casta diva' especially –

others seem less well executed. I say seem because on the recording we have not the trappings of stage and costume nor the fine acting that Callas gave us in this role to take our minds off the vocal inequalities. Those things by which Callas' Norma will surely be remembered in operatic history – the biting scorn of her scenes with Pollione, the moving outburst when she is thinking of killing the two children, the exciting moment in the last scene where she announces war against the Romans, all these are fully captured on this recording."[13] Desmond Shawe-Taylor shows no inclination to disassociate himself from the much of this: "By present-day standards, she passes the test brilliantly enough for it is impossible to think of any contemporary who could hold a candle to her in this role. She is in fact a very considerable artist who possesses about half the qualities needed by a great Norma. Her great virtue, now a very rare one, is the authority of her style; she sounds grand and imperious and noble, and in her declamation of recitative and melody she always pays scrupulous attention to Romani's text as well as to Bellini's notes. She is one of the very few singers of today who can mould a phrase with the distinction of a fine string player, as she demonstrates near the opening of Act 2 when she takes over the D minor melody 'Teneri, teneri figli' from the cellos and invests it with a finely restrained pathos. What, then, prevents us from counting her among the very greatest of Normas? Simply the defects of pure vocalisation which she shows no apparent desire to correct: the uneven scale, the sudden sour, unwanted sforzando, the ungainly scooping with which she can mar an exquisite phrase and most of all that heavy pulse in the voice which is always liable to make its appearance in forte singing above the stave and elsewhere too. For a demonstration of what is wrong with even the best of our contemporary singing, turn to one of her duets with Stignani and in particular to those passages in which the two voices sing a succession of rising thirds. As the powerful and warring tremulos of Callas and Stignani climb the scale, they set off a battle of overtones which is not only guaranteed to produce distortion of any known methods of reproduction but sounded distorted, as I remember, even in Covent Garden. Can anyone doubt that such barbarous sounds would have horrified the Victorians as they would have horrified Bellini himself or his great admirer Chopin? To show how the thirds ought to sound, we must go back to the old Ponselle-Telva 'Mira, o Norma' or the still older 'Ah si, fa core' by Lilli Lehmann and her niece." Maybe Mr Shawe-Taylor should have gone back even further, to Queen Victoria and one of her daughters. He does, however, finally decide that "the whole set, whatever its incidental faults, is filled with dramatic tension and grandeur; most of all where Madame Callas sweeps us away with the great sequence of numbers which culminates in the expansive Finale."[14] Much the most favourable review comes from Dyneley Hussey of **Musical Times**: "The beauty of Bellini's music rests in its firmly shaped yet sensuous melodic line and everything depends upon the realisation of that beauty by the singers. This is magnificently achieved by the two sopranos in the present recording and it is on them that the main burden of the opera lies. Maria Callas does nothing so well as this most exacting of all Italian soprano parts. The steadiness and beauty of her tone which rarely spills over the edges of a note, the shapeliness of her phrasing and the expressive colouring of her voice makes this one of the outstanding performances of our time. And she is beautifully matched by Ebe Stignani ..."[15]

As Callas re-recorded the opera six years later and both versions were scrupulously compared in all further re-issues, let us now turn to the stereo *Norma* of 1960. The critical response was similar to the earlier stereo release of *Lucia* and Andrew Porter in **Gramophone** sings its praises and argues its merits as if his life depended on it: "Better or worse than the 1954 recording? The answer cannot be put in a word any more than it could in the case of *Lucia*. But those who heard Callas sing Norma at Covent Garden in 1953 and then again, slim, in 1957 will know the difference. The facts are that in 1954 the voice above the stave was fuller, more solid and more certain, but that now the middle timbres are more beautiful and more expressive; and further, that an interpretation which was always magnificent has deepened in finesse, flexibility and dramatic poignancy. The emphasis you give to these facts must be a matter of personal opinion but I cannot help wondering whether those people who so readily declared their preference for the early Lucia had really listened to both performances right through or merely compared the showy bits. Certainly Callas' voice lets her down again and again often when she essays some of her most beautiful effects. The F wobbles when it should crown a heart-rending 'Oh rimembranza'; the G wobbles in an exquisitely conceived 'Son io' – and yet how much more moving is it than the simpler, if steadier, messa di voce of the earlier set. There are people who have a kind of tone deafness to the timbres of Callas' present voice, who don't respond to one of the most affecting and eloquent of all sounds. They will stick to the earlier set. But I know that it is the new one which I shall be listening to again and again, not unaware of, not even unflinching from, its faults, but still more keenly responsive to its beauties."[16] Desmond Shawe-Taylor takes this view in choosing the new *Norma*, with its strong supporting cast and better sound. He writes: "Callas herself is the heart of the matter and I do not see how it can be denied

Recording the second *Norma* [La Scala, September 1960] with Franco Corelli and Nicola Zaccaria

that her vocal powers show here a certain decline. For a long time her sustained upper notes have resembled a slow trill; now they often are that. Below, the tone is usually veiled, seldom beautiful or pure in the abstract but often fascinating in context. And though I cannot help wilting under those huge high tremolos, I come in the end to admire and almost to love the lower regions of Madame Callas' voice because of the incomparable art, now richer than ever with which it is applied. There are refinements and subtleties which come closer to the world of some great Lieder singer than to that of Italian opera as we know it today. Of the same order is her exquisite fining-off and shading away at the end of many phrases and cadences; for instance, in the first two phrases of 'Deh non volermi' in the finale or in the 'Mira, o Norma' duet with Adalgesa. This opening scene of Act 2 is indeed the high watermark artistically of the whole set."[17]

With all this, Harold Rosenthal was totally at odds and in **Opera** could not conceal his bitter disappointment with the new set: "This is one of the saddest notices I have ever had to write. I do not have to tell readers that I have for years been an ardent admirer of Maria Callas. In recent years as her vocal weaknesses have grown and that wobble and other blemishes become more apparent I have been prepared if not to overlook them at least to accept them as Callas had so much else to offer in her interpretations. But I cannot but believe that she was unwise to sanction the release of this new *Norma*. There are of course some exciting moments as in the trio and some exquisite ones as in the 'Mira, o Norma' duet and some memorable ones (the change of vocal colour when she appeals to Pollione to leave Adalgisa for the sake of his children); and certainly the middle of the voice can still sound beautiful as indeed it does in both the Norma-Adalgisa duets. But elsewhere there is much that is ugly and ungrateful to the ear. Example follows example where the singer's intention is all too clear but where the voice will just not obey that intention. The downward scales no longer consist of separate notes threaded together and the upper voice sounds thin. While Callas' characterisation of Norma has deepened and developed I still find her savage and often less subtle earlier recording more exciting and that's the one I would prefer to play."[18]

It remains to be seen, therefore, which of these positions holds good. The first set to be reissued [in May 1978] was the earlier 1954 recording which Alan Blyth, writing in **Gramophone** finds curious because he thoroughly seconds Andrew Porter's preference for the stereo version with its superior sound and supporting cast. But whilst urging its release, he readily agrees that "the Callas *Norma* of 1954 was indeed truly great, capturing the majesty and greater security of the young Callas' utterance, rising to dramatic, tragic heights in the great second act finale, supported by Serafin who is here more in command of the tensions in Bellini's writing than he was in 1960."[19] When the stereo set came two years later, Harold Rosenthal stuck to his guns and, notwithstanding its miserable supporting cast, still preferred Callas' earlier recording "for there is the Callas we all want to remember."[20] J.B.Steane, writing in **Gramophone**, on balance shares this view, making a subtle distinction between Callas' Norma and *Norma* with Callas, where he prefers the later recording. More remarkable is the consistency he finds between the two recordings as far as interpretation and style are concerned. Where there is clear blue water between them is in a matter of sound and voice: the former, a huge improvement, the latter "loosened, thinned and hardened".[21] When the old arguments were again rehearsed for the CD issue a decade later, relative positions are largely maintained. Alan Blyth in **Gramophone** summed up the importance of these performances: "For a generation of opera goers Callas was Norma and nobody since has come near challenging her hegemony in a role for which her timbre, declamation and dramatic understanding so peculiarly suited her. Now a new generation of record collectors can hear in much improved sound what all the fuss was about, how Callas in phrase after phrase can imprint Norma's predicament on our minds, how in a few bars of 'Casta diva' she can capture her audience by the plangent, intimate quality of her tone, how as the opera progresses she can unfold you Norma's tragedy. Above all, hers is a wholly commanding yet wholly feminine account of the part, its many subtle overtones allowing us to forgive the occasional uncertainty when pressure is exerted on the voice. Yet I'm disappointed that EMI did not opt for the second recording where Callas is vocally more fallible but the reading is deeper, even more expressive, certainly more touching; and with a superior supporting cast and infinitely finer sound. Nevertheless, anyone wanting to hear why Callas has always been considered a unique phenomenon need look no further than this CD issue of the first recording, for her talent, genius if you like, is at its most potent here."[22] Three years later when Alan Blyth's preferred 1960 recording was finally issued on CD, John Steane in **Gramophone** repeated his view that the two recordings are not nearly so different as was originally thought to be the case, that vocal deterioration and deepened interpretation had both been overstated. Noel Goodwin said the same: "What her voice lost in the interval between 1954 qnd 1960 is compensated by greater experience in interpretation – finding, for instance, the added warmth and feeling in the early scenes, the anger and deeper resignation of the last."[23] Ten years later to mark the CD reissue on the 20th anniversary in 1997 of Callas' death, Michael Tanner opted for the 1954 recording, "less subtle but more secure, it showed Callas in full cry, in the intensity of her emotions and the completeness with which she can express them. The supporting cast too is remarkably strong."[24] JB Steane was more equivocal, letting other factors decide, like the better supporting cast and superior sound.

This surely clinches it. Callas, who gave a lifetime of performances of the work on stage, would surely have been gratified not to say a little amused to know of the head-shaking and hand-wringing over the years on the subject of her quest for perfection – a perfection finally recognised in the **G.C.G.CD G.2000,** which gets itself out of a tight corner by recommending both! 1960: the all-out choice, 1954: the historical choice, quoting all the familiar arguments. Very recently, however (February 2000) even that has been somewhat turned on its head by Hilary Finch in Radio 3's **Building a Library** when she chose 1954 over 1960, most unusually backing the superiority of the supporting cast. Honours therefore are about even on Maria's Norma: in any event, the "Casta Diva for all time".

★ ★ ★

PUCCINI ARIAS

33CX1204

With five complete operas behind her and a burgeoning international career of glamorous proportions, Callas recorded not one but two recital discs for EMI in September 1954. The first consisted of 11 arias from Puccini operas. Her overwhelmingly successful Tosca (notwithstanding some previously stated doubts from some quarters) and the composer's popular appeal no doubt prompted this release. All the same, Maria Callas was known to have had little taste for Puccini's music and the queen of La Scala, as she now emphatically was, never sang a note of it in the famous Milan opera house, though, responding to Walter Legge, she later committed the four remaining great roles to disc – Madama Butterfly (1955), Mimi (1956), Turandot and Manon Lescaut (1957). This recital disc meanwhile was, on the whole, rapturously received and constituted a veritable demonstration, if one indeed was needed, of her astonishing versatility. Let's begin with Philip Hope-Wallace in **Gramophone**: "To each and every aria she brings the stamp of individual artistry, something of character acting and a concern for the dramatic and musical shaping of the aria. What she often lacked (however) was a lovely natural bloom on the voice or a heart warming spontaneity. Compare her Manon to Tebaldi's (on Decca). The latter has much more opulent and sheerly, sensuously beautiful tone, plus much easier delivery. Yet Callas phrases the opening exquisitely, not matter-of-factly as Tebaldi does but dreamily as Spani used to. And the anti-climax? Tebaldi's strong and steady, Callas' exciting but is quickly invaded by a slow, heavy, pulsing vibrato which I can only say I find very distressing. This happens again and again at climaxes. For me, it spoils Mimi's finale 'Senza rancore' on which the diminuendo is unsteady; it spoils Liu's pathetic final 'Liu non regge piu', a phrase which such singers as Schone or Schwarzkopf make ethereally beautiful. As Turandot herself, Madame Callas makes a magnificent assumption: one feels the presence of a great Princess and the whole scena is carried through with enormous authority. At one place she is definitely inferior to Eva Turner but this must be the most exciting effort since that famous old 10-inch 78 even if the pulsing vibrato aforementioned does make it seem rather a hard-won victory. At the other end of the scale (figuratively) listen to the artistry with which 'O mio babbino caro' is phrased, especially toward the end; and the fresh meaning and pathos put into Butterfly's 'Che dira? Chiamera Butterfly della lontano'. It seems one can so seldom have everything: the voice in perfect bloom and ease, yet the temperament to make for a full range of artistry; or only in exceptional cases."[25] With this interesting account of Callas' qualities, he concludes that, though impressive, the recital will divide opinion. There is little doubt whose side Harold Rosenthal is on: "Only an artist with Callas' gifts and artistry would attempt such a recital: Turandot and Liu, Lauretta and Butterfly. Although the vibrato is much in evidence, so is this singer's wonderful ability to sing phrase after phrase with real freshness. The 'In questa reggia' must be one of the most exciting pieces of singing to have been recorded for many a day. The Suor Angelica piece has been sadly in need of a satisfactory according, though Magda Olivero's had a lot to commend it. Mimi is the one part which I do not think comes off."[26] (An interesting observation because within two years he would be raving about her Mimi in the complete recording.) Conversely, the remaining heavyweight to pronounce, Desmond Shawe-Taylor, backed Philip Hope-Wallace, finding the "slow, heavy pulse in the voice almost intolerable in such moments as the final note of 'In quelle trine' nor do I care for her muscular treatment of Liu's two pathetic songs." But he goes on: "the big aria of Turandot herself is so splendid that I wish she could be persuaded to record the whole opera; and the versatility and artistic subtlety shown elsewhere in this record is certainly astonishing. The most unexpected success is her 'Un bel di'. One scarcely thinks of the imperious Callas in the role of Butterfly yet from the first note she is absolutely convincing. She brings the well-worn aria freshly to life by sharply visualising (just as Butterfly is supposed to do) every detail of the imaginary picture of Pinkerton's return."[27]

At the first reissue 25 years later, Rodney Milnes in **Opera** finds Callas in stunning form: "Her voice is under firm control, the variety of dramatic expression bewildering. When after the death of Butterfly, Mimi's first aria starts, you can hardly believe it is the same singer, so light and airy is the tone. The ensuing Farewell is one of the great Callas items: the way she gives the impression towards the end that she is ashamed of having betrayed such depth of emotion in what was supposed to have been a calm leave-taking shows extraordinary insight. 'In questa reggia' also has rock steady intonation, those unearthly undertones springing from the consonants and the thought behind the words conjure up a living character before you." However he is not so happy about Suor Angelica, Liu and Lauretta: "At the end of 'Senza mamma' (which she overplays, missing Angelica's simplicity) a top A suddenly flaps wildly out of control and the close of Liu's first aria – Callas, surely, could never have been a Liu – is sadly bumpy. While the humour and self mockery of the *Schicchi* aria are charming, the singing as such is unsteady."[28] – an assessment clearly at odds with his predecessor's. Alan Blyth can't agree, finding Callas "almost perfectly cast making us feel the poor girl Liu suffering for love in the way she gives certain phrases an anguish not encountered in other readings." He then goes on to compare the performances in the recital with those in the complete sets which followed: "Perhaps they are more intense but here as one aria succeeds another we are able to hear just how Callas varied her characterisation to suit each role: the delicate vulnerability and simple eagerness of Cio-Cio-San, the winning smile and ardour of Mimi, the desperation of Manon are all felt as individual and personally accented creations yet the applied intelligence never obscures the spontaneity of the expression."[29] When it comes to J.B. Steane's turn for the CD, he is overwhelmed: "It is indeed one of the great recitals. Phrase after phrase, one character after another: everything is special. Random moments: Butterfly's 'Va, gioca' to the child, simple, unexaggerated and unlike many whose histrionics would make it howl for life; Lauretta's 'O Dio, vorrei morir', an appeal with heartfelt longing;

Manon's 'Terra di pace', touchingly sweet-toned and wistful. Wonderful too (even when they're expected) are the metamorphoses, Butterfly into a completely different Mimi, Angelica into Lauretta, Liu into Turandot."[30]

These very special performances surely give the lie to her protestations about Puccini. It can't have been that she disliked his music; it is sung with such beauty and love. But the structure of his works militated against the sort of heroine which dominated the great bel canto operas and which were Callas' 'raison d'etre'. Too many heroes, perhaps, got in the way.

Chapter Three

1954–55

LA FORZA DEL DESTINO
I PAGLIACCI
OPERATIC ARIAS
IL TURCO IN ITALIA
MADAMA BUTTERFLY

FORZA

There can't have been many cognoscenti at the time who could have guessed the identity of Callas' first Verdi recording. *La Forza del Destino* was a very strange choice. Of course the music is glorious but it never excited much dramatic interest, for Callas at least. Curiously, it was the fourth role she ever sang in Italy, at Trieste in 1948, to plug a hole maybe. She sang only two solitary performances six years later in May 1954 in Ravenna, most likely to run into the recording that summer. It is a rambling work, the lovers spending most of the opera apart. The Callas complete recording was the very first ever (before her older rivals Tebaldi and Milanov, of whom more later) to the delight of Philip Hope-Wallace, who reminds us of the opera's glories, including the finest Verdi tenor/ baritone duet of them all. His welcome to the set is not unreserved (he wouldn't otherwise be a critic) and his greatest praise is for the tenor, Richard Tucker: "Callas gives a blazingly exciting performance and for sheer dramatic aptness plus the musicianship to bring up, new minted, some coin you know well, you should try straightaway ... the prayer outside the monastery gate and also the rising, serene melody of Leonora's dying words, 'Nella terra promessa'. Here is greatness. Why, then, any reservations? Simply because she twice at least spoils (for me) truly heavenly moments by loud, perilous and heavily beating sforzandos on high notes, a steadiness and the purity of which are not merely a desirability but a true artistic necessity. I cannot understand how any soprano so manifestly an exceptional artist can bear to oblige with such variations of quality. Needless to say, the 'Maledizione' which follows the last, climactic phrase of 'Pace, pace ... ' is hair-raising. All in all, she does triumphantly present the Leonora of whom Dyneley Hussey so well wrote: 'To our intellect she may remain a lay figure: to our emotions, she is a living human personality'"[1]. Mr Hussey himself, in **Musical Times**, paid this tribute: "Although Callas' tone is apt to spread under pressure, (this singer) makes a superb Leonora. Her voice has that exciting energy which generates dramatic tension. What she most lacks is the pure, silvery quality of tone which made Destinn's singing of Verdi's music so memorable."[2] Milanov as well as Destinn had long been famous in the role and knew how to 'ravish the ear' as Harold Rosenthal put it when the Yugoslav soprano's recital and highlights discs were released much about the same time as Callas' 'beating sforzandos'. However, Rosenthal, who had succeeded Lord Harewood as editor of **Opera**, continued: "The Greek diva is still supreme as the singing-actress of our time, colouring the familiar phrases with some new meaning, and living and breathing Leonora's emotions for us in the most exciting manner possible. Even the rather dull opening scene takes on new meaning in her hands while her death scene is truly great."[3] The recording gave rise to a

"Fellow perfectionists" Maria Callas and her recording producer, Walter Legge, during a session for *La Forza del Destino* [La Scala, August 1954]

consideration by Desmond Shawe-Taylor in his **Gramophone** Quarterly Review (September 1955) of the relative merits of the two sopranos. Callas he found better in life than on record, her faults of voice reproduction being mercilessly exposed and apparently exaggerated by the microphone. (This problem has already been noted. One of the reasons, perhaps, why Callas' recordings have steadily grown in stature is that improved technology [digital remastering and the compact disc] has done greater justice to her recorded art, initially hampered by indifferent techniques in the LP era.) Mr Shawe-Taylor could only comment on what he found in 1954: "I can well imagine that in the theatre she may be an impressive Leonora in *Forza* but I must confess that I found her new Columbia recording of the opera very exhausting to listen to. True, she is always an artist who gives an individual turn to phrases that usually pass unnoticed; but what is the good of that when there is no real beauty of sustained tone when the higher notes develop an alarming judder and when there is so much singing off pitch as in the G major cadenza for instance at the end of the first inn scene. What a relief it is to the physical ear and to the musical sense to turn from this effortful performance to the long stretches of *Forza* that are included in Zinka Milanov's admirable HMV recital. On the strength of this record, Milanov clearly establishes herself, I feel, as the leading Italianate dramatic soprano of our day with a voice of beautifully even texture from top to bottom, a firm if not impeccable technique and an ingrained sense of style."[4]

Within six years both Tebaldi and Milanov had entered the lists with complete recordings, the former with "golden gravity but rather tired ... and unimaginative"[5], and the latter floating her famous soft high notes. But as Harold Rosenthal (in **Opera**) points out in Milanov's "incomparable account of the beautiful music Verdi provided for Leonora, the voice of course does not sound a young voice." And indeed it does not. She simply recorded it too late (1960); outstanding in my opinion is di Stefano who according to Harold Rosenthal "sings much better than he has done for a very long time."[6] J. B. Steane in **Gramophone** for the first Callas re-release a year after her death wrote: "I believe that Callas considered 1955 the year in which her powers were at their height. Certainly her recording of *La Forza del Destino* comes from the period when this was so. Her voice still had body, loosening of the high notes was not too far advanced and she sang it with the full fervour and command of her mature genius. The *Forza* Leonora moreover was one of the roles best suited to her. Her very low notes have a thrilling individuality of timbre and strength of character; she has only to sing 'Padre, signore' for us to recognise instantly that tragic intensity of hers that was so powerful and so personal. Of course there are troubles: the B flat of 'invane la pace', the quiet G flat in the final trio, the pianissimo E at the end of the duet with Father Guardiano. Callas is easily replaceable as far as the climaxes of the big arias are concerned. Where she is incomparable is in the way any phrase whether of aria or recitative is liable to light up suddenly as we have never known it to do before."[7] Alan Blyth in **Opera** recalls Lord Harewood's praise in 1962: "'Callas' performance was one of unparalleled musical sensibility and imagination, a size of phrasing and grasp of total musico-dramatic picture which are unique.' So it still seems as she finds the tone and colour to etch each successive phrase into one's mind. From such a brief aside as 'Oh, mio rimorso' in the first scene, through the arching phrases of the second act aria and the anxious thoughts as she prepares to enter the monastery, to the beseeching 'Pace,pace', the performance has the usual marks of Callas' unerring interpretative powers, intense and convincing, and the harsh, wobbly notes are happily few and far between. She manages, in sum, to present a noble, impassioned creature, cruelly treated by the fate of the title – 'Fatalita' indeed."[8]

Ten years later on CD, Richard Osborne fully amplified this view when also considering another formidable Leonora, Leontyne Price. "It was a role to which Callas was particularly well attuned. Leonora's ardour, sincerity and desperate vulnerability are etched by this great artist into her every utterance. *Forza* begins with a subdued conversation and ends with the great trio and Callas is unforgettable in both; whenever she is before the microphone – throughout Act 1, in the great scene with the Padre Guardiano and in Act 4 – we are aware of the greatness of *Forza* as music-drama. There are some flaws in execution but fewer than might be expected given the rough patch Callas (generally in fine fettle around this period) had gone through in the spring of 1954. Walter Legge, whose advice Callas respected and whose authority she acknowledged, told her that, unless the wobble was sorted out, EMI and Angel would have to issue sea-sickness pills with the records. In the event, they weren't necessary." Osborne then goes on to stress the point (raised earlier *vis à vis* Shawe-Taylor's comments) which may help to explain why many of Callas' recordings were so critically received in the 'Fifties when they were first released: "Callas is helped by the new digital remastering, and by CD; her voice never really sat comfortably in 1950s vinyl which bucked and jabbered at her emissions as surely as any dyed-in-the-wool canary-fancier. The sound is now clear and true. So, even if you opt for a rival CD version of this opera, the Callas set is unmissable."[9] Though not, it has to be said, according to

G.C.G.CD G.2000 which does not include the set amongst its recommended recordings of this works. Nor did Roger Parker choose it when comparing the available versions of the opera on CD in Radio 3's **Building a Library** on 20th September 1997: "A Callas interpretation can rarely be ignored and this one will always command respect, even from those who might be sceptical of her talents." Including himself, perhaps?

* * *

I PAGLIACCI

Shortly before recording this Verdi role which had little place on the stage for her, Callas recorded another role which had no place whatever: Nedda in Leoncavallo's *I pagliacci*. It was one of four roles (the others being Mimi, Manon Lescaut and Carmen) to be recorded complete which she never sang at La Scala or anywhere else. True to form, Philip Hope-Wallace questioned the wisdom of this: "Madame Callas is surely not very suitably cast as Nedda, often more effectively taken by a contrastingly light, womanly and sensuously pleasing type of voice. Madame Callas – it goes without saying – acts the role excitingly enough. Her taunting of Tonio is tigerish. She, in a rough way of speaking, 'spits out' her words with tremendous effect. In the love duet, she is one of the few Neddas I can recall who actually sings clearly the third syllable of 'non mi tentar' which Victoria de los Angeles, for instance, lets slip, and in the play scene she admirably suggests the mounting horror behind Columbine's playful ripostes. But though the ballatella is sung with a proud swing, I think it is conceived on far too robust a scale. Too many of Madame Callas' high notes turn into perilous and wobbly shrieks."[10] These would seem to have troubled Harold Rosenthal, his fellow critic in **Opera**, rather less: "I think that Serafin has made this set into the definitive Pagliacci. The freshness of the music, which after all has become very hackneyed, is one of the joys of the set; another is the Nedda of Callas which is a most convincing characterisation. Her scene with Tonio is one of the most vivid pieces of operatic acting I can recall, and the way she reserves a different voice for Columbine is another sign of her fine theatrical sense."[11] So it would appear that her lack of stage experience in the role did not in any way hamper her dramatic instincts.

This recording thereafter was always reissued alongside its traditional companion *Cavalleria rusticana* (considered previously). It was one of the first

"An unbeatable line-up" – Di Stefano, Callas, Gobbi, Serafin – with Rolando Panerai and Nicola Monti, recording *I pagliacci* [June 1954]

sets to reappear in mock stereo and was amongst five recordings by this time available. As Richard Osborne wrote in **Gramophone**: "One has heard Neddas who are more soubrettish than Callas (eg. Lucine Amara) or more purely radiant (eg. Caballe or Carlyle). But there has been none more urgently or pressingly feminine than Callas. It's odd that of all the many Neddas on record Callas is the only one to create real tension at the idea of Canio reading her thoughts; the only one to give meaning (as well as brilliance and charm) to her mood as the birds fly overhead; and – a crucial point – the only Nedda to greet her lover with delight. With Callas there is radiance in the single word 'Silvio' and only then a suddenly dawning apprehension."[12] Alan Blyth in **Opera** echoes Harold Rosenthal of 20 years before in praising both Serafin's and Callas' contributions, the latter "seconded by Gobbi's brilliantly manevolent yet half-sympathetic Tonio. Needless to say, their encounter bristles with life and at the end of it Callas can, with the single word 'lurido', conjure before one's eyes her hatred for the deformed clown; then seconds later, in her surprised, whispered 'Silvio', all her heart's desire. Her lightening of her tone for Columbine is another signal of vocal artistry. She and Panerai, lustrous and full-voiced, make their love scene into the erotic affair it should be."[13] Returning to review its CD appearance a dozen years later in **Gramophone**, he notes how despite having never sung the role on stage "she lives the character more vividly than anyone. She differentiates marvellously between the pensiveness of the aria, the passion of the duets, and the playfulness of her commedia dell'arte acting."[14] Richard Fairman of **Opera** agrees: "Her portrayal of Nedda is earthy and passionate in a way that makes one appreciate the role afresh and he concludes that more recent glossy recordings may be in better sound but for a pair of idiomatic and impassioned performances, this is as good as you can get."[15] His editor wasn't convinced however; in Radio 3's **Building a Library** in June 1996 Rodney Milnes described Callas' Nedda as an 'alley cat'. Chaqu'un à son gout – as the **Gramophone Classical Good CD Guide 2000** s recommendation of this recording finally made clear! Following Callas' swiftly changing moods of hatred for the one and love for the other, "in the immediacy of emotion of di Stefano's Canio, it is the tenor's turn to evoke pity and display anguish. Di Stefano does it as well as any Canio on record without quite having the heroic tone for the latter part of the opera. It is impossible to choose between the two Tonios, both pertinently cast. But Gobbi plays the part more menacingly."[16]

⋆ ⋆ ⋆

OPERATIC ARIAS

The pleasantest of surprises followed. After her beautiful Puccini recital, a programme of lyric and coloratura arias was committed to disc. Let me say straightaway that this is my favourite recital by far, greater in my opinion than both the Verdi and Mad Scenes recitals of 1958. All of these discs contain music not recorded elsewhere in the complete sets. But she sang much of what was on the '58 discs on the stage at some point in her career, live performances which are now available on CD which does not, however, apply to this earlier disc which gives us our only taste of Callas in *Adriana Lecouvreur*, *La Wally*, *Mefistofele*, *Dinorah* and *Lakme* (though the last two we have live from concerts). Alec Robertson, back on the scene, gives it a very warm welcome even if he does nit-pick to begin with: "That heavy beat of the voice is just faintly present at the end of the first aria from *Adriana Lecouvreur* and perhaps the climax of 'Poveri fiori' is too strenuously done. For the rest of the verismo

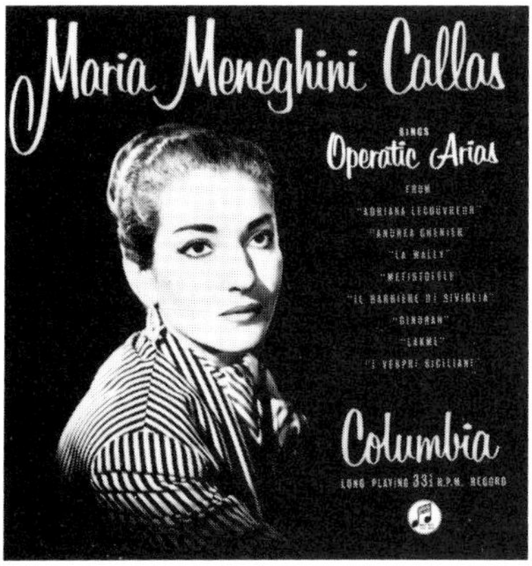

33CX 1231

items there is great tenderness and simplicity, deep emotion, and the most lovely moulding of the vocal phrases. Madame Callas' characterisations of Adriana, especially in the entrance aria and of the temporarily insane Margaret in the aria from *Mefistofele* are nothing less than superb, and altogether there is some of her finest singing yet recorded. But it will need a good reproducer to do it justice. In the florid arias, she makes a curiously gentle but very inventive Rosina in the first half of the famous aria. In 'Ombra leggiera' she competes, of course, with the flute and very successfully but the trills lie in an awkward part of her voice; and in any case she should not be wasting her time over this foolish piece. Her chromatic scale in 'Dov'e l'Indiana bruna' is beautifully done and she sails up to the region known as 'in alt' with the greatest ease, reaching an F at the end of the Bolero, though this aria needs more sparkle in it."[17] He added to what he called this very good and amazingly versatile recital the hope that he would now hear Callas as Senta or even Isolde which could well be a most revealing experience – forgetting presumably that she had already had enormous success in the latter role earlier in her career.

In **Opera**, Harold Rosenthal is impressed: "This amazing artist continues to challenge comparison with the past by singing a mixture of florid and lyric arias. As Adriana and La Wally, she is superb, hardly less so as Margherita; but the *Chenier* is not up to standard and I want a more voluptuous voice here. The *Vespri* Bolero makes us want to hear her in the whole opera and the Rosina aria is a revelation; taken slower than usual and full of meaning and wit, this is really something."[18] Mr Rosenthal must have forgotten that Callas' Bolero had indeed been heard in a staged *Vespri*, at the 1951 Maggio Musicale Fiorentino, and so good as to finally persuade the Scala's Sovrintendente, Antonio Ghiringhelli, to open its doors to her. I am surprised, too, that he is unhappy with 'La mamma morta', the performance chosen for the 1994 award-winning film 'Philadelphia' 40 years after it was recorded. It must presumably have some merit. And though Harold Rosenthal finds *La Wally* superb, I am mortified that this most glorious piece escapes Alec Robertson's attention altogether. If anyone asks me what is special about Callas, I play that. One note is enough. Even Alan Blyth writing about the reissue in 1974 fails to mention it in his otherwise appreciative review: "Her insight into the different predicament of these late-Romantic heroines is uncanny and the voice was here at its freshest. Just for an example take the passage in the *Mefistofele* excerpt starting 'Ne andro sola e lontana', here so sadly, so eloquently articulated; this is Callas at her inimitable best, and the following climax shows hardly a trace of the usual 'beat' when she applies pressure above the stave. She is still more touching as Adriana, a role she did not sing on stage."[19] He describes the coloratura items as essential Callas – "An even more mischievious 'Una voce poco fa' than on the complete set, an irresistibly beguiling 'Shadow Song' and a performance of the Bolero that is in some ways a compendium of Callas' most magical traits."[20] Harold Rosenthal, twenty years on, remains impressed: "Una voce poco fa' is stunning, full of wit and innuendo"[21] and this time the Bolero has him regretting that Callas did not record the role of Elena in full. How right he is!

Two different critics have a go when the LP is again reissued in 1980. Rodney Milnes, the less happy, disagrees with his editor about her Rosina, at least to begin with: "The sloppy, unrhythmical Rossini sounds odd today and not even Callas can do much with the wooden items by Cilea and Giordano. But the *Mefistofele* aria is another locus classicus of the conjunction of technique, intelligence and worthwhile words and notes. Although the Rossini sounds over-decorated, here for once is a Rosina who sounds as if she could be a viper when cornered. Maybe the Meyerbeer and Delibes items were recorded last and the soprano was tired, for although the coloratura technique is dazzling, there are moments when the pitch sags slightly. Only the top E mars the stunning *Vespri* Bolero."[22] Then it's J. B. Steane's turn, so much more sympathetic and appreciative. Referring to "hard, unsteady, uncomfortable" high notes even in 1954, he asks "when genius is involved, and it assuredly is, do these and other faults matter now (1980) when, after all, this is all that is left to us to know the genius by? What matters now is the sound of that sad voice starting 'Poveri,poveri' with such restrained passion, so full of feeling in the achingly beautiful aria from *La Wally*, so imaginative and inner in the *Mefistofele*. All of these are sung in an unforgettable way and it is intensely moving to hear them again in this reissue. The coloratura arias too have their attractions: 'Una voce' well characterised and with some light, neat and rather magical downward runs, and the *Lakme* 'Bell Song' reflectively done. The 'Shadow Song' is less successful. But whatever the criticisms, nobody who missed the original should miss the reissue."[23] It seems to me that Steane's priorities are absolutely right.

10 years later, Alan Blyth was thrilled with the CD version which "allowed us to hear the unique voice and art with much greater faithfulness; to use the old cliché highly applicable here, Callas seems to be in the room with you dispensing her old magic. The intensity of 'La mamma morta', the pathos of 'Poveri fiori', the sauciness of Una voce', the breezy joy of 'Merce, dilette amiche' are all there to be admired afresh in the new medium. But the plum of the recital is undoubtedly that haunting piece 'L'altra notte', where the blank tone given to 'L'aura a fredda' and the desperate expression of the whole sum up all that is most truthful and perceptive in Callas' singing. Against that have to be placed the occasional sense of strain at the top in the Bell Song from *Lakmé* and elsewhere. Yet what singer with more reliable high notes could bring such variety of feeling, so many different colours of tone even to this lighter repertory? I know of none."[24] And neither do I.

★ ★ ★

IL TURCO IN ITALIA

Callas' next complete recording, in marked contrast to her Nedda before it, was very much a consequence of her work on stage. In October 1950 in Rome, she gave four performances as Fiorilla in Rossini's *Il Turco in Italia*. Five years later, a new production by Franco Zeffirelli at La Scala was mounted for the diva, then at the height of her powers. The EMI recording preceded this by some nine months with an identical cast, save for the tenor. Gianandrea Gavazzeni presided in the pit throughout and was enormously impressed with Callas who worked as hard to master this comic role as any of her great tragic roles. And without exception she captivated the critics. Dyneley Hussey in **Musical Times** wrote: "This is a soprano's opera and admirably Madame Callas sings, whether she is wheedling or scolding or just being sentimental. There are faults in her production, but this is a performance of great vitality and charm."[25] And the often-sceptical Philip Hope-Wallace: "All through, Madame Callas acts vividly, chiding, boasting, melting; one can 'see' the performance, and when in typical Rossinian style she is given a 'key' figure, each repetition of it carries, so one thinks, a slightly different meaning. I found myself teased by memories of these little phrases for hours afterwards, though neither of her big arias contains anything quite up to the best of the *Barber*. On her own and when in lighter voice, Madame Callas is admirably the Rossini heroine, and she has such go and gusto in the ensembles, one

"An incomparable Fiorilla" – Maria Callas at La Scala in April 1955

forgives the crowing and the occasional bagpipe skirl. Spontaneous? Never – in the Galli-Curci blithe, canary style. But an artist!"[26]

Harold Rosenthal was almost as enthusiastic: "Callas is coy, arch and spiteful in turn, and sings with gusto and enjoyment, if not with charm."[27] He is more expansive when the set was reissued 25 years later: "When the 1950 Rome production was reviewed in the February 51 issue of **Opera**, it was the first occasion on which a full-length review as well as a full-page photograph of Callas appeared in our pages. Our then Rome Correspondent wrote that Callas was the surprise of the evening in that she sang a soprano leggiera role with the utmost ease in what one imagines as the style adopted by sopranos at the time this work was composed, making it extremely difficult to believe that she can be the perfect interpreter of both Turandot and Isolde. Yet here she is in the recording made nearly five years later displaying a delicious sense of humour notwithstanding that she will be remembered primarily as a great dramatic, even tragic singing-actress."[28] Richard Osborne in **Gramophone** agreed wholeheartedly: "It is Callas who carries the piece on record. She, outstanding among the cast, has flair and guile with which to shade and project Rossini's deceptively placid vocal lines in the recitatives, arias and racy duologues. She also has the score's obvious comic high point when Fiorilla denounces her old husband in terms which Norma herself would be hard pressed to improve upon, before the music begins to dance and spit with comic derision motioning itself forward to the more emancipated world of Rosina and 'Una voce poco fa'. Otherwise, Callas has no star numbers though she handles the wry, laconic minor key love ditty 'Se il zefiro si posa' – a wheedling vaudeville number in the Neapolitan style – with consummate hidden art."[29] Later, on CD, he had more to say: "'Our *Turco* was so refreshing, so lovely' claimed Zeffirelli. 'From the beginning Callas knew it was going to be a hit.' And yet he had to work hard to bring out on the stage the comedienne in Callas, that quality which was later to irradiate on record her Rosina and, in a more savage dimension, her Carmen. The set contains some classic things above all in Callas' several confrontations with her Selim, the wonderfully grave Rossi-Lemeni and her ageing husband, Geronio. Their hilarious duet in Act I is a locus classicus of Callas' art, an extensive array of bel canto rhetoric lined up ready to be deployed with surgical precision. These fleeting appropriations of the classical tragic style are used by Rossini with an understated comic relish that Callas perfectly comprehends."[30]

It was Callas' association with this recording that provoked a moment of madness at the King's Theatre, Edinburgh during the 1957 Festival. Tickets had long since been sold for *La sonnambula* (and *L'elisir* with di Stefano) so we, two penniless students, not to be outdone, bought, at enormous expense, the only seats left for a Rossini opera we didn't know, with a soprano we didn't care for. The records now make it abundantly clear what we were missing.

* * *

MADAMA BUTTERFLY

As we have seen, record purchasers in 1953 were given a splendid Christmas present and two years later history repeated itself. The great *Tosca* was now followed by an epic performance of *Madama Butterfly* about which it is not easy to find adequate words. A previous plan to record *Butterfly* and *Manon Lescaut* alongside Cetra's *Gioconda* and *Traviata* nearly precluded the necessity of finding any words at all. Mercifully, it came to nought, so I may now quote J. B. Steane from the April 1997 Gramophone 20 years after Callas' death: "Callas' *Butterfly*! That I would keep till last in the dreaded shipwreck, earthquake, house on fire, or whatever. One can emerge from this, as I did reviewing it in October 1987, convinced that not only is it the best of all Callas' recorded works but that she is the best of all recorded Madama Butterflies and that *Madama Butterfly* is the greatest of all operas."[31] These sentiments are precisely shared by Michael Tanner who wrote at the same time: "If I could only choose one Callas recording this would be it, even though she didn't much like Puccini and actually only sang three performances of the work. Still, this is a miracle of creation of character, and one of the most powerful recordings of any work, ever. She is given tremendous support by Karajan. Listen and marvel."[32] Yes, indeed! But it had not always been thus. Two *Butterflies* preceded Callas: Renata Tebaldi, "by far the best since Destinn" said Alec Robertson which I myself, whilst on anti-terrorist duty in Cyprus, heard floating out over the blue Mediterranean; and Victoria de los Angeles, with Callas' regular partners di Stefano and Gobbi; I bought the latter on the strength of the tenor's golden-voiced Pinkerton. It was some time therefore before the full impact of Butterfly's death hit me and only then when I heard Callas. And I'm pleased to note that even Alec Robertson thought this "tremendous, a generous outpouring of tone equalled only by Tebaldi and as the opera ends one is filled with a sense of having heard a great performance of the part." For the rest he is predictably equivocal: "Callas gives consistently the best sung performance I have heard from her. At her entrance she takes the optional top D flat and the voice develops that slow beat sometimes noticed elsewhere; but this happens on no other occasion and she can, like Tebaldi, give a cutting edge to her tone when that is dramatically called for. There are some points that Callas misses. Tebaldi's singing of 'Dolce notte! quante stelle' brings the scented starlit night before us but Callas puts nothing behind it at all and she is, for a moment, as casual in 'Un bel di' at 'Chi sara', etc. Such moments are, however, few and the only other one worth mentioning is when the cannon is fired and she, like de los Angeles, gives no hint of what that means to her. Tebaldi alone registers, as she quits the high G Sharp, the unbearable tension of that moment. However, Callas' singing of 'Che tua madre, with the cry 'Ah! morta' at the end, is magnificent and so is her outburst of joy and faith after the cannon is heard. It is wonderful, in contrast to these great outbursts to hear

Maria Callas as Madama Butterfly, Chicago, November 1955

how she whitens her tone to suggest the youth of Butterfly."[33] I can only add that Callas' cry of 'Morta' is indeed magnificent. From this very point, the opera assumes a desperate greatness which never lets you go. But right from the famous entrance, Callas' Butterfly has a very special allure. Just listen to how she spins out the climactic B flat beginning 'ove s'accoglie il bene' with ravishing love. Dyneley Hussey of **Musical Times** found her "an appealing Butterfly, at once passionate and childlike."[34] Astonishingly, when we turn to **Opera**, it is Harold Rosenthal who registers the jarring doubts: "I think it is a great pity that Callas recorded this performance before she had sung the role on the stage in Chicago for I am certain that she is an artist who needs time to grow into a role and unfortunately there is something rather tentative about this performance. Butterfly is a child bride and although Callas tries in the first act to whiten her voice, she soon becomes the domineering character of this recording; one feels that it is she and not Pinkerton who has done the kidnapping. Of course, as is usual in a Callas performance we get moments when her great artistry suddenly illumines a phrase with some new meaning or reveals some hidden nuance we never knew existed. But on the whole this is something of a disappointment and I still find de los Angeles' Cio-Cio-San the most moving and convincing portrayal on record."[35] Mr Rosenthal's opening observations above are very interesting but, in Callas' case, not very convincing. Of course, many of Callas greatest roles on stage are superbly represented on disc. But four she never sang on the stage are also first-class and others she recorded first are, like Butterfly, outstanding – Amelia, in *Ballo*, for example. Conversely, other stage performances like the *Barber* and *Rigoletto* fell far short of the recordings. Rosenthal, too, is not correct when he says Callas has to grow into a role – consider, for example, the greatness of her first Lady Macbeth, Abigaille in *Nabucco*, Elena in *Vespri*, or Armida. In any case, to return to *Butterfly*, she gave only three performances of Cio Cio San on stage, hardly time to eradicate 'tentativeness'!

As it happens, by the time of the first re-issue 20 years later, he has retracted somewhat: "Callas gives as complete and convincing performance as one could hope for, lightening and even whitening her voice to create the child bride of Act I, and then developing into the trusting wife and mother, and finally the disillusioned woman."[36] The field had also widened considerably with a great performance conducted by Sir John Barbirolli, new stereo versions by Tebaldi and de los Angeles, and another Karajan recording with Freni and Pavarotti. But Alan Blyth was undaunted: "'E un immensa pieta' (it's heartbreaking), says Sharpless near the end of Butterfly and in the most direct sense those were my sentiments as I listened to this set. As it progresses, Callas and Karajan raise what is so often a mere tear-jerker into the deep tragedy Puccini surely intended, reminding us what a masterly score this is. Indeed, my well seasoned and wary ears were quite overwhelmed by the experience. If I knew someone who doubted the validity of opera as music-drama, I would sit him down to listen to the last 20 minutes of the set, text in hand, to receive an object lesson in what it is all about. From the false happiness of 'E qui, e qui!' through the stunned empty tone of 'forse portrei cader morta sull'attimo' and the expansive generosity of 'sotto il gran ponte del cielo' to the searing intensity of the suicide and Karajan's heart-rending last chord, the performance is quite tremendous. But there is more, much more, to Callas' interpretation and I could quote enough examples of her penetrating vision of what Butterfly means to fill the rest of the page. Let me suggest but three: the way she suggests at 'Ieri son salit tutta sola in segreto' (Act I) all Cio-Cio-San's absolute faith in following her destiny and forsaking her religion, the gentle simplicity of 'Mio marito m'ha promesso' and, a little later in Act II, at the end of 'Che tua madre' the impending tragedy of the repeated 'Morta!' Callas made this set when she was at the absolute peak of her vocal form and she is the mistress of every vocal change needed to express Butterfly's changing mood, even to the white, little girl timbre she uses in the first act, which sometimes sounds too twee; that and the sour D flat at the end of the Entrance are my only adverse criticisms of her interpretation. Karajan supports Callas at every turn of the drama with a tauter, more through-conceived direction than he brought to his later stereo version, where the slow tempo seems to have turned to self-indulgence and rhythmic flabbiness. But for once my heart was not in comparative listening. Whenever I turned away to test reactions to other sets, I longed to be back with Callas and Karajan, and blow recorded sound that is less than lustrious. Even on this occasion my old love Scotto and Barbirolli could not shake my new allegiance, although Scotto comes much nearer to Callas' very personal interpretation than does Freni, good as she is, taken in isolation too."[37]

Ten years later for the CD release we are back with J. B. Steane and his peroration on the incomparable greatness of Puccini's score and Callas' performance of it: "Like every other artist worthy of playing the role, Callas presents the development of the woman from the child. Where she is unusual, if not unique, is that she takes no exterior view of Cio-Cio-San (which then presents a pretty childlike vulnerability), but enters the girl and finds there not the weakness of childhood but the strength. There is a natural childlike shyness, a natural childlike impulsiveness, as well as hurt and trust. But the keynote is firmness of mind: a simple factuality which sees right and wrong with the clarity of that miraculously rinsed and lightened voice. Everything here is in place. For instance, in 'Un bel di' where, in his review of the recording when it first came out, Alec Robertson found the expectancy of 'Chi sara?' too casual, Callas feels the strength of the whole utterance as residing in the calm of certainty: Butterfly is re-telling what she so often has seen in her mind and she tells it with the clarity and factual sureness of a child, exact over the details of a favourite story."[38] Noel Goodwin in **Opera** had the courage to admit that he had not much sympathy with the work (how very sad) but was nevertheless appreciative of "the fetching quality of Callas' Butterfly which develops all the way from childlike simplicity (but without coyness) through trusting assurance to final tragic stature."[39] – a stature unaccountably and somewhat scandalously ignored in the **G.C.G.CD G.2000**.

Chapter Four

1955–56

AIDA RIGOLETTO LA TRAVIATA

AIDA

Only one opera now – Verdi's *Aida* – separated me from my own moment of truth with the same composer's *Rigoletto*. However, like *Madama Butterfly*, my appreciation of it was to be postponed while, in the wake of their *Trovatore*, I savoured the excitements of the Milanov/Bjorling *Aida* which was released about the same time. And neither I nor Philip Hope-Wallace were disappointed: "Glories and weaknesses summed up, I do think Milanov a finer Aida than either Tebaldi or Callas, with more variety, quality and tonal allure, even if no more drama than either of those ladies and something which at its best takes us right back to singers like Rethberg or Destinn."[1] This assessment is even more enthusiastically echoed by Harold Rosenthal in **Opera** who said that of the three available recordings it was "far and away the most satisfying musically and vocally, Milanov singing magnificently, with great feeling and beauty of tone."[2] He tells us that "Callas is not a born Aida – we knew after her stage performances in the role in London in 1953 and there are one or two really horrible notes; yet on the whole she gives a performance of the title role which for dramatic intensity and moments of heart-rending pathos can have few equals. Of course, we all know what Tebaldi can do with the music and what Milanov can also do with the arias; indeed, of those three ladies, only Milanov has a true Aida voice."[3] Philip Hope-Wallace is more ambivalent hovering between "ecstacy and irritation", and slightly preferring Tebaldi of the two. But he continues: "Callas is a great artist. I believe that any time she would be so considered and having recently heard her Lucia from the second row of the stalls, I aver that, faults or no faults, one is in the presence of a tremendous singing-artist whose will power and art are brandished at you in such a way that faults 'mean' nothing. Often in this Nile scene in the silence under the moon, she will caress a phrase as lovingly as Kreisler or Mischa Elman, fining her voice, colouring it, giving the words a heart-felt meaning which could – that hallmark of his histrionic genius – surprise us. There are dramatic points wonderfully brought off which Tebaldi, ever steady and appealing, hardly makes us notice. Yet Tebaldi is so much steadier and produces tone which is so infinitely more sympathetic that one cannot, in the long run and for repeated playing fail to prefer the suave Italian to the agitating American-Greek soprano. At least so say I, with my ears unable to rid themselves of the memory of the toppling yowl of Madame Callas' high A and high C, even if real tears stood in my eyes when she cried to Tito Gobbi :'Padre, son maladirmi; schiava non son', which is marvellous: an artist – but how incomplete."[4]

The passage of time has dealt rather more kindly than most with Callas' recorded Aida, its weaknesses receding as its essential strength and greatness grow. And rightly so because it was in a role like this that the truth finally dawned that, as Callas always maintained, a beautiful voice simply isn't enough.

Sharing a joke during the recording sessions of *Aida* at La Scala with Richard Tucker and Fedora Barbieri [August 1955]

Even in 1956, Dyneley Hussey of **Musical Times** recognised this: "The Scala *Aida*, directed by Tullio Serafin, is a great performance, splendidly recorded. Callas' dramatic power and her ability to shade the beautiful vocal line here find the best imaginable medium for their display and the occasional ugly tone which sometimes mars her singing is rarely heard. Apart from the high C in her opening scena, her singing in the third act and in 'Ritorna vincitor' can bear comparison with memories of Destinn, even to the silvery high A's."[5] These qualities were apparent later to Alan Blyth in his perceptive review in **Gramophone** at the first reissue in 1978: "When Callas makes her first entry in Act I I momentarily query her greatness with a voice so initially harsh and uninviting. I wonder if we have overdone the claims on her behalf since her death. As soon as she starts 'Ritorna vincitor', however, the estimates seem under rather than over the top. Here the much exposed aria, in which every prima donna has her fling, immediately lives afresh. Here at once is the slave-girl who is aware of her other identity as the king's daughter. Here is the young woman torn between love for her soldier and longing for her homeland. The hatred she registers in spitting out the words 'dell Egizie coorti', the change of colouring at 'Sventurata! che dissi', the obedience to the marking *triste* at 'I sacri nomi', the withdrawn quality of 'numi pietà', all illuminate the music, give it dramatic relevance in a way none of her successors (and few of her predecessors, let me add) has equalled. These instances of verbal and musical insights could be multiplied throughout a role with which the singer was not perhaps entirely happy on stage. To list them all would not only be tedious ... and I would point only to the sudden outburst of pride, asked for by Verdi, when she realises Amneris is her rival in their duet in Act II and the marvellous floating tone at 'O fresche valli' in 'O patria mia'. J.B. Steane has commented how Callas "yearns sadly" in this aria; in context, it is even more evident. Almost inevitably, above A, the voice develops an uncomfortable beat. That makes the high C near the end of this aria a trying experience, but all is at once forgotten when the final rising phrase F-C-A is also perfectly made."[6] He concludes that even with stereo versions under Muti, Leinsdorf, Solti and Karajan, the Callas mono recording tells us more about Verdi's greatness than any of them (an interesting observation on the composer's most spectacular work which I had the opportunity to relish first hand in my fruit-carrying professional debut with Amy Shuard and the Covent Garden touring company at the New Theatre, Oxford, only four years after this recording). Steane has no reason to retract one iota when the CD version comes up and is struck particularly by the vividness of the duets with Barbieri and Gobbi. For Max

Loppert in **Opera**, Callas' Aida is quite simply the most moving most completely characterised on record. At the 20th anniversary reissue, Michael Tanner agreed entirely that her portayal "is registered with unequalled fullness"[7] and for J. B. Steane it is one of her finest studio performances even if ultimately he were forced to part with all but one of Callas' Verdi recordings, he would (interestingly) take a drowning look at *Aida* and cling to *Un ballo in maschera*, – both of which are recommended in the **G.C.G.CD G.2000**: "The tensions between Aida, Radames and Amneris are rivetingly portrayed and explored and the gradual build-up to Aida's and Radames' union in death is paced with the sureness of a master composer. Callas' Aida is an assumption of total understanding and conviction; the growth from slave-girl torn between love for her homeland and Radames, to a woman whose feelings transcend life itself represents one of the greatest operatic undertakings ever committed to disc. Alongside her is Fedora Barbieri, an Amneris palpable in her agonised mixture of love and jealousy – proud yet human. Tucker's Radames is powerful and Gobbi's Amonasro quite superb – a portrayal of comparable understanding to stand alongside Callas' Aida. Tullio Serafin is quite simply ideal and though the recording cannot compete with modern versions (it was never, in fact, a model of clarity), nowhere can it dim the brilliance of the creations conjured up by this classic cast."[8]

It was, after all, one of the roles which Callas sang most – thirty-three performances between her debut in Turin in 1948 and her final appearances at the Verona Arena in 1953. It opened the Covent Garden Coronation Season on 4th June 1953 under Sir John Barbirolli. Three years earlier in Mexico City, Callas caused a sensation when she closed the Act II Triumph Scene with an interpolated E flat in alt: repeated the following year and not heard anywhere since.

* * *

RIGOLETTO

Thus it was in my young, untutored opera-loving days that the first ten complete Callas recordings were as ships that hardly passed in the night. That they were now to be transformed into mighty ocean-going liners of the first magnitude is thanks to the arrival of the eleventh – *Rigoletto*. The huge impression it made on me rendered it unlikely that I would attach even the slightest importance to any carping in **Gramophone**, **Opera** or anywhere else. But, assuredly, carping there was which in the cool light of nearly half a century must now be noted. This time Philip Hope-Wallace was more critical than Harold Rosenthal: both thought the Callas set superior to Decca with Hilde Gueden but the former was impressed by Erna Berger's beautifully tuned and stylish Gilda on HMV. No mention was made of that magnificent E flat with which Callas brought the second act to such a stunning conclusion. Instead "Callas' lightening and fining of her voice and also keeping it much steadier than usual, though not always illuminating that cupped up hooty tone, seems bent on showing restraint – her death is lovely. But her 'Caro nome' is all the same a much more elaborate and prima donna-ish affair than Erna Berger's. Not that she ever sounds bored or perfunctory; quite the contrary, a world of significance invests every syllable of the wonderful old aria. But where Berger opted for simplicity, Callas embroiders with extra trills and also that cadenza with the 'bird tweetings' at the top which always seems to me to hold up the dreamy flow of the aria and so spoil it. Nevertheless, as usual, some features of the agility of Callas' 'Caro nome', the glissandi and the span of some phrases on a single breath where an ordinary canary leggiero would merely peck, are so striking that once heard, this rendering is never likely to be forgotten."[9] No, indeed! For Harold Rosenthal, Callas is "intelligent, moving and musicianly. She lightens her tone and generally produces a girl-like quality of voice. The 'Caro nome' is done as a showpiece, but the 'Tutte le feste' and ensuing scene with Rigoletto is Callas at her best while the death scene is hardly less good."[10] Dyneley Hussey of the **Musical Times** did not agree: "It cannot be said that Callas' versatility really includes the qualities for a first-rate Gilda. Despite some lovely notes in the cadenza high up in the leger-lines, her 'Caro nome' sounds muscle-bound. She makes a good effect in the more dramatic moments but never really convinces one that this is the Gilda of Verdi's imagination."[11]

Alan Blyth commenting on the first reissue in 1976 is fairly receptive of Philip Hope-Wallace's strictures 20 years previously. "Gilda in Maria Callas' care is far from the usual pale innocent but a girl obviously infatuated with her supposed student. Her 'Caro nome' is (again) a performance once heard never forgotten, Gilda's rapture implicit in the strikingly articulated coloratura. The exchanges between father and daughter particularly in recitative passages are etched into the mind with the kind of vocal 'face' of which she and Gobbi are masters. On the other hand, where effortless legato is called for there is, as Philip Hope-Wallace pointed out exactly 20 years ago, this 'tendency to labour phrases which, with a perfect cantabile, should 'sing themselves' and the singers

"Io t'amo." Callas and di Stefano record *Rigoletto* at La Scala in September 1955

are hardly helped by Serafin's ponderous tempi. Here I sometimes prefer McNeil and Sutherland whom I praised here recently. Still for subtlety and feeling, Callas and Gobbi win hands down. If you doubt it, listen to the whole of the final scene, musicality and eloquence going hand in hand."[12] Harold Rosenthal maintained his earlier position by recalling some of Callas' laboured singing but also praises her duets with Gobbi. The temperature is very markedly upped by Alan Blyth for the CD release: "That one recording should continue to hold sway over many other attractive comers after 30 years is simply a tribute to Callas, Gobbi, Serafin and Walter Legge. Whatever the merits of its successors and there are many, no Rigoletto has surpassed Gobbi in tonal variety, line, projection of character and understanding of what Rigoletto is about; no Gilda has come anywhere near Callas in meaningful phrase nor achieved such a careful differentiation of timbre before and after her seduction; no conductor matches Serafin in judging tempo and instrumental detail to a nicety, nor benefited from a chorus and orchestra bred in the tradition of La Scala; no producer has equalled Legge in recording voices rather than the space around them. And di Stefano? Well, he may not be so stylish a Duke as Domingo and some others, but the 'face' he gives his singing, and the sheer physical presence he conveys, not to forget his forward diction, are also unique in the complete recordings of this opera."[13] The chief beneficiary from this review is Serafin whose conducting of the score had hitherto been variously described as slow and dull, stately and classical (1956), ponderous and plodding (1978). Noel Goodwin clinches it in **Opera**: "Callas becomes a young woman who grows up literally overnight and the difference between her singing of 'Caro nome' and 'Tutte le feste' is there to prove it, closely abetted by Serafin's incomparable feeling for pace and line."[14]

But J. B.Steane gave it only the classic recommendation in his Radio 3 **Building a Library** assessment in September 1996, though he described it in Gramophone a year later for the 20th Anniversary issue as "one of the most striking examples of voice adaptation on record, for Callas is not one of nature's Gildas."[15] She gave only two stage performances of the role – in Mexico City in 1952, which were not remarkable. But the recording most certainly is and it remains the top recommendation in the **G.C.G.CD G.2000**. Repeating the praise he lavished on the CD issue of the set in 1987, Alan Blyth concluded; "Nothing in this world is perfect and there are small drawbacks. Serafin sadly makes small cuts in the first Gilda/Rigoletto duet and omits entirely the Duke's cabaletta as used to be the practice in the theatre" – a fact which a hugely disappointed JB Steane in **Building a Library** failed to take on board. "Gobbi could be said not to have quite the weight of voice ideally called for by a Verdi baritone role. Finally, the recording although immeasurably improved from the previous issues of the set, still has one or two places of distortion obviously present on the original tape. In every other way, this remains a classic performance on record and one that should be on every Verdi collectors's shelf."[16]

⋆ ⋆ ⋆

LA TRAVIATA

The next issue in the Scala series, *La Traviata* (released in September 1956) caused a furore, the shock waves of which are still felt today. The greatest Violetta of her time and probably of the century, Callas performed the role 63 times in opera houses all over the world: Florence, Cagliari, Mexico City, São Paulo, Rio de Janeiro, Bergamo, Parma, Catania, Verona, Venice, Rome, Chicago, La Scala, New York, Lisbon, Covent Garden and Dallas. Yet from the EMI recording of 1955 conducted by Serafin with di Stefano and Tito Gobbi, Callas was missing. Philip Hope-Wallace, for one, could not guess why. The answer in fact was simple. She recorded the opera with Cetra in September 1953 which, under the terms of the contract, precluded her re-recording of the role for five years. Walter Legge of EMI, impatient to have his Scala *Traviata* available along with the many other versions on LP, could not, or would not wait until 1958 and went ahead without Callas. The repercussions were enormous. Although it wasn't Serafin's fault, she broke off relations with the conductor and did not sing under him again until 1957, in a concert performance of *Norma* at the RAI studios in Rome. The EMI recording with Antonietta Stella singing instead was not a success. Described by Philip Hope-Wallace as a young singer with a sumptuous voice, he found Stella as yet an immature artist with faults too numerous and impolite to list here. Harold Rosenthal in **Opera** thought she was "so dull" and Dyneley Hussey in **Musical Times**: "Never came within yards of being a good Violetta."[17] Nevertheless the set gave rise to a detailed comparison of available Violettas at the time – Albanese, Tebaldi, Carteri and Stella. It is highly significant, surely, that Desmond Shawe-Taylor in his **Gramophone** Quarterly Review opted for Stella: "The most radiant, the most truly Violetta-like timbre of all; and much of her singing is very beautiful, notably the floated and hushed opening of 'Dite alla giovine'....All in all, I would plump for this Columbia Traviata, though I cannot help hoping that some dazzling new Violetta will soon appear in the world to make my selection seem out of date."[18] Sadly and tragically, thanks to Walter Legge and EMI, he was to wait in vain. Taking place only three and a half months after Visconti's epic production at La Scala, the Columbia *Traviata* (which Legge, probably fearing the worst, left to the inexperienced Walter Jellinek) only added insult to injury. Di Stefano's Alfredo, having left in a huff after the first night on 28th May 1955, was back before the microphones on September 15th, alongside Tito Gobbi who, as was usually the case, had not participated. Of the singers, then, only Callas' Violetta, the great glory of the evening, was missing. So, of course, was the conductor, Carlo Maria Giulini, but he was not contracted for any of the EMI Scala recordings, whereas Serafin, ironically *persona non grata* within the theatre itself, emphatically was – business-as-usual, no less. The set has never been reissued in the UK, which speaks volumes, and is a waste of di Stefano and Tito Gobbi in two key roles. Worst of all, of course, is that a decent studio recording of Callas' great Violetta was never made. Possibilities there were in abundance, all squandered after her glorious Covent Garden performances in 1958 when she recorded [instead?] arias and scenes [albeit superbly], and in 1959 and 1960 when she made stereo versions of *Lucia*, *Gioconda* and *Norma*. Later as the years passed when a mature Callas Violetta became an urgent necessity, EMI did what they could with live performances in Lisbon and La Scala but the sound is so bad as to preclude any kind of safe recommendation *vis à vis* other versions, according to Michael Oliver in **Building a Library** (February 1998). Altogether it was a dreadful miscalculation, initially because coming over a year after her contract with EMI, the Cetra recording should never have been made in the first place and then later when EMI failed to make good this great hole in their catalogue.

Although the Cetra recording was eventually released in the UK over two years later in 1958, Desmond Shawe-Taylor got his hands on it in the summer of 1955 (just after the Callas/Visconti/Scala production in fact). He found it "on balance preferable to HMV (Carteri) and Decca (Tebaldi), though far from perfect. Mme Callas excels in the light conversational exchanges of the first act, in the poignant phrases of her dialogue with the elder Germont and in the last act, where it would be difficult to decide between her and Mme Tebaldi, for both here are deeply moving. Callas' florid singing is more accomplished than Tebaldi but it suffers from the occasional roughness and the unsteadiness on sustained high notes which are the familiar drawbacks of this most interesting singer. An example of the latter is the singing of the long high C's in 'Sempre libera' which are so uneven as to suggest a slow trill; on the other hand, Mme Callas negotiates one appallingly difficult bar near the end of Act I with a precision which I have never heard equalled, not even in the Melba or Sembrich versions of 1904 … the recording and orchestral playing (under Gabriele Santini) are first-rate."[19] It was also very warmly welcomed by Philip Hope-Wallace in **Gramophone** who acknowledged Callas' supremacy amongst available versions: "I doubt if anyone could rival her dramatic insight into the role. For one thing she has the extraordinary gift of vocal suggestion, to colour her voice to imply all the irony of the part;

Callas' January 1953 Violetta in Rome, with the baritone and tenor (Ugo Savarese and Francesco Albanese) of her Cetra recording later that year

where Violetta must pretend (so often the point) to be cheerful, pretend to be recovered when the wing of death has already stroked her, Mme Callas brings to it what Gerhardt brought to Brahms or Feuillère to Dumas. If all this is not part of *Traviata* as well as sumptuous sounds, then the opera is surely only a compendium of scrumptious tunes. I admit that Callas' voice really does let her down once or twice. One obvious point is the wonderful moment near the end of the second scene when she bids the puzzled Alfredo a passionate farewell (thinking to leave him for ever). The music pulses back and forth before suddenly soaring into the overture tune 'Amami, Alfredo'. The soprano has a tremendous chance to go 'all out' for sheer vocal grandeur. It is not forthcoming from this Callas-Violetta. But then, do any of the others (in complete versions, that is) begin to put so much meaning into fioriture, as in 'Sempre libera' in the first act or achieve such alternations of hectic gaiety and sudden pensive asides? Note, in the last act, the trill at the words 'Orason forte'. As for some of her phrasing, I can only hark back to my threadbare comparison with a master violinist; the reprise of 'Dite alla giovine' in the duet with Germont père or the apprehensive rise of the tune 'Che via? Morir mi sento', where she positively seems to wince at the dreadful situation. Very lovely, too, is her dominating of the ensemble with the big swinging line of 'Alfredo, Alfredo, di questo cor non puoi comprendere..' which concludes the unhappy evening party chez Flora; and as here Mme Tebaldi is also very beautiful, comparison again looms, for the latter soprano is technically surer. But is she so meaningful? Callas, as Mr Shawe-Taylor, I think, said, "sounds as if she had written the libretto herself". It is "only a waltz tune" to be sure; yet what feeling it carries. The final trio and death scene are very beautiful, too, but then so they are on Decca. You must decide for yourself: just as our parents and grandparents argued whether Bernhardt or Duse took the palm as *La Dame aux camélias*, so opinions will divide today. I shall put it thus: I find Tebaldi more beautiful and more moving in a conventional way, but Callas the more haunting."[20] But the supporting cast and conducting badly let her down and technically the recording was sub-standard, factors about which Hope-Wallace is too tolerant. Harold Rosenthal in **Opera** is more pragmatic: "There are many things Callas does superbly – the beginning of 'Dite alla giovine' is sung in a manner reminiscent of Melba; in fact, the whole of the Violetta/Germont scene is memorable for drama and feeling with which the soprano colours her words and phrases. The 'Amami, Alfredo' passage can seldom have been sung with such intensity; and the reading of the letter in the last act and the short passage after the 'Parigi o cara' duet is both thrilling and heart-rending. About 'Ah fors è lui and 'Sempre libera' I have reservations; and I am certain the bel canto lovers will find little satisfaction here."[21] He concludes his review by warning correctly that the Cetra is as good as you are likely to get. Unfortunately, it wasn't good enough.

At its first re-issue in 1973, Richard Osborne found "even from the first utterance, Callas' performance can hardly fail, at key points, to etch itself into the memory: the potent blend of brilliance and darker emotion in the whole of the first scene."[22] In its most recent reincarnation (March 2000), Alan Blyth reminds us yet again of the plodding conductor and insensitive male singers. "But all is not lost for in Act III Callas, relatively uninspired till then, rises above her surroundings to give us a death scene of poignancy, with her letter reading, 'Addio del passato' aria and final moments evincing all her gifts as a singing actress, and in better voice than either of her later renderings (Lisbon or 1955 Scala). With this transfer (Warner Fonit Cetra) in excellent sound at mid-price it's worth hearing, even if the shattering Violetta of 1955 and 1958 is not yet present elsewhere."[23]

Chapter Five

1956–57

LA SONNAMBULA
UN BALLO IN MASCHERA
IL TROVATORE

LA SONNAMBULA

The first Scala release in 1957 was Bellini's wonderful *La Sonnambula*. Nothing could have been more appropriate or ultimately ironic. Visconti, in their Scala production, had Callas look more like an exquisite ballet dancer than any kind of opera singer, her Amina full of grace and innocence. In all, she gave twenty-two performances at La Scala, and later in Cologne 'en route' to Edinburgh where the ghastly row over the 'fifth' Festival performance in this of all operas triggered off a series of crises which ended her operatic career and changed the course of her life. Her resentment against La Scala over

With the cast of *La sonnambula*, recording at the Basilica of Santa Euphemia [March 1957]

Edinburgh must have fired her exasperation over the Rome *Norma* debacle (in the New Year when she walked out of a Gala performance), the flames of which were eagerly fanned by an American society hostess and her wealthy Greek shipowner friend.

In his review of the recording in **Gramophone**, Andrew Porter wrote: "Here we have Callas' Amina which for two seasons has delighted audiences at La Scala and very wonderful it is. The voice is not perfect. There are once or twice hints of that second note underlying and sullying the proper one and there are some sharp, wobbly notes. But there is also much exquisitely beautiful singing – lovely tone, movingly tender phrasing, gloriously delicate and virtuosic moments such as at some awkward arpeggios in 'Sovra il sen'. I had used the words 'spellbinding and sublime art' about Callas' interpretation of the role. It is very intricate and fired by poetic intellect." He then quotes the composer's librettist on the subject of his heroine for all that he says is relevant to Callas' performance. "'Although it may seem at first sight easy to perform, it is perhaps more difficult than many others deemed more important. It calls for a singer-actress who is playful, ingenuous and innocent, and at the same time passionate, impetuous and affectionate: who has one cry for joy and another for sorrow, different timbres for reproof and for pleading; who displays in every movement, in every glance, every sigh, a certain stylisation mixed with realism'...and thus does Maria Callas perform it. I need hardly point out how strikingly she colours every phrase, note and word. After a couple of playings, almost every line of recitative sticks in the mind with the exact colour and expression that she gives to it". He then compares Callas with Pagliughi whose recording was released the same month, who in fact he finds altogether the more "playful, ingenuous and innocent heroine. Between them, perhaps, but not separately, they would embody the perfect heroine." Like Andrew Porter, both Dyneley Hussey and Harold Rosenthal attended the controversial Festival performances Callas gave that summer in Edinburgh against doctors' advice. The **Musical Times** critic noted "the many lovely details in her performance that make one forget her shortcomings in the actual quality of vocal tone."[2] Likewise, the editor of **Opera** (pictured right with the diva at the Festival) quickly overlooked the vocal difficulties there in the light of "the wonderful study she made of Amina in the recording."[3]

When the set was first reissued (in December 1978), Harold Rosenthal reminded himself and us of those very details which made her Amina so "subtle and appealing – a gazelle-like, pathetic figure, miles removed from Norma, Medea, Ifigenia and the rest; Callas creates a truly believable character.

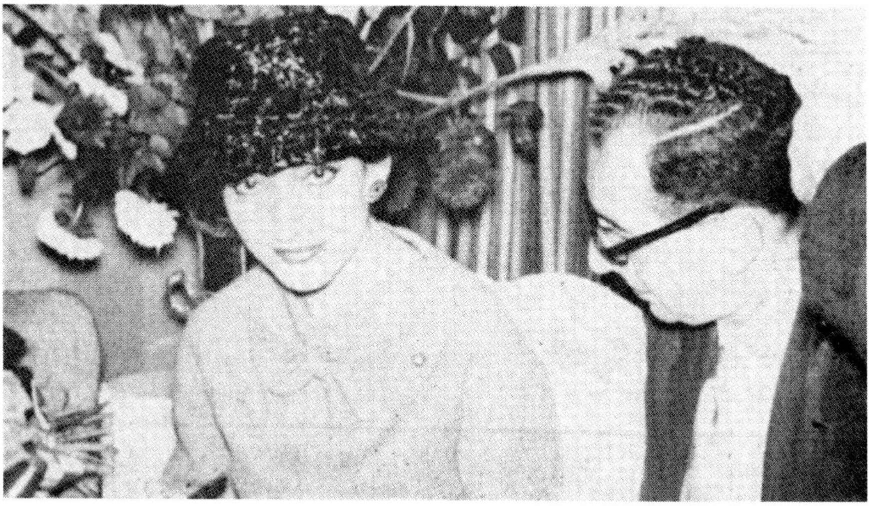

Harold Rosenthal with Maria Callas at the Edinburgh Festival, 1957

Her singing of 'Come per me sereno' in the first act is hauntingly beautiful, and indeed quasi-recitative passages, for example the few lines between Amina, Elvino and the notary before the latter draws up the wedding contract, showed just how she was able to invest seemingly unimportant words with dramatic intent. Listening to how she colours a phrase to her mother after being rejected by Elvino, injecting it with tragic meaning and the simple words 'L'annelo' tear at the heart strings."[4] He concludes that despite some mediocre support and conducting, the set is certainly not to be missed. Alan Blyth, in **Gramophone**, compares the studio reissue with the newly released Bernstein live performance of 1955. "They are very different interpretations in many respects, but in one they are similar, and that is in Callas' delicately moving account of the recitatives, particularly that before 'Ah! non credea mirarti'. The seeming hopelessness of her dream, 'Vana speranza' is touching indeed, and just as in the first scene, her little accentuation on the first syllable of 'tenero amore' speaks unmistakably of Amina's love and 'Il cor soltanto' of her faithfulness. These are treasurable moments in a treasurable reading, more relaxed than that for Bernstein two years before and thus possibly better suited to this little village near tragedy"; but, he adds, "I do miss the way Bernstein in the set pieces urges on Callas to ever greater flights of vocal fancy. There you feel the sadness that hits Amina when she is suddenly rejected by Elvino. I would say that she was also in marginally fresher voice in 1955 but the difference in that respect is definitely small and you here have, of course, the benefit of a clear recording."[5] Ten years later, Blyth was even more impressed because digital remastering highlighted the way Callas adapted her tone and manner to the heroine in hand. On CD, this effect was greater still. "We seem in the very presence of the shy, vulnerable Amina and the sequence of recitative in the second sleepwalking scene as Amina tries to capture her seemingly lost happiness is almost unbearably moving. Its key lies in the unique quality of Callas' voice and the apparently simple way she uses it. I doubt if even Pasta, the first Amina, could have made it so touching, and then 'Ah! non credea mirarti', the line so finely etched in piano, crowns one of the great operatic achievements of the gramophone. When we think of this singer's totally commanding and dramatic Tosca and Norma, this achievement is all the more remarkable."[6]

Little wonder it is a top recommendation in the **Gramophone Classical Good CD Guide 2000**, despite J. B. Steane's 1997 20th Anniversary qualms about the freshness of Callas' voice so essential to the role: "La Sonnambula, first performed in Milan in 1831, was once the most popular opera in England. Dramatically, it is a tepid mix which might be subtitled 'The Mistakes of a Night' if that did not suggest something more amusing than what actually takes place. Musically, the promise of a brilliant finale keeps most people in their seats until the end, and there are half-a-dozen charming, sometimes exquisite items on the way. But it is all a little insubstantial, and much depends upon the performance, especially that of the soprano. The name of Maria Callas is sufficient to guarantee that there will be a particular interest in the work of the heroine. As usual, her individuality is apparent from the moment of her arrival. Immediately, a character is established, not an insipid little miss, but a woman with a potential for tragedy. This is the pattern throughout and much has exceptional beauty of voice and spirit. Nicola Monti has all the sweetness of the traditional lyric tenor. Nicola Zaccaria sings the bass aria gracefully, and carrying off her small role with distinction is Fiorenza Cossotto at the start of her career. The orchestral playing is neat, the conducting (Votto) sensible, and the recording clear."[7]

The release of this recording, along with *Ballo* and *Trovatore* which followed later in 1957, however, all with Callas and two with di Stefano, prompted the Shawe-Taylor broadside reported on page 19. Not one of these he found wholly satisfactory: "Callas' singing in the Bellini is far superior to the unhappy performances which she gave at the end of the festival last year. It abounds in subtle touches and inflections on single phrases, even words; but the general effect is studied, not spontaneous, and altogether inferior to Pagliughi on the

Cetra set."[8] In fact, he prefers the Scala *Ballo* recording of the three and rejects the new Callas/Karajan *Trovatore* in favour of Milanov/Björling, like so many other critics of this period. It is now time to examine these.

⋆ ⋆ ⋆

UN BALLO IN MASCHERA

Stage and studio activity coincided again with the recording of *Un Ballo in Maschera.* Callas and di Stefano opened the 1957/8 season at La Scala in an epic production – their last collaboration. The obvious frisson between them is captured well on disc, even if the live event is more potent still. The EMI recording has enjoyed much, though not by any means, unanimous acclaim. J. B. Steane and Patrick O'Connor regard it as Callas' finest Verdi role on disc, and in June 1999, the set, well over 40 years old, was Hilary Finch's recommended version on Radio 3's **Building a Library**. But it got off to a rather poor start. Andrew Porter, who reviewed it in **Gramophone** was disappointed: "Callas brings all her dramatic power and imagination to the role of Amelia but I find her tone monotonous. It is constantly plangent and rather bitter. The dolent timbre is effective in 'Morro, ma prima in grazia' (though the last note wobbles), but there is no gentle tenderness, no floating beauty of sound to afford contrast. She is, however, very fine in the sotto voce warnings to Riccardo in the last scene."[9] Harold Rosenthal finds Callas at her best in "the more dramatic portions of the work especially her scenes with Gobbi. At other moment she sounds tentative and displays a lack of line in the great sweeping curves of Verdi's melodies."[10] Dyneley Hussey in **Musical Times**, for his part, thought Callas' "Amelia more successful than her Leonora"[11] in the *Trovatore* set out at the same time.

All three critics preferred Toscanini's recording for its vigour and vitality. But unexpectedly, Desmond Shawe-Taylor thought the new Scala set scored certainly in "richness of sound and general theatrical impact. Callas and di Stefano make a really exciting thing out of the love duet; and there is vein of gaiety and high spirits in this tenor which makes his Riccardo a more credible study than that of Jan Peerce."[12] Harold Rosenthal points out when the recording was first reissued in 1979, Votto (Callas' conductor) "worked with Toscanini at La Scala but gives little evidence of having learned anything of his mentor's fiery and dramatic approach to Verdi."[13] This, however, is in direct contrast to J. B. Steane's assessment at the same time in **Gramophone:** "In an unforgettable performance, a feature that I found I had forgotten was Votto's conducting. Sensitive in its feeling for rubato, it responds to the warmth of this most fervent score and it doesn't obtrude. At this date such virtues are gratefully acknowledged; especially the last, for I find that listening to modern operatic recordings can be like sitting in on a novel kind of production where a follow-spot moves to and fro between different sections of the orchestra. Here the spotlight focuses on the stage, and the opera unfolds with much vividness. With Callas and Gobbi in the cast, some exceptional dramatic power is assured, but in this opera the soprano and baritone stand on either side of the tenor and if di Stefano had not risen to the occasion the recording would have been seriously spoiled. Of course, he's not ideal: the first scene does not introduce through his voice a character of inherent nobility and dignity, and his singing style is still marred by his way of lifting up towards the high notes and of opening the tone out on uncovered, broad vowels. But he does give himself, heart and soul, to the role. His portrayal deepens, from the vitality of the opening of its smartly observed dotted notes, through the 'Di tu se fidele' in which he is more sensitive than most to the deeper moods, through the

All smiles for the recording of *Un ballo in maschera* at La Scala in September 1956, di Stefano and Callas with their conductor Antonino Votto

unforced laughter of 'E scherzo', the ardour of the love duet, to the great moment of renunciation before the last aria, where all is felt and nothing is cheapened. This is a stalwart performance. The real distinction of the set, however, remains the work of Callas and Gobbi. Here, too, there are a few limitations ... but the individuality and strength of vocal character make the Library Scene, for example, intensely memorable as in no other recording of the opera."[14]

This turn-around is not untypical of what has happened to many Callas recordings over the years – *Rigoletto, Aida, Norma, Tosca.* Initially, a rather sceptical 'Fifties warmed up in the 'Seventies to a positively glowing 'Eighties and 'Nineties. Alan Blyth, on the CD version, now grasps the lead offered by Steane with a vengeance: "This reissue of *Ballo* is a welcome reminder of the special qualities of its principals. Votto has been underrated as its conductor; his direction has a truly Verdian elan. This is one of Callas' most compelling assumptions. Certain phrases ... remain uniquely accented and convincing. Her Amelia has more character, presence and sheer spinto quality than that of rival sopranos. With di Stefano and Gobbi, all three principals are superior to their successors in creating the tension of a live performance against a studio one. In that respect, this is the recording I have always turned to most often, in preference to sets conducted by Abbado and Solti."[15] We have already noted that J. B. Steane in the 20th Anniversary issue chose Callas' Amelia as his favourite of all her Verdi complete sets. Michael Tanner felt much the same: "*Ballo* needs a heroine who can go berserk and also express the most tender emotions ... Callas is incandescent, again partnered by di Stefano and Tito Gobbi, each of them in roles in which they surpassed all competition."[16]

In addition to the **Building a Library** recommendation, it is the historical choice in the **G.C.G.CD G.2000**: "*Ballo* manages to encompass a vein of lighthearted frivolity (represented by the page, Oscar) within the confines of a serious drama of love, infidelity, noble and ignoble sentiments. None of the more recent recordings has quite caught the opera's true spirit so truly as this one under Votto's unerring direction. Callas has not been surpassed in delineating Amelia's conflict of feelings and loyalties, nor has di Stefano been equalled in the sheer ardour of his singing as Riccardo. Add to that no less a singer than Tito Gobbi as Renato, at first eloquent in his friendship to his master, then implacable in his revenge when he thinks Riccardo has stolen his wife. Fedora Barbieri is full of character as the soothsayer, Ulrica, Eugenia Ratti a sparky Oscar. It is an unbeatable line-up."[17]

★ ★ ★

IL TROVATORE

Hardly was the ink dry on *Ballo* when another Verdi opera appeared, and not just another but my early favourite, *Il trovatore*. Of course, I could not readily contemplate it ousting my first love, Milanov, until ... until, sitting in Wakefield market in the 'Sixties with a record programme on the car radio, 'D'amor sull'ali rosee', begun by Leontyne Price and then taken over by Callas' art. Another defining moment of truth. With her stunning 'Tu vedrai' which followed, all arguments were over as J.B. Steane was to confirm much, much later in 1997. Callas' great Verdi roles all have slavish admirers: Aida, Amelia, Gilda, Violetta, the *Forza* Leonora. But for me, her *Trovatore* Leonora is incomparable and always will be. And I am not alone. First, Philip Hope-Wallace in **Gramophone**: "The role of Leonora is one in which I have much admired Mme Callas. Her assumption is that of a great lady, as it should be; and in the two big arias I have heard her phrase the music like a virtuoso violinist with a mastery which marked her off from most other Leonoras of the common sort. Most of that grandeur is evident in this recording. But to enjoy Mme Callas you have – if I may commit an Irishism – to like her in the first place. If you can accept that half-closed throat and the occasional curdling skirls and a sagging beat on the top notes, all will seem magical. She again brings to the most hackneyed music a gift of recreating it as if it were being sung for the first time. She feels a sense of words as, for example, neither Tebaldi nor Milanov seem to sense them at all. On the other hand, considered from a purely tonal angle, the purely sensuous side of her singing offers little here to compare with the ravishing sounds which issue from their Leonoras. But the actual spanning and placing of the phrases are lovely and in the rapid and difficult cabaletta to 'Tacea la notte' Mme Callas who is far more nippy with her shakes and gruppetti, though sticking to a fairly safe pace, shows up as a much more practised coloratura singer than either of her rivals. In the scene with the count which comes after the Miserere, Mme Callas is altogether astonishing in her realisation of the drama in her dynamic phrasing, making her rivals sound really like also-rans in a steeplechase. Altogether, provided you like Mme Callas' strange vocal production, you are likely to forget the other two 'complete' Leonoras. Only in one place does she a little disappoint me; that is in her moment of amazement in the Convent scene, 'E deggo – e posso crederlo?,' not nearly as thrilling as expected. But the working up of the ensemble thereafter is exceptionally clear on this new issue. Indeed I do not recall a *Trovatore* in which so many of the words came through so clearly."[18]

A break from recording *Trovatore* at La Scala in August 1956 for Legge, Callas, Panerai and Barbieri

Harold Rosenthal is similarly impressed: "Callas has always been an outstanding Leonora and here her aristocratic performance reaches truly tragic heights in the last act. Probably for the first time in living memory, the Leonora remains with Manrico during the singing of 'Di quella pira' and she sings a few bars between the two verses of that aria."[19] Desmond Shawe-Taylor being his more predictable self was less impressed: "*Il trovatore* is very masterfully directed by a first-rate conductor, Herbert von Karajan ... but not all Karajan's virtues can alter the truth that, in Verdi, singers count more than conductor; the splendid tone and noble style of Björling and Milanov outweigh, I feel, the relatively dull conducting of that set."[20]

Twenty years later Rosenthal rather curiously attributes the reissue of this and other Callas recordings to the 1973/74 world tour with di Stefano; maybe though he does so for personal reasons to enable him to atone for his unkind observations on the condition of her voice at that time. He overlooked the fact that the reissues started with *Tosca* before the tour started. Be all that as it may, Rosenthal again reminds us that Callas' Leonora is "one of her truly great and aristocratic assumptions. The tragic overtones she brought in the 'Fifties to the heroine especially in the last act, plus Karajan's similar way with the music, combine to shed a new light on this old warhorse."[21] Alan Blyth in **Gramophone** is equally impressed: "One has to go no further than the lovely floated passage 'Come d'aurato sogno' in her first act entrance to be reminded of just what Callas' magic was really like: an ideal shaping of the Verdian phrase, a full, vibrant, expressive instrument to execute the thoughtful phrasing. Admittedly, as the succeeding aria shows, the tone was never entirely sweet or properly equalised throughout its register; instead there was an instinctive feeling for the matching of text and music, a distinct presence felt, even on records conveyed, even in the cold of studio."[22] On CD in 1987, Richard Osborne, Karajan's biographer, pays tribute to "that charismatic duo, Callas and Karajan, whose rare acts of co-operation took the world by the ears in the 1950s. Leonora was one of Callas' finest stage roles and this recording is wonderfully intense, with a dark concentrated loveliness of sound in the principal arias that puts one in mind of Muzio and Ponselle at their best. Walter Legge always managed to team Callas with the right conductor for the work in question. Often it was Serafin, but Karajan in *Trovatore* is as compelling a prospect as de Sabata in *Tosca*."[23] J. B. Steane in the 1997 20th Anniversary re-issue nearly overlooks its compulsive greatness until the cabaletta 'Tu vedrai' and all that follows in the last act.

Callas gave twenty performances of this great Verdi role, whose haunting melancholy suits the diva to perfection. Her debut in Mexico City in 1950 was sensational and her ravishingly poised singing transfixed audiences in Naples, La Scala, Covent Garden and Chicago, where in 1955 her partner, Jussi Björling rated her the finest Leonora of all. The recording made a year later fully justifies its top recommendation in **G.C.G.CD G.2000:** Richard Osborne reiterates his 1987 tribute to Callas' Leonora and adds: "This opera is one of music's great essays in sustained rhythmic intensity; dramatically it deals powerfully in human archetypes. All this is realised by the young Karajan with that almost insolent mastery of score and orchestra which made him such a phenomenon at this period of his career. There are some cuts, but equally some welcome inclusions (such as the second verse of 'Di quella pira', sung by di Stefano with his own unique kind of slancio). Although the EMI sound is very good, one or two climaxes suggest that in the heat of the moment, the engineer, Robert Beckett, let the needle run into the red and you might care to play the set in mono to restore that peculiar clarity and homogeneity of sound which are the mark of Legge's finest productions of the mono era. But whatever you do, don't miss this set."[24]

Chapter Six

1957–58

IL BARBIERE DI SIVIGLIA LA BOHÈME LA SCALA RECITAL TURANDOT LA GIOCONDA

IL BARBIERE DI SIVIGLIA

Earlier in 1956, the year that produced these miracles from the studio, Callas experienced her only failure on stage – Rossini's *Il Barbiere di Siviglia* at La Scala. Used to the loving care afforded by Visconti, Zeffirelli, Margherita Wallmann and others, this production, even with Giulini in the pit, didn't work. The distinguished cast, including Luigi Alva, Tito Gobbi, Nicola Rossi-Lemeni and Melchiorre Luise, were left fatally to their own devices. Happily, this was put absolutely right in the studio early in 1957 and released a year later. On the threshold of the stereo age, the recording had the extra advantage of the Kingsway Hall's lustrous acoustic, with London's Philharmonia Orchestra

Tito Gobbi and Luigi Alva listen as Callas makes a point during a recording session of *Il Barbiere di Siviglia* at the Kingsway Hall, London (February 1957)

in attendance. Philip Hope-Wallace, who believes a *Barber* needs to be seen as well as heard, welcomed it somewhat caustically: "Madame Callas, to whom tragic scorn and resignation come easily, is at home also in Rossinian comedy and can be very funny, as in *Il Turco*. She elects to make Rosina, not a minx, and certainly not a canary, but rather a sly boots, a puss cat whose 'Dunque io son' for instance positively purrs where others flute or trill." But what this recording fails to do, he says, is sparkle. "When we first hear Callas singing, very gingerly indeed, as though in agonies not to sing sharp, it can hardly be called a thrilling foretaste. The voice sounds dull and tired and her little scream of surprise occurs after the window has been slammed shut. Callas' 'Una voce' is sung, not in the soprano version in F, but in the original mezzo which takes the diva down to rather hollow caverns and ends, as if to put her stamp on the disc, with a sour wobbler. Her rendering is the antithesis of a showpiece. Rosina is here communing with herself, in a reverie, almost humming into the microphone and cooing as gently as a dove. It is slow, unflashy very nearly perfect in staccato ornaments (though not quite) and though I felt terribly disappointed at first not to get the lift which a glittering Rosina can here give you, I could see that it might grow on you and make other Rosinas later sound like vacuum-brained minxes."[1] In his review of the stereo version a year later, Hope-Wallace said that he felt exactly the same about the set as before: "Callas is the most calculating of Rosinas, often brilliant, clever and witty, but without much gaiety, real spontaneous gaiety. She also does the things she often does; following passages of radiant violin-like phrasing with curdled, hollow or wavering and ill-supported singing."[2] On balance, I would say that her Rosina is indeed growing on the critic!

Harold Rosenthal is more impressed, saying it is easily the best *Barber* to date, if not entirely satisfactory: "The ever versatile Callas makes a clever, calculating Spanish minx of the part. Her singing of all the recitatives and her big duet with Figaro 'Dunque io son' are the highlights of her performance. 'Una voce' is sung in the mezzo key and is not treated as a display piece for the prima donna; and in the lesson scene we have what the composer wrote."[3] Alan Blyth in **Opera** at its first reissue is conscious of some of the irritations of the Scala performance still showing through in the EMI recording. "But her singing, qua singing," he continues, "is some of the most accomplished even she has ever committed to disc. I think particularly of the way she plays with phrases and the fioriture in the duets, and her stupendous cadenza to 'Contro un cor'. In his original review, Harold Rosenthal remarked that she sang the 'Una voce' and the lesson scene in the mezzo key, which is true, but she often varies the vocal line to suit herself when the original notes lie too low. Indeed one could fairly describe it as a Callas edition, neither one thing nor the other. Such textual points matters little when her performance is so full of verve and spirit."[4] In **Gramophone**, J.B. Steane is warmer still; he finds Callas as superb in comedy as she is supreme in tragedy. "Her Rosina shows its character in small things as in great. An incidental 'Perché' in recitative is stamped with individuality as is the 'dolce amorosa' of the big aria."[5] The whole set he finds delightful in every respect. With the CD in 1987, Noel Goodwin in **Opera** sees Callas' Rosina as a mite controversial because Callas "never for a moment seeks the soubrettish approach. She prefers to convey a shrewdness of intention as to the young lady's future which turns to honey at the allure of Alva's youthful Almaviva."[6] And who wouldn't asks Alan Blyth in **Gramophone** who finds Callas' portrayal "has mellowed. Even though the diablerie can still be felt, even in a line of recitative as it should be, this Rosina can melt sweetly." He rejoices at this thirty-year-old set which is sung and played with such character, and recorded so naturally which "only goes to point up its excellence in all departments, masterminded by the irreplaceable Walter Legge."[7]

Ten years later, for 1997 anniversary, Michael Tanner notes her glorious sense of mischief, expressed in superb timing, especially in the recitatives. J. B. Steane applauds her "comic mastery, delighting (no doubt) in the exercise of woman's power, relishing a game in which she is to be an expert player. This is the spirit that informs her Rossini recordings. Here in *Il Barbiere* she shows mastery of the deadpan poker-face that gives nothing away and her 'Una voce poco fa' has a lovely example of the comedian's art of switching off the smile ' ... ma!'"[8]

* * *

LA BOHEME

The startling versatility of Callas' art sustained another twist in her next portrayal. Even those who now accepted a Lucia/Tosca/Rosina all in one might well have been caught napping with the arrival of her Mimi. In the celebrated hands of Tebaldi, de los Angeles with Beecham or even Toscanini's Albanese, wouldn't this be one Callas part too many, with her distaste for Puccini and no appearance in the role on stage? But that's to reckon without her genius and Harold Rosenthal welcomed the Columbia *La Bohème* as the most completely satisfying of all. Other voices, he said, are the more obvious choice for this music but "Callas is Mimi and her sensitivity and feeling for words and phrases create for us a fragile, moving character."[9] This is absolutely echoed in **Gramophone** by Philip Hope-Wallace: "The quality at the top (of the voice) is here rubbed bare of all bloom; she does not seem to be able to soar as de los Angeles can and, if that is something you demand of a Puccini heroine, then Callas may disappoint you. Under pressure, all the spinto roles in fact show the usual tendency to beat or hover. But how richly does this singer make amends – by sensitivity of another sort, by the luminous meaning she gives to the words (all crystal clear which you can't say of de los Angrles) and a variety of tonal nuances she gives to the detail (superior in that to the unchanging beauty of Tebaldi). No blurting mars this brilliantly realised brilliant Mimi; no conventional vocal pathos at, say, 'Sono andati' on the death-bed (and why should that statement be made in a voice ringing with drama, yet it nearly always is?) The absolute sense of fitness which goes into her contribution to the wonderful pattern which makes up the supper at the Cafe – the tone is like a wonderful oboist, endowed with speech, and at a hundred tiny points of characterisation, this Mimi comes alive and later haunts you in a most extraordinary way. As against that if you want a pure welling up of tone – as distinct from some subtle artful diminuendo – you won't get it. She is at her squalliest, and Votto at his slowest, in the Mimi-Marcello duet near the start of Act 3. The last notes of a marvellously feeling yet unsentimental 'Addio di Mimi' would have given Melba a fit, so wavering are they; and yet I found Callas' Mimi one of the most moving I have ever heard."[10]

Edward Greenfield had the pleasure 20 years on of comparing both Callas and Tebaldi reissues, the latter being the Italian diva's stereo version which had superseded the original mono, the first Italian opera ever to appear on LP. The mono Callas, he said, was "a tribute to the enduring qualities of what is on any count one of the most strikingly individual portraits of Mimi ever put on record. You may say that it is simply Callas scaling down a flashing-eyed personality to suit the character of Puccini's archetypal little woman. But Act 3 will tell you far more than that. It is an extraordinary example of Callas the supreme singing actress, agonisingly intense from her first solo onwards, until after a superbly shaded 'Addio', the quartet starts rather fast and relatively light, with Callas magnificently conveying the heroine's drained emotions, the momentary consolation of temporarily returning to Rodolfo wonderfully touched in."[11] Rodney Milnes in **Opera** prefers the "sheer sensuousness of Tebaldi's singing to Callas' steady, if less than seductive voice, even though she makes much of the conversational exchanges after 'O soave fanciulla' and all of the last act."[12]

Two further critics in **Gramophone** and **Opera** greet Callas' Mimi with renewed enthusiasm when it appeared on CD. First Michael Oliver:"Mimi was not an obvious role for Callas and she knew better than to attempt a girlish charm or naive innocence that were not in her repertory (that was second nature to Beecham's de los Angeles). One misses those qualities in the first two acts, passionately and beautifully sung though they are, but in the Third and Fourth she is incomparable: a great singing actress at the height of her powers. Time and again she makes one realise how full Act Three is of poignantly recollected intimacies: remembering how she felt Rudolfo's gaze on her as she pretended to sleep beside him; recalling her bonnet, his gift, left under their pillow; even in the two syllables with which she asks whether he is sleeping 'Dorme?' – all these are so filled with expressive inflection, yet without a hint of studied effect, that the entire act is wrenchingly pathetic. And the final scene is built of no less beautifully observed details: the shy

Musetta with Mimi for the recording of *La boheme* at La Scala in August/September 1956.
Anna Moffo, with Maria

smile of greeting to the other Bohemians, the wisdom of a woman who has learnt much in a very brief while in her recognition of the flighty Musetta's essential goodness, the fining down of the voice to murmur as she asks Rodolfo if he still remembers their first meeting."[13] And Max Loppert: "Callas' Mimi demands and rewards the closest attention. Extraordinary how she could scale down to the Mimi of Acts 1 and 2 without ever sounding dainty or quaint – if we expect here a lusher, more placid quality of voice and personality, a less vibrant alertness of response, may this not be simple force of habit? Act Three is, of course, more natural territory for the singer's dramatic powers yet every phrase is kept in scale with what has been established about Mimi earlier in the performance. Callas' gift for welding musical and dramatic detail of previously unsuspected expressive potential proves just as enthralling in her Mimi as in her 'real' roles. The ability, for instance, to imbue names with a special current of meaning makes something new and wonderful of 'Mi chiamano Mimi, ma il mio nome e Lucia': in the weighting and accenting of that line, in the different caress given to the utterance of those two names, the whole character flares to life."[14] Finally, in 1997 J.B. Steane paid tribute to her special identity with the role: "Far more than a dutiful lightening of voice is involved in the creation of this gentle but full-hearted Mimi."[15] Competition from the classic Beecham and 1972 stereo Karajan sets, however, proved too strong to warrant a **G.C.G.CDG.2000** recommendation.

* * *

CALLAS AT LA SCALA

Out of the blue, Andrew Porter gave a warm welcome to a "wonderful" La Scala recital which "not only gives us Callas at her most spell-binding and enthralling, but also four beautiful arias not otherwise obtainable in the British catalogues" – Italian too, in all probability, he might have added as *La Vestale* was a curiosity, even at the Scala. After rehearsing at length Ponselle's supremacy in this area, he found Callas "perhaps not quite so superb; the tone misses the mysterious beauty of Ponselle's. But then Callas is superb too; makes much more of the words; and certainly characterises 'Tu che invoco' more fully, more intensely. She is magnificent in the dramatic and tender passages which follow, that Ponselle did not record."[16] Of the *Medea* aria, he found it an "exciting" preview of the complete recording to be released three months later. The *Sonnambula* and *Puritani* scenes from the complete recordings he found predictably

33CX1540

enticing. In **Opera**, Harold Rosenthal echoed these sentiments entirely: "It is for the *Medea* and *Vestale* excerpts that Callas admirers will want this disc ... the *Medea* excerpt whets our appetite for the forthcoming complete recording. Callas makes the Act 1 scena here both moving and exciting. In the *Vestale* excerpts Callas has real dramatic intensity and feeling for words. Her performance of the dramatic section of 'O Nume Tutelar' is magnificent – possibly the best thing she has done on disc so far"[17] – praise indeed! Thirty years later when the arias appeared on CD, Alan Blyth said that "'Dei tuoi figli' has more dramatic feeling in her accounts of the complete opera. But there are classic examples in 'O Nume tutelar' of her refined and intimate mezzo voce line, like no one else's, and all the *La vestale* items show just how moving and tender her stage portrayal of Giulia must have been"[18] – sadly, in the absence of a good studio recording, we will never know.

Indeed, far more important is what the critics didn't, and probably couldn't, say about this disc at the time of its release in June 1958, that 'high noon' of Callas' career when, very ominously, regular stage appearances and complete recordings suddenly became things of the past, following the diva's traumatic break with La Scala. To begin with, the four arias were recorded three years previously, along with the two *Sonnambula* arias the release of which Callas refused to sanction, and rightly so. They did not appear until a year after her death. J. B. Steane found the Act I aria "often rather preferable to the performance Callas gave in the complete set, rather more relaxed...taken with easier, fresher vocal quality",[19] as did Alan Blyth, who found "particularly wonderful the articulation of the recitative to 'Ah non credea', the very epitome of the sad, apparently maligned Amina. In 'Ah, non giunge', though, she is a trifle careful. Comparison with the confident, free account of the Bernstein performances at La Scala shows just how much happier the voice could sound in stage performance, studio inhibitions turned aside."[20] Reviewing them on CD in 1987, J. B. Steane considered "the recitatives masterclasses in themselves, though (to him, too) it seems a shame that we are left with an oddly formal, even severe 'Ah, non giunge'".[21] Serafin's cautious editing is tame beside Votto's complete recording, and at least we have that! *La Vestale* was not so lucky;

three arias were more than enough for Walter Legge which was just about all he would later come up with for *Macbeth*, *Anna Bolena*, *Il pirata*, *Nabucco*, *Don Carlos* and *Ifigenia* – all sung gloriously complete by Callas on stage. Callas' is a great recorded legacy, but it could, and should, have been greater still.

★ ★ ★

TURANDOT

With three Puccini roles now recorded with such distinction, Walter Legge was keen to complete the cycle with *Turandot* and *Manon Lescaut*. This was duly accomplished in 1957. *Turandot* was the first to be released, a fiendishly difficult part with which Callas enjoyed much success in her early career – too much so it might be said because, after 24 performances in 18 months, she wisely abandoned it. Resurrecting it in the studio must have revived many memories, not least her three-month trip to Argentina in 1949, embarking on the very day she married Battista Meneghini, to sing the icy Princess in the Teatro Colon in Buenos Aires. Her fiery dramatic instincts gave the role a special distinction, recognised at once by Harold Rosenthal: "Turandot is a Callas role par excellence. Although there may have been Turandots with larger, more steely and powerful voices than this, I doubt whether any soprano has invested the part with more authority or just that right mixture in imperiousness and coldness that combine to make the character one of the most difficult to portray in all opera. As is usual with a Callas performance, phrase after phrase takes on a new meaning, and the posing of the riddles has a terrifying calculation about it."[22]

Philip Hope-Wallace, however, is at his most equivocal: "Madame Callas has her own exciting qualities, but lacks steel girder strength and steadiness in the taxing upper ranges of the appalling address 'In questa reggia' before the riddle-posing. The timbre is sometimes hollow and plummy in the easier positions; the emission is wavering and sounds both strained and ill-supported in the upper reaches; and her Turandot is here, to my ear, totally unsatisfying – no matter how often elsewhere I may applaud this and that stroke of dramatic truth and imagination. Many people have been looking forward to Madame Callas' Turandot just because something infinitely aristocratic and tragic, inherent in the timbre of the voice at its best, makes one want to hear her interpretation of the ice-bound princess: and, to be sure, by the same token, all she does is memorable whether for good or ill. I do not necessarily think that the role needs ultra heroic treatment in the manner of Eva Turner... with clarion tones and tireless 'top'. I am perfectly prepared to accept a frailer, gentler icemaid: if only the actual vocal means could seem secure. Of the acting ability – vocally imaginative enunciation of the text – there is never a doubt; the scene between princess and slave where Turandot asks what it is which gives Liù strength is marvellously 'real' and subtle; and in the Alfano pastiche parts which bring this unfinished opera to a conclusion of sorts, Madame Callas brings her own interesting personality sharply to bear, adding stature to the diminishing dramatic interest. But if it's secure and grand singing you want in this role, I have to say that I think you will do better to seek elsewhere."[23]

By 1979, when this recording was first reissued, there were attractive alternatives, including Joan Sutherland and two by Birgit Nilsson but both Alan Blyth in **Opera** and Edward Greenfield in **Gramophone** respectively remained loyal. Blyth: "Callas' performance in Act II, though evidently one that taxed her resources even by 1957 to the limit, is one of her greatest. She tells the unhappy story of Lo-u-ling with such immediacy that you feel that she has been justified in her frigid reaction so far to all men; then she builds the narration to a searing climax by the usual intensity of her tone, and her fury at the Prince's solving of the riddles is truly frightening, as is her insistence on the torturing of Liù."[24] Greenfield: "The start of 'In questa reggia' brings a sudden generation of electricity that has one gasping but hearing this riveting performance afresh has brought it home to how much it is Serafin's *Turandot* as well. His electrifying energy owes much to the influence of Callas, even in scenes that the icy princess does not take part. And she herself sounds at her most incisive and compelling. In the theatre, the role must have imposed an almost intolerable strain on the voice. But on record there is no doubt about it: despite the very occasional unsteadiness on top, it is one of her greatest roles. Her singing time and again implants an unforgettable nuance on well-known phrases to make them her own for ever."[25] The same critic was even more impressed with the CD version when it was released in November 87: "To have Callas the most flashing-eyed of all sopranos as Turandot is – on record at least – the most natural piece of casting. Other sopranos may be comparably icy in their command, but Callas with her totally distinctive tonal range was able to give the fullest possible characterisation. With her, Turandot was not just in implacable man hater but a highly provocative female. One quickly read something of Callas' own underlying vulnerability into such a portrait, its tensions, the element of brittleness. Equally, in the final arioso of

Alfano's completion, 'Del primo pianto', the chesty way she sings 'Straniero' in the opening phrase, addressing Calaf, is unforgettable in its continuing threat. With her the character seems so much more believably complex than with others. It is sad that, except at the very beginning of her career, she felt unable to sing the role in the opera house but this 1957 recording is far more valuable than any memory of the past and, for me, one of the most thrillingly

Due prima donne: Liù and Turandot [Schwarzkopf and Callas] at the Scala recording in July 1957

magnetic of her recorded performances."[26] Max Loppert in **Opera** was likewise transfixed: "From the first, her Turandot's psychological make-up develops a startling intensity and depth of colour. After countless hearings of the Scala set and now again in its new CD format, I find such small features emerging and re-emerging in ways that can only reaffirm Callas' incandescent artistry, her genius. For me, it has long been, and on re-issue remains the first choice version; altogether the spacious zestfulness of its big moments has not been equalled."[27] All this is a far cry from Jeremy Sams' facetious remarks on Radio 3's **Building a Library** on 29th May 1998: "She doesn't really have the vocal big guns but her psychology and poetry score highly with a marvellously controlled palette of colours at the start of 'In questa reggia', showing compassion towards her ancestors, horror at her predecessor's scream and disgust at Calaf. But the top of the voice loses its fingertip control and she sounds like any other wobbly old soprano."[28] Again, 'chacun à son goût'. A year earlier for the 20th Anniversary issue, J. B. Steane, commenting on her recorded Puccini roles, thought that he "could let Turandot go, for those unstinting high notes are hard work for singer and listener alike; yet, along with those, would be lost probably the most thoughtful, least 'set', characterisation on record."[29] It remains the historical recommendation with Sutherland's stereo version in **G.C.G.CD G.2000**, where Edward Greenfield repeats his 1987 appreciation of "Callas' magnetic Turandot amply supported by Elisabeth Schwarzkopf's comparably characterful and distinctive portrait of Liù, far more than a Puccinian 'little woman', sweet and wilting. Even more than usual one regrets that the confrontation between princess and slave is so brief. Next to such supreme singers it was perhaps cruel of Walter Legge to choose so relatively uncharacterful a tenor as Eugenio Fernandi as Calaf but at least his timbre is pleasingly distinctive. What fully matches the singing of Callas and Schwarzkopf in its positive character is the conducting of Serafin, sometimes surprisingly free, but in its pacing invariably capturing rare colour and atmosphere and mood as well as dramatic point. The Ping, Pang and Pong episode of Act 2 has rarely sparkled so naturally, the work of a conductor who has known and loved the music in the theatre over a long career. The conducting is so vivid that the limitations of the mono sound hardly seem to matter. As the very opening will reveal, CD makes it satisfyingly full-bodied. Though with its rich, atmospherics stereo the Mehta set remains the best general recommendation, it is thrilling to have this historic document so vividly restored."[30]

★ ★ ★

LA GIOCONDA

Callas' great career had opened on 2nd August 1947 in the Verona Arena where she sang *La Gioconda*. It was there that she met Tullio Serafin, her conductor, who was to have such a huge influence on her career, principally in terms of her artistry and repertoire but also initially in finding her some work. A young Greek-American in post-war Italy was not likely to be anyone's first choice and the great Italian maestro coached her Isolde, Aida, Norma and Brunnhilde and most significantly, of course, her Elvira in *I puritani*. This splendid start made it likely that Gioconda, a role she sang a total of thirteen times, would always have a particular place in her heart and it was indeed her first complete recording – on the Cetra label in September 1952. It did not reach British shores until 1958. Of our two friends in **Gramophone** and **Opera**, Harold Rosenthal was by far the more enthusiastic: "The set dates back some six or so years to the time when Callas had only recently forsaken Wagner and Turandot, and was still singing Aida and Gioconda frequently. It

In Verona [July 1952], Maria with her husband, Battista Meneghini, for the Arena performances of *La gioconda*. She committed it to disc a month later for Cetra in Turin [her first complete recording]

also dates back to the days when her voice was larger, but her art had not reached the refined stage that was later to become its hallmark. Callas has always, however, possessed that feeling for words, that vibrancy and urgency which make her interpretations exciting and interesting; and what she does with this famous old warhorse is a revelation. Her last act duet with Barnaba contains some of her most exciting singing-acting on disc."[31]

In 1952 at the time of the recording and its release in Italy, Desmond Shawe-Taylor also referred to it favourably in his Quarterly Review (January 1954) vis à vis a recent performance of *Gioconda* in New Orleans by another famous interpreter of the role – Zinka Milanov. Hearing the last act of the Cetra set, he found it "most interesting to compare the very different handling of the music – the high point, by the way, of Ponchielli's uneven but thoroughly enjoyable score. I must say that, though Callas occasionally over-works her chest voice, she is in superb form, moulding the phrases and enunciating words with a passionate verve and conviction which bring everything to life, and fascinating in the brief passage of coloratura – not Milanov's strong suit. If the rest of the Cetra *Gioconda* is on the same level, then that is one more reason for deploring the non-availability of the Cetra catalogue in England."[32] Philip Hope-Wallace, however, was much taken with the recent Decca recording: "On the problem of Callas versus Cerquetti, I find I have to eat my words (honest I hope). I said that I actually preferred Cerquetti's 'Suicidio!' to Callas' which at that time I knew only out of context on a 7-inch EP. In context, though plummy at the start and tremendously laboured, it is undeniably more exciting than Cerquetti's more rapid and firmer, less melodramatic version. In spite of some painful high notes and unevenness of effect, Callas' Gioconda is a marvellously vivid figure; everything is made memorable, convincing; everything is 'dared' at its most exciting. I don't want to seem to be going back on Cerquetti, but an aria such as 'Suicidio!' as the climax to a growing interpretation can sound quite different and much more artistic than when cut from its context." Andrew Porter made it clear (**Gramophone** February 1959) that, in or out of context, he "preferred Callas to any other – Milanov, Turner, Farrell, etc.; having had occasion to broadcast a record of the aria recently, I listened to several versions in succession, and all others sounded tame after this one."[33]

I am particularly interested to be reminded of Hope-Wallace's enthusiasm for the 'excellent' Decca set because, when I heard it on the radio not so long ago, I thought it the coarsest recording of any Italian opera that I had ever had the misfortune to hear. Critics! No wonder they so exercised Samuel Beckett.

However, whatever the whys and wherefores, Callas made a stereo version of the opera in September 1959 in the full flood of her passionate affair with Aristotle Onassis and it certainly shows! Philip Hope-Wallace for one, whose second thoughts are most gratifying: "Can any reader help me towards the remainder of the Victorian poem which contains the line 'She found that La Gioconda was rather beyond'er'? Not, of course, that Madame Callas finds any such thing: *au contraire.* I simply cannot imagine anyone getting more out of the role than she does this time – not that sounding 'gioconda' (ie. joyous) is quite her forte. But just listen to the passage beginning 'O mio madre' and ending 'per lui...per lui',etc. 'Pure' singing? By no means. Indeed there is much constriction and at least one heavily beating climax. And yet the total effect is 'riveting' – to use a hackneyed adjective to describe the effect of rather banal music suddenly being burned afresh on to one's imagination. Compare this same passage with the 1952 Cetra version reviewed two years ago; same singer, same conductor. Both make an infinitely more artistic effect now. It could epitomise the whole recording. Of course you may say that artistry is not the prime consideration here; beef à la Barbieri (the rival Laura in the earlier set) is what most Gioconda fans today insist on. But it cannot always have been so. Generations of bel canto singers lavished their art on this superlative old Grand Opera. Obviously, it still has a public of kinds. Since in an excess of unwanted goodwill I gave the old Decca set under Gavazzeni the big hello, I have been assailed by doubts and waking in the night thinking I have heard an accusing voice say, 'You didn't half start something ...' Well, there they are: not one, but three versions to choose from, with my blessing now lighting (as Gioconda's blind mother would say) on this latest. And it is as a portrait of Madame Callas' voice (blemishes and all) and a souvenir of her exceptional dramatic gift that the new set will most commend itself",[34] [though Hope-Wallace is more guarded when reviewing the stereo version the following month: "Callas does at times sound a little thinner and more strained than one would ideally like."][35] Harold Rosenthal is equally impressed: "In her second recorded Gioconda, Callas recreates one of Italian opera's most demanding and rewarding roles in her own very personal terms. Sometimes the actual singing will distress the bel canto fans – so does Hotter's as Wotan, but who would want to exchange his Wotan for any other? So who would want another Gioconda? The ensemble at the end of Act I, the duet with Laura in Act 2, and the 'Suicidio' aria and the final duet with Barnaba, reveal not only the many facets of Callas' art, but the highly complex character of La Gioconda. A pity that such a performance...did not receive the orchestral

Callas records *La gioconda* for the second time, La Scala, September 1959

interpretation it deserved. Antonino Votto's reading is very dull."[36] On the last point, we shall see.

Both recordings were re-issued, first on LP. Their relative merits continued to be argued in **Gramophone** by JB Steane in December 1974: "The Cetra recording is a relatively primitive production. But Callas was aflame with greatness at that time: her singing had a unique force and concentration, and the world was under compulsion to take notice. This is a scalding Gioconda. It works by strong contrasts, broad phrasing, intense declamation; above all, by something utterly personal and inimitable in the timbre, in the fierce thrust and strength of the chest notes, and a depth of feeling that permeates the whole role, present in any phrase of recitative as much as in the great arias. Then, when that aria comes, it is certainly the high spot of the whole recording, and even better, I think, than her later and more famous performance in the EMI set. Both recordings of Gioconda were conducted by Votto, but the tightening and tidying which in many ways improve the later one, leave Callas less scope in the 'Suicidio'. Subtler shading, suppler rhythms, and a searing intensity of emotion distinguish the performance on Cetra, and for this alone the reissue is valuable."[37] Reviewing a very recent re-issue (March 2000), Alan Blyth was very impressed indeed: "Callas is in overwhelming voice throughout, mixing love, fury, pathos, desperation in equal measure and she imprints on our minds the woman at the end of her tether so marvellously described in the score. Above all, it is what she does in welding text and notes, and her complete emotional identification with the part that makes Callas' Gioconda the most emotion-laiden in the work's history. Most of the supporting cast are excellent. Apart from his penchant for cutting the score, Votto makes the most of the work's many strong points and overlooks its weak ones. The refurbished sound is admirable. Don't miss it."[38]

When the EMI stereo set followed five years later, Alan Blyth, also in **Gramophone**, was captivated by "an exciting reissue and not only for Callas' superlative performance. On these records one realises that in the right hands this opera comes close to equalling late Verdi in taut construction, for its tragic story has been matched in music of immediate, full-blooded vigour of universal appeal. We must thank Callas for so completely identifying herself with Gioconda's fate. Indeed, it may be that her own unhappy personal life helped her as much as anything to portray the emotions of the heroine. At any rate, she depicts the ballad-singer's love, jealousy and eventual magnanimity with all the considerable powers of vocal characteristion of which she was capable. Happily when this set was made she was in magnificent voice, even delivering a top C at the end of the last act trio without a wobble, and throughout moulding her phrases with refulgent tone and filling them all with the impassioned overtones Ponchielli calls for. Nothing is more arresting than her final benediction on Laura and Enzo 'Quest'ultimo bacio', infinitely moving and tender. She is just as successful earlier in the part in throwing insults and fury at her rival Laura, and the great slanging match has never sounded more truthful." And far from finding, as Rosenthal did, Votto's conducting dull, Blyth concludes: "Votto did nothing better on disc than this Gioconda, bringing out the subtlety of the composer's orchestration and the charm of the ballet music... there is no doubt in my mind that this is the recording to have. Nobody could fail to be caught up in its conviction."[39] But by this time (1980), Rosenthal had changed his mind: "In the past I have never really got on with La gioconda either in the theatre or on records, but this reissue has given me much pleasure, far more than when I first heard it in 1960, though even then I was bowled over by Callas' performance of the title role, and that of a young mezzo-soprano, just beginning her career, Fiorenza Cossotto as Laura... Antonino Votto was never a scintillating figure but always a good sound routinier, and sometimes more as in this *Gioconda*, which is certainly the best thing he did on records."[40]

The CD version, Alan Blyth states, makes the case even more strongly: "This was perhaps the most successful of Callas' remakes. She seems to have been in good and fearless voice, and the role's emotions were obviously enhanced by the traumas of her own life at the time: 'It's all there for anyone who cares to understand or wishes to know what I was about.' Here her strengths in recitative, her moulding of line her response to text are at their most arresting. Indeed, she turns what can be a maudlin act into real tragedy; that is the alchemy of a great artist. The whole of the beginning of the scene is a magnificent and heart-rending soliloquy in which soul, verbal acting, and tone are bound together into a totally convincing whole. She completely identifies herself with Gioconda's fate throughout with absolute conviction and not a trace of artifice."[41] Richard Fairman of **Opera** completely concurs: "An essential addition to any library of Callas' recordings, the fourth act of which is among the pinnacles of her recorded achievement. The aria 'Suicidio' opens up an enormous black pit of despair; but it is her singing in the long passages of recitative and arioso, where feelings must be articulated at a faster rate, that is worth the price of the whole set. Even simple phrases like 'Enzo sei tu!' and 'Ebben, corri al tuo voto' pin down specific emotions with remarkable precision. The yield of these passages in terms of operatic depth and passion is so rewarding that one quite regrets the arrival of Laura and Enzo, even though they have come to sing the work's big climatic trio … altogether, this is Callas' set: she brings a logic and dramatic certainty to her role that are unequalled by the rest of the cast."[42] J. B. Steane paid this tribute in **Gramophone** reviewing the complete 20th Anniversary issue: "I have left *La Gioconda* till last and slightly wonder why. The opera was not one with an enduring place in her career and, of the two recordings, 1952 sounds immature by comparison with the EMI in 1959 which misses the best of her voice by just a few years (in such a narrow space of time is all of this confined). Yet the role is surely made for her. One senses a personal identification, and the writing requires of its singer just those tones of tenderness and abandonment in which Callas was supreme. One does not have to accept her estranged husband's belief that she left for him at the end a coded message with portentous reference to the opening words (yet as with other shivery mysteries, part of us inclines to think there may be something in it); it is not fanciful, however, to sense a strong emotional involvement. It also comes to mind because I was recently playing the marvellous 1925 recording by Rosa Ponselle, the centenary of whose birth came round in January 1997. Callas had not the vocal glory of Ponselle, who may not have had the imaginative intensity of Callas. But between them they seem to me to share the supreme honours of our century in their shared repertoire; and in terms of gramophone history, as a soprano who recorded, all in all, more than 30 operas hardly one of which can be dismissed without loss, Callas stands alone."[43] Michael Tanner adds his word: "This set, made just after Callas had fallen for Onassis, contains a kind of artistic credo; she is on amazing form, and no one who listens to her here will ever forget her."[44]

Needless to say, it is the overwhelming recommendation in **G.C.G.CD G.2000**: "Ponchielli's old warhorse has had a bad press in recent times which seems strange in view of its melodic profusion. his unerring adumbration of Gioconda's unhappy predicament and of the sensual relationship between Enzo and Laura. But it does need large scale and involved singing – just what it receives here on this now historic set. Nobody could fail to be caught up in its conviction. Her strengths in declaiming recitatives, her moulding of line, her response to the text are all at their most arresting. Indeed she turns what can be a maudlin act into true tragedy. Ferraro's stentorian ebullience is most welcome. Cossotto is a vital seductive Laura. Cappuccilli gives the odious spy and lecher Barnaba a threatening, sinister profile, whilst Vinco is a suitably implacable Alvise. Votto did nothing better than this set, bringing out the subtlety of the Verdi-inspired scoring and the charm of the 'Dance of the Hours' ballet. The recording sounds excellent for its age."[45]

Chapter Seven

1958–59

MEDEA
VERDI HEROINES & MAD SCENES
MANON LESCAUT

MEDEA

Callas recorded the last of her great roles, Medea, in September 1957. Only one further complete recording remained – *Carmen* – and that was seven years off. The release of one other set – *Manon Lescaut* – was delayed because of Callas' doubts, quite needlessly as it turned out. Alec Robertson. who last reviewed a Callas recording four years before, was riveted by the diva's legendary Medea: "'Io son Medea'. Callas is indeed Medea and that is enough: it could not be more. From the moment she discloses herself to her faithless husband, his bride to be and her father, to her tremendous cry at the end of the opera, 'I go now to the Styx, the sacred river; there will my shade await you', this great singer runs through the gamut of human emotions; love and tenderness, hate and scorn, rage and anguish, cruelty and hypocrisy; a princess and a magician who, in spite of her revolting crimes, gains our unwilling sympathy. Only a great character could hate and murder on this scale. And so in Medea's superb arias, in her recitatives, in her duet with Jason, at all points Callas gives the finest performance I have ever heard from her. At one or two moments, she cannot make us forget the cruelly trying nature of the vocal part, but her voice is in splendid order, her attack magnificent: and she gives us some spine-chilling moments when she glories in the horrible death, by poison which burns the flesh off the body, that she has brought to Glauce and Creon, or when she cries to the Black Furies to come to her aid as she determines to kill her children."[1] Harold Rosenthal echoes this entirely in **Opera**: "It need hardly be said that Callas sweeps all before her in an interpretation of the title role that ranks as possibly the greatest thing she has yet done. Apart from two uncomfortable B flats, one in her first act aria, her voice is in excellent condition. The attack and the various colorations the voice assumes as the mood of the protagionist changes, show us once again that this singer has no equal today. Outstanding moments include her words to Jason in the first act, 'Ricordi il

At a recording session at La Scala for *Medea* in September 1957

giorno tu' (Do you remember the day, the first time you saw me?) – womanly, insinuating, tender; after the great outburst at the opening of Act 3 which send shivers down the spine as she calls down the curse of heaven on Jason; the savage fury in her words when she hears from Neris that Glauce has received the poisoned diadem she has sent her and will place it on her brow;

and all the final scene where she summons the Furies to her aid to complete her task."[2] Dyneley Hussey of **Musical Times** also rushed to pay tribute to Callas' achievement; "Medea is 'a part to tear a cat in' and there is no one more expert in that exercise than Madame Callas. She has no difficulty in matching up to the heroic demands of the character nor in extracting the utmost from its moments of pathos."[3]

Three months after the recording was issued, Callas gave five performances of Medea at Covent Garden, her first staged performances for over seven months. A certain *Medea* mania prevailed, giving rise to the following paragraphs in Desmond Shawe-Taylor's Quarterly Review in the July **Gramophone**: "This has been for the vocal collector a Maria Callas quarter. Not only her complete recording of Cherubini's opera but her two latest recital discs have proved to be of the most extraordinary and absorbing interest, even by her own high standards. If the gramophone had not been invented, a few generations would have speculated vainly about the voice, technique and style of this astonishing singer. We read of famous prima donnas of the past that there was a certain harshness in Pasta's voice, for example, which was never quite subdued but that the artist's genius and taste triumphed over all such drawbacks, and such reports are freely used by the more intemperate admirers of Maria Callas to demonstrate the stupidity of those who venture upon any criticism of their idol. But what we can never tell about those old singers is just how harsh their tone was or just how serious were the flaws in their technical equipment; there is a point at which mere words break down in assessing such things, if only because we can only guess the standards against which these weaknesses were measured. We may, however, legitimately suppose the general standards of vocal tone and technique to have been a good deal higher in Pasta's time than today, if only as a result of comparing the types of music written for the voice then and now. Consequently, the harshness and imperfections of Pasta may well have been much less marked than those of Callas: more akin, perhaps, to those of Destinn, another glorious artist some of whose records disclose unmistakeable technical weaknesses. That Maria Callas is a glorious artist, an interpreter of genius, there can be no doubt: the force and variety of her declamation, the subtle coloration of her tone and the exquisite taste and skill of her phrasing place her in a category entirely her own. Even when her physical powers fail her – when her loud high notes become fearsomely strident and unsteady, or when some pianissimo thread of tone comes dangerously near snapping altogether – we are never in a moment's doubt as to the rightness of her musical and dramatic intentions. Seldom could we wish a word otherwise delivered, or a phrase otherwise shaped: within the limits of her physical powers, all is perfection – and no cold perfection either, but a fiery or delicate or quite pathetic realisation of the innermost musical and dramatic idea. It is this power of the imaginative penetration, coupled with sheer hard work and complete dedication to the task in hand, that has enabled Mme Callas to revive a whole succession of forgotten operas, and to reveal the qualities in them that amazed and captivated our grandparents. I have found that my admiration for Cherubini has grown with each repetition. At first we may find the music too formal, but the sheer skill of the composition and especially the variety of figuration in the accompaniments become a source of deep pleasure, while as soon as Mme Callas appears she sweeps all before her. Serafin gives a noble and classical reading of the score; Mirto Picchi does well as Jason and Miriam Pirazzini makes an affecting thing out of Neris' G minor lament. Only Renata Scotto is sadly disappointing as Glauce, delivering her brilliant C major aria near the beginning as though she had barely learnt the notes."[4] Alec Robertson, when he returned nine months later for the stereo version, sprang to Scotto's defence: " I cannot believe, all else apart, that any artist would dare appear in the same opera as Callas with a half-learnt part, nor does her singing, though she is not perhaps in very good voice, give me that impression." But he does share Shawe-Taylor's rather eccentric view that Callas' "marvellous performance is the best sung that she has ever given in a complete opera."[5] Mr Robertson reviewed only five such; had he listened to the remaining seventeen, one wonders?

After 20 years, J. B. Steane revives the superlatives: "At this date the criticisms do not matter: what has to be said, preferably in letters of fire against the sky is that here is one of the great performances on record. The concentration, the sensitivity to all shades of changing moods, the sheer individuality of the tone and its ability to embody such depths of emotion, all of these qualities of Callas' art fit her wonderfully well for the role of Medea. The capacity for anger and sorrow, and for grandeur in both, also suits; and perhaps most moving of all, most aptly matching the material with the interpreter, is the scene where Medea proved herself a great actress, pleading with such intensity that we, the audience, are deceived as well as Jason, the plea coming from an inner source deeper than she herself knows. The irony of that true love for the children can surely never have been more touchingly and terribly communicated than it is in Callas' performance here. However, John Ardoin in his Callas Legacy points out that this Medea compares poorly with performances at La Scala and Dallas; indeed he believes that it was a mistake to have attempted a recording of the opera when the singer was fatigued and under strain. For myself, listening to it again after many years, I cannot imagine a more intense and striking performance."[6] Interestingly though, another ten years later on CD he is less sure of its greatness: "Callas does not do full justice to herself or to the part. It was of course one of her great roles but she sang it better on other occasions, some of which have appeared on 'unofficial' releases. It followed closely on the 1957 Edinburgh *Sonnambula* which itself had been undertaken during a period of stress; though she gives unstintingly of voice and spirit, there is a want of freshness and even, till the final act, of those moments of sudden insight which were so regularly the mark of a great Callas performance. That last act does indeed bear the authentic stamp. Medea's opening phrase, her invocation to the gods, has tremendous concentration and a vivid sense of presence. The fierce internal debate finds expression in subtle inflections. The harrowing cries of 'Lontan!' give way to the exhaustion of 'Son vinta gia' and the aria 'Del fiero duol' calls on that fine reserve of dark colours in the lower and by this time most beautiful part of the voice. Later, hearing of her rival's grateful acceptance of the poison coronet, the vindictive prayer 'La uccida' leaps into a clear spotlight and provides at least one example of the power she had of making a phrase in recitative carry the dramatic weight of a whole aria."[7]

These reservations may account for the fact that **G.C.G.CD G.2000** does not recommend the set, or, indeed, any other. For the 20th Anniversary release, J. B. Steane felt it should be "essential Callas, though, as recorded, he, too, finds that it is not really until the last act that this baleful presence becomes fully potent, culminating in the famous last words ('See you in Hell' or to that effect). Curiously, the first words as recorded are relatively ineffective, considering the dramatic build-up to Medea's entry and Jason's obliging cry of recognition ('Ah, qual voce!')."[8]

* * *

VERDI HEROINES

It was indeed rather absurd of Desmond Shawe-Taylor in his Quarterly Review of July 1959 to describe *Medea* as the best of Callas' complete opera sets. Following within a month of the well-known vocal difficulties at the 1957 Edinburgh Festival, it was in fact a Medea at half throttle. Certainly many of her live performances more vividly conveyed the frenzy of this demented woman, not least that of November 6th, 1958 when Callas learned that she had been sacked from the New York Met by its manager, Rudolf Bing. This unfortunate event was but one in string of serious mishaps to bedevil the great career. The infamous walk-out in Rome on 2nd January 1958 triggered an increasingly fraught atmosphere which poisoned her working relationships, notably at the Scala. The enormous success of previous seasons had facilitated the series of EMI Scala recordings, most, though not all, being made in the theatre itself, and it can be no coincidence that her departure from her artistic home drew the recordings to a halt. What did emerge from the company's studios instead were a couple of recital discs of rare distinction – Verdi in one (*Macbeth, Nabucco, Ernani* and *Don Carlos*) and in the other mad scenes from *Anna Bolena, Il Pirata* and *Hamlet*. Whilst they were widely admired at the time, they were no real substitute for complete studio recordings of some of her greatest roles, the absence of which has since been deeply regretted. EMI later recognised this by issuing live CD sets of three of them.

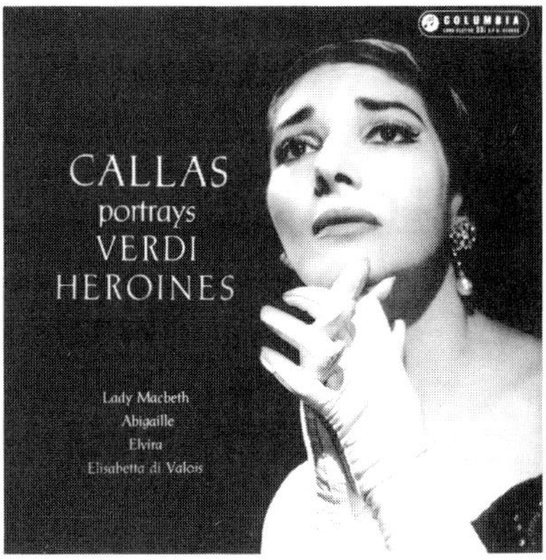

SAX2293

The first recital disc offered arias by four Verdi heroines and became famous for the *Macbeth* scenes. Philip Hope-Wallace, for the mono version, was guardedly enthusiastic: "Madame Callas has seldom had such a field day and her dramatic instinct is well nigh perfect in interpreting these wonderful pages, each characterised convincingly and differently. There are some very curious hollow sounds in the middle and bottom of her compass; in the *Don Carlos* the word 'aval' might almost be breathed into a milk jug, so cupped is it. And where this superlative artist wishes to put a world of tenderness into the word 'Francia', her means almost (but not quite) defeat her intention. The note is 'cawed' rather than floated... but we cannot argue endlessly about this. Either you mind the flawed production of some notes and it spoils your pleasure in the total effect (in any case abundantly exciting) or you don't notice anything at all. I will say that the last off-stage arpeggio in the sleepwalking scene is, for this singer, remarkably steady; though one can't say the same for the end of 'Tu che le vanità'. The phrasing of 'Ernani, involami' is most musical; it is a pity the cabaletta has to sound so fierce and macaw-like, with a very rough trill and an escape from it which would have made Ponselle raise her eyebrows.

Exciting? Yes. But so was Bianca Scacciati and others of that ilk, often quoted as the beginning of the end. However, the *Macbeth* scenes for which Verdi so much insisted on dramatic truth rather than smooth vocalisation are very effective."[9] When, a year later, he reviewed the stereo version, he was surprisingly critical of the performance of 'Tu che le vanità', saying it "needed a greater weight, majesty and spaciousness of control, in the manner of Margherita Grandi's famous record. Especially in the stereo version, one feels Mme Callas' voice to be unequal to this test. It is as if a quite gentle-voiced lyrical mezzo-soprano were trying to tackle hoch dramatisch music, a dove playing the hawk."[10] Desmond Shawe-Taylor does not agree, and I don't blame him. He begins: "Mme Callas is here at her best, notably at Lady Macbeth's counting of the hours ('Una! due!'), and in the soft ascending and descending arpeggios to the high D flat at the end (Her audible retreat is capitally managed at this point). The excerpt is preceded by Lady Macbeth's opening scene (here, surprisingly, Mme Callas makes less of the reading of the letter than Margherita Grandi used to do) and by the fine, gloomy aria 'La luce langue', in which her repetition of the words 'Nuovo delitto!' ('A new crime!') is given a haunting intensity of colour. Mme Callas excels in the gentle G major section of the *Nabucco* aria where she achieves delicate lacy decorative effects, but concludes this scene with some of those fierce notes which make one quite afraid to play the record until everyone is out of earshot! 'Tu che le vanità' from *Don Carlo* is more consistently done, and the central section recalling the distant happiness of Elisabetta's life in France is given with much pathos. Throughout, Nicola Rescigno and the Philharmonia provide beautifully sensitive accompaniments (how inexplicable it is that this conductor should once have been booed at Covent Garden!)"[11] Dyneley Hussey of **Musical Times** entirely agreed: "Her Sleepwalking scene is superbly sung and deeply moving."[12] Harold Rosenthal in **Opera** is, on balance, enthusiastic: "Who else in our day has, or can, sing Lady Macbeth's music like Callas? Who can invest the recitative to the *Ernani* aria with so much meaning? And who can surprise us again and again with a new inflection to word here and a phrase there? And there are some hauntingly beautiful moments too: I seriously question whether even Grandi ever demonstrated quite the demonic qualities and dramatic power of Callas. Let us hope we will hear this Greek soprano in this role in London soon."[13] – sadly, not to be.

Twenty years on, their younger colleagues largely dispensed with the original objections. Alan Blyth in **Gramophone**: "One marvels afresh in the Lady Macbeth extracts at the vividness and presence of the recitative, even more of the psychological detail brought to the sleepwalking scene which is really a compendium of all that Callas could achieve in shaping words to capture the mood of the moment, the stifled sound on 'immaginar', the searing expression at the reference to the perfumes of Arabia, the sensuality brought to the repeated 'a letto'. There are also three other quite different characterisations: a vengeful, cat-like Abigaille, a gentle Elvira, a loving aristocratic Elisabetta. The *Ernani* aria, no easy piece, is gently but ardently voiced and Ernani's name tenderly breathed. The cabaletta, Rescigno the conductor tells us, was recorded in a single take and, in a positive sense, it sounds it, having the right touch of elated spontaneity. Elizabeth's great scene is shaped in a single span, yet with the expected mastery of phrase and word. In 'Opera on Record', Lord Harewood commends this performance as being of the 'utmost delicacy and beauty' – just so. There is great art here and throughout this wonderful recital."[14] For Rodney Milnes, this would be his Desert Island Disc – "Throughout superb, it would take a page to describe the variety of dramatic ideas expressed in just the first few lines of the Sleepwalking scene and there is similar detail in the letter reading and opening aria, where Rescigno supports the thought behind the notes with subtle rubato. In 'La luce langue', too, everything racing through that tortured mind is expressed through, never over, the notes. The contrast with the girlishly eager Elvira and the momentarily nostalgic Abigaille could hardly be more telling, and the disc ends with a truly regal Elisabeth de Valois. If there had to be only one Callas record – heaven forbid – I think this would have to be it."[15] These tracks were reissued in 1987 as the principal items of a Verdi I CD, being joined, as was the pattern, by another four Verdi arias from the LP issued in 1972. Richard Osborne was impressed: "This fine disc is dominated by a great Shakespearean sequence. Callas was born to sing Lady Macbeth – Verdi's famous letter on the role seems to anticipate her at every characteristic including some that may be thought less than flattering. And it is impossible not to thrill at the chilling triumphalism of the early arias or the infinitely subtle dramatic intelligence and complex vocal mastery in the Sleepwalking scene. No wonder Toscanini wanted to direct her in the work. He never did; but here as elsewhere, Rescigno proves to be a most reliable accompanist. The long *Don Carlos* scene is comparably fine in its presentation of a variety of moods and it is marvellous to have glimpses of Callas' Abigaille and Elvira, roles she never recorded complete."[16] No further comment!

⋆ ⋆ ⋆

MAD SCENES

A companion disc of Mad Scenes from *Anna Bolena*, *Il pirata* and *Hamlet* followed quickly: two great scenes from recent triumphs at La Scala and a little-known masterpiece of French opera. Almost (but not quite) all of Philip Hope-Wallace's previous reservations about the diva were thrown to the winds: "This is a most remarkable record not only for extra material (pure gain) but for its astonishing vividness and dramatic poetry. It will, I judge, intensify all the same the controversy which this exceptional singer already incites. Those who cannot admit any faults will no doubt be able to overlook the one or two (to my ear) almost intolerable blemishes. On the other hand those who doubt the claims made by the fans for her interpretive powers would surely be won over by the exquisitely poignant and delicate art exhibited by many of the quieter passages. And yet ... the pity of it; that a singer who can sing the phrase 'des larmes de la nuit' as she does, cannot also, like Melba, cap it with a perfectly attacked and held climactic high note. The attack here is not as insecure as elsewhere but when the voice is used at full pressure the attack seems to me always perilous. Perhaps that is exactly what the Callas fans like; but can they possibly like the insecure sostenuto in nearly all loud high notes? Mme Callas starts all these three great scenes singing like an angel, but by the end of them, she is often more apt to be sounding like a bird of prey in a rage.

SAX2320

But nobody could get more dramatic truth or tenderness out of Ophelia's mad scene [one of the most exquisite things Callas has done, said Andrew Porter of the stereo version]. To be noted (and never forgotten too) is the extraordinary inwardness of the veiled or hummed snatches of folksong and at the other end of the scale, the positively maniac marcato rhythm, suggesting with extreme realism these rather alarming transitions from simple sadness to mysterious unexplained glee which are alas to be noted among the unbalanced. Altogether Ambroise Thomas is made to seem greatly increased in stature and though I think he would have found that final note unendurable, he would surely have been grateful for much else. The Anne Boleyn scene takes the soprano again through the whole gamut of emotion: tender recollection, alarm, dismay, fiery resignation and in all moods Mme Callas is intensely identified with the music which is very typical of Donizetti's grand manner and yet at one point he includes a quote from 'Home Sweet Home'. This is just the sort of thing the actress in Mme Callas does to perfection. Note too the 'genuineness' of her amazement on learning of her brother's detention. Oh, it was well worth presenting the entire great scene thus with admirable support from Covent Garden singers and fine recording. [Andrew Porter said he was asked if the mezzo, Monica Sinclair, was Simionato].

Il pirata, too, gives Mme Callas a chance to show her versatility in mood painting. The longing for the absent Ernesto, and the prayerful recollections recall 'Casta diva' and the crashing finale is thrilling, though pierced with some terrifying top notes. All very thrilling, and yet in a way, though the singer shows her genius revivifying this kind of music, I cannot but wish she could apply her art in some field of song (such as German Lieder) where high C's con tutta forza simply do not occur. But as far as the present record goes, I can only commend, with the usual cautions. It has been a thing of much wonder to me."[17] Harold Rosenthal rated the disc as "possibly the best solo record that Callas has made and one which is full of interest giving us as it does virtually the last twenty or more minutes of *Anna Bolena* – a complete assumption and the British singers give her admirable support. I doubt whether Thomas' mad scene has ever been as dramatically realised as here, though I do not doubt it might have been better vocalised. The Pirata is quite different again and those who are out to find fault with the singing as such will probably be affronted by some of the top notes. However, I am reminded of what Chorley wrote about the great baritone Ronconi: 'He possessed such wonderful dramatic powers that one virtually forgot his limitations.'"[18] The disc moved Desmond Shawe-Taylor to paroxisms of praise – he had finally arrived at the shrine: "If asked to name one record which contain the essence of her genius I should be inclined to choose her recent disc of Mad Scenes. The choice of music is as unconventional as it proves rewarding and in each case the soprano brings to life these forgotten specimens of a genre long considered fit only for mirth and parody. To add to our pleasure, the record is technically well made and generously planned, with subsidiary characters and chorus present where required, and without the cuts which were inevitable in 78 versions of the *Hamlet* music and which would have been unavoidable in the Bellini and Donizetti scenes too, had these ever existed on 78. In such a case, the often inconvenient LP 'recital' comes triumphantly into its own. Two years ago I was lucky enough to see Visconti's brilliant revival of *Anna Bolena* at La Scala, with Callas as the tragic Queen of England and I have been hoping ever since that we should have a worthy recording at least of the final scene in the Tower of London where the Queen is not entirely mad, but rather vacillating between sanity and a world of illusions. We here have no conventional mad scene with flute obligato but a long chain of ariosos, arias and recitatives, the shifting emotions of which are wonderfully conveyed by Mme Callas, who at one point achieves a sequence of softly rising turns which is remarkably accomplished simply as a feat of the vocalisation. She is no less successful in the concluding scene from *Il pirata* which shows all Bellini's tender melodic sensibility, and in the *Hamlet* scene, the slow cantilena which will astonish those who may have thought Thomas a negligible composer."[19]

With the first reissue, J. B. Steane, recalling many of the sentiments above of his predecessors in **Gramophone**, wrote: "Now 20 years later when she is no longer in our midst we are more ready to take the rough with the smooth; we flinch as the high C's approach but we find much more than we have perhaps remembered to be beautiful in sheer qualities of tone as well as artistic intention. The tone moreover is so full of humanity that it is difficult and perhaps irrelevant to think of it as a sound to be objectively assessed. Some loose vibrations, some strident high notes, even some lazy trills: they are faults now as they were then. But as one recalls so many phrases from this recording that have remained vivid over the years, the wonder of it remains uppermost."[20] Rodney Milnes in **Opera** could only add his superlatives: "If anyone were ever to have any doubts about Callas' genius, her record of Mad Scenes would surely be the one to sweep them away. In the Bellini and Donizetti excerpts, it is not just the musical-verbal inflections that take the breath away, but the way she invests Anne Boleyn and Imogene with towering dramatic stature – this, if anything is, is grand opera. But what is even more startling is the way she shows just as unfailing a command of music in a completely different style; in the *Hamlet* scene her tone is lighter, more flexible and her technical assurance is stunning."[21]

For the CD reissue 10 years later, EMI added four bel canto items in an effort to give greater value for money in the new format. Alan Blyth described it as a 'sensible conflation'. But a further 10 years on in 1997 however, EMI had second thoughts and the new reissues resumed their previous LP selection at mid-price. This made much greater sense and the chronology of Callas recording career was restored; mixing old and new tracks was no longer good news. Nevertheless, Blyth makes a strong case for the later pieces, though he admits that the original mad scenes show up the marked deterioration in the voice between 1958 and 1961.

These two exceptional discs reflected the dramatic course of Callas' career on stage. It may or may not have been recognised at the time but her five glorious performances of Violetta at Covent Garden in June 1958 marked a watershed. The previous season she had appeared in a total of 29 performances as: Amelia, Violetta, Lucia, Tosca, Anna Bolena, Imogene at: La Scala, New York Met, Lisbon and Covent Garden. Suddenly the engagement book was empty except for two performances each of *La traviata* and *Medea* in Dallas, five performances of *Medea* at Covent Garden and two concert performances of *Il pirata* in the Carnegie Hall, New York. In their stead, a new pattern emerged of recitals, logistically convenient and financially remunerative, as Meneghini in particular realised. The very first took place at Birmingham, Alabama and was repeated in nine cities in North America – Atlanta, Montreal, Toronto, Cleveland, Detroit, Washington, San Francisco, Los Angeles, St Louis, and Kansas City. A further 23 then took place in Europe between 1959 and 1963 in Madrid, Barcelona, Hamburg, Stuttgart, Munich, Wiesbaden, Amsterdam, Brussels, Bilbao, Berlin, London, Essen, Bonn, Dusseldorf and Copenhagen. Such an arrangement is not uncommon when an artiste acquires world renown. Melba, Gigli and today the Three Tenors are examples. With Maria Callas, other factors, too, were significant: difficulties with her voice and opera house managements after a fiercely intensive career began to militate against stage appearances; and her lifestyle transformed by her love for Aristotle Onassis, causing the break with her husband, compounded the upheaval. Between 1960 and 1963, she sang only a total of 13 performances – as Norma, Paolina and Medea (La Scala and Epidavros). Likewise, the intensive run of complete recordings were replaced by a series of recital discs. A huge surprise was her first collection of French arias, the performances of which gripped critics by the throat. But before that came a rather wonderful reminder of the old days – Puccini's *Manon Lescaut*.

* * *

MANON LESCAUT

Puccini's first great success, *Manon Lescaut*, was recorded immediately after *Turandot* in the summer of 1957. Callas had reservations about her performance and delayed its release for over two years by which time she had confined her recordings to remakes and recitals. Her fears however were groundless and her Manon, with di Stefano at her side as des Grieux, has long been widely admired. In July 1994, the 37 year old set was the recommended version of Michael Oliver in BBC Radio 3's **Building a Library**, where only Callas' Manon really contemplated death. Of the viable rivals, in my opinion Kiri Te Kanawa's lustrous tones suggested a glorious sunset; Licia Albanese's blowzy hysteria, a sedative; and Tebaldi's heft, a twenty-mile hike. But William Mann in his original **Gramophone** review of December 1959 understood Callas' doubts and weighed up the pros and cons fairly and perceptively: "Where Manon is upon us, a promising set becomes a really stimulating one. It is the old story again. Callas' high notes, not so much in the first act as later, are acid in quality and develop what is a beat if not a wobble. But her singing of Manon's more vivacious passages is beautifully poised and dazzling; she characterises Manon in every move – the gentle, rather preoccupied girl in her first meeting with des Grieux, the spoiled darling at the beginning of the second act, the woman knowing herself in the wrong but still promising to do better next time though everybody else knows she won't, the kept woman

Maria Callas with the almost complete cast of *Manon Lescaut*, recorded at La Scala in July 1957

throwing scorn at her protector. And so her performance continues, through the slightly comic quick trio in which she tries to collect all her treasures before decamping, through the forlorn degraded convict of the third act, to the death in the American desert which Puccini had the creative audacity to make an act for two characters alone, a symbol of solitude which makes its point on the gramophone more impressively than any proscenium-bounded stage can ever do. Comparison with Tebaldi is here unkind, because Tebaldi is always herself, warm and opulent and slightly fuller toned. She makes a really lovely noise in all Manon's expansive cantabile music, and that in turn is beyond Callas' reach; but the opera is more than vocal euphony, and the much more is where Callas displays herself at every moment of this opera as a great artist of the gramophone, an interpreter who removes veils from our eyes, and a singing actress who like all great singers of this century, transforms a gramophone from a wooden box into an experience. Altogether, there is no doubt that this recording is musically and dramatically more desirable than its rival Decca set; and for that we have to thank Callas and the conductor who has done so much to make her the artist she is. I am fairly sure that Puccini would thank them too."[22]

Harold Rosenthal again echoes these sentiments: "Callas has never sung Manon on stage, but unlike many artists who record roles they have never performed in the opera house, she succeeds in creating a vivid personality, a real flesh and blood figure. The differing aspects of Manon's character are admirably realised, and although Callas has not the beautiful, rich creamy tones of Tebaldi (the typical Puccini soprano from the purely vocal point of view if ever there was one), she makes Manon a far more credible character than that singer."[23]

With the reissue 20 years later, Edward Greenfield was ecstatic: "Having complained from time to time that EMI's reissues of Callas' greatest recordings have taken something of the brightness and attack from the sound as originally presented, I am delighted to welcome this superb set of *Manon Lescaut* as an improvement even on the original. Nowadays the EMI policy is against electronic stereo transcriptions and in favour of a straight mono transfer. When I first tried my old copies of the original Columbia issue, I was a little taken aback by the relative stridency and boxiness at the start. That has now been effectively tamed without any loss of clarity. The level is marginally lower but the agonised fortissimo at the very end of the opera is if anything even more impressive than before with an extra degree of refinement. It is that final scene – normally on stage a great anti-climax after the musical and dramatic intensity of the embarkation scene of Act Three – which immediately comes to mind when one recalls the Callas set of *Manon Lescaut*. It has lived up to all my memories this time with the great monologue of 'Sola, perduta, abbandonata' leading on inexorably to the final duet with des Grieux. But what had rather slipped my memory was the quality of di Stefano's performance, and even more strikingly the mastery of Serafin's conducting." After some comparisons with other available sets expected to be an easy choice ahead of this old offering, he writes: "As it is, not only is the performance with Callas more compelling (di Stefano more individual and better focused than Domingo) but the recording allows you to hear more detail even while it is less obviously atmospheric."[24]

Rodney Milnes of **Opera** is equally impressed: "The changing moods of Puccini's Manon, from less-than-ingenuous ingenue in Act 1, to bored sophisticate playing a role in the second act, through the broken spirited invalid of the finale, are more than matched in one of Callas' most vivid recorded performances. In minutely judged variation of tone colour, weighting of certain words, use of portamento and rubato, she creates so fully rounded a character in sound alone that it is hard to believe that she never sang the role on stage. Even so, this is far from being just a 'Callas recording'. Di Stefano's open, ardent tone and excellent diction make him an outstanding des Grieux, one who really sounds as if he means what he is singing." He concludes: "An exceptional performance, then, in forward, clear sound that is fair for its age – 1957, with the release delayed for nearly two years because of worries over a handful of ugly top notes from Callas. They may have been worrying twenty years ago but today seem small price to pay for an otherwise classic interpretation."[25] Only six years ahead lay the digitally re-mastered issue first on LP where Edward Greenfield again exuded: "This time the digital re-mastering has kept the sound more open (again with no false stereo enhancing) and bringing out far more inner detail. The very start had me sitting up at the clarity of the triangle in the opening tutti and the voices, though placed rather close, are caught with new fidelity. Callas may present a rather formidable portrait of a young girl in Act 1, but here the final act, with its long duet and the big aria, for once is far more than an epilogue to the rest, rather a culmination, with Callas at her very peak. Di Stefano, too, is in superb form and Serafin's pacing of the score is masterly."[26] The CD, he added, "brought the usual advantages of absence of background and ease of finding places, this time with ample banding. But while Callas' supreme assumption remains unique, anyone just wanting this early, richly coloured Puccini opera on CD will almost certainly find the Sinopoli/DG more congenial when, with all its improvements, the sound here necessarily remains very dry and unatmospheric."[27] J. B. Steane, welcoming the 20th Anniversary issue described Callas' Manon as "a subtle study in character-development, from the 'simplicita' (Puccini's repeated direction) of the opening, through the sophistication and mature commitment of the middle scenes, to the desolation of 'Sola, perduta, abbandonata'."[28] The set's dry sound did not preclude its historical recommendation in **G.C.G.CD G.2000**: "This performance is unique for reasons relating especially to Callas, already stated above by Edward Greenfield. Admirably partnered by di Stefano who wipes the floor with most of his rivals past and present; in Act 4 he has a concerned tenderness for Manon that others can only sketch, his debonair charm in 'Tra voi belle' is incomparable and (rarest of virtues among tenors) he never sings past the limits of his voice. Fioravanti as Lescaut and Calabrese as Geronte sing well if not very characterfully."[29] Reviewing the very latest recording [April 2000, on Deutsche Grammophon with Maria Guleghina], Michael Oliver finds "plentiful vociferous excitement but in an opera that seldom calls for it. One older one stands out as *hors concours*: Callas with Serafin, fascinating throughout, unbearably moving in Act IV, with di Stefano outstandingly sympathetic as Des Grieux."[30]

Chapter Eight

1961 – 65

FRENCH RECITALS
MOZART, BEETHOVEN, WEBER ARIAS
VERDI ARIAS CARMEN
ROSSINI & DONIZETTI ARIAS

GREAT ARIAS FROM FRENCH OPERA

The genesis of the French Recital disc of 1961 could fairly be said, I think, to have taken place in the Rome Opera House on the 2nd January 1958 – the notorious occasion when the great diva, suffering from a cold, suddenly found herself *persona non grata* for walking out on the President and his wife during a performance of *Norma* which she said she could not complete. Within a fortnight Meneghini decided to punish the vengeful Italian establishment (on his wife's behalf) by arranging the Gala of the Century at the Paris Opera. There she met Aristotle Onassis for the second time and, within a year, had moved into a neighbouring apartment on the Avenue Foch.

SAX2410

Far from being the surprise claimed, therefore, this recital was virtually inevitable and artistically a triumph. Lionel Salter in **Gramophone**: "Were this not Callas who is accorded a divine right to do whatever she thinks fit, one would regard this as a very rum record indeed, with the same artist singing dramatic soprano parts like Chimene, coloratura arias like 'Je suis Titania', and mezzo or contralto roles like Carmen and Dalila. Andrew Porter, in an informative and erudite programme note however, points out that there is plenty of precedent for sopranos singing Carmen and that in French opera there is a tradition of the 'falcon', a kind of dramatic mezzo and a dramatic soprano combined. Well, it's still very extraordinary. I can only say that if you know anyone who is adversely critical or sceptical of this unique artist (and we all do know someone) you should force him or her to sit down and listen to her 'J'ai perdu mon Eurydice' (in French, for once). Instead of the fruitfully sung cavatina we are usually fobbed off with, here is a gripping dramatic experience – the distracted Orpheus of the story beside himself with grief and desolation. Gluck's broken phrases, and the anguished cries 'Eurydice' followed, after an agonising pause by the flat despair of 'Mortel silence ...' have rarely appeared so heart-rending. Callas' phrasing, coloration of words and subtle variations of speed (admirably accompanied by George Pretre) all contribute to the overwhelming effect. She hasn't the weight – or the sheer beauty of tone – of certain favourite contraltos in this aria; but anyone who cares for dramatic truth rather than mere voice production would cheerfully swap all your Ferriers and Berganzas for this. Anguished intensity is also the prevailing emotion in the Massenet 'Pleurez, mes yeux'; yet at the next moment this astonishingly versatile artist can convey the breathless ecstasy of Juliet's young love, Alceste's ringing invocation of the powers of Hades, or the passionate vibrancy of Carmen. Her Carmen, at least in the Habanera, is a purring tigress, as against the fatal seduction of Supervia or the blandishments of de los Angeles; in the Seguidilla a characteristically Spanish hardening of tone is legitimately employed. When, however, it comes to pure singing, as against characterisation, the diva is less successful. 'Je suis Titania' is amazingly clean and accurate in all its fioriture, but the tone is somewhat constricted; and several arias are blemished by the strident top notes which are her weakness – the climax point of 'Depuis le jour' has a particularly ugly wobble as well. But opera is more than just a canary-fancier's holiday; and all who appreciate dramatic insight as a major factor in operatic performance will relish this disc."[1] Desmond Shawe-Taylor in fact found 'Je suis Titania' positively painful; but other arias, he said, were "unforgettably eloquent, notably 'J'ai perdu mon Eurydice', the two excerpts from Samson and 'Pleurez, mes yeux'. It would be hard indeed to find a better example of the grand manner and the singer's spacious, unhurried delivery of this noble Massenet aria."[2]

Harold Rosenthal in **Opera** hoped the recital presaged a new direction in her stage career: "If ever a record was designed to display the amazing gifts as well as the vocal faults of this great artist, this is it. The arias for soprano voice reveal the now familiar wobble on top notes and some other ugly sounds. The mezzo-soprano arias, however, are superbly well sung and show the beauty of Callas' middle voice. Hearing these arias at about the same time as the recently reviewed *Norma*, one can only hope that this great and intelligent artist will decide to embark on the mezzo-soprano repertory for stage performances. Indeed one can visualise a whole new career: Carmen, Dido, Delilah, Eboli and many other parts. The whole fascinating question of distinction between different kinds of voice, especially in French opera, is admirably summed up in the excellent sleeve notes by Andrew Porter." He makes the same observation on Orfeo as Salter and finds Callas' Carmen and Delilah both "subtly and almost suggestively sung; and the change from these to the girlish, innocent Juliet is yet another proof of her amazing versatility."[3] A mezzo career, however, was never in Callas' mind: she was a soprano, and this disc, with its companion which followed a year later, reflected her domestic arrangements (a new home in Paris) as much as artistic considerations.

When the recital was reissued 20 years later Richard Osborne was inspired to write a most eloquent tribute: "This recital vividly and movingly demonstrates how sure a medium for the expression in music of the great human passions Callas was. The range is astounding, so much so that hearing the record is both an inspiring and an upsetting experience, not merely because of the sense of the early loss of so great an artist but because the plights of these great human archetypes are themselves so uplifting and disturbing as Callas presents them to us. How rousingly Callas sings Alceste's great invocation and how desolate is her vibrant yet stunningly understated account of Orpheus' great lament. I once saw Ileana Cotrubas openly weep at the sound of Callas' voice on a gramophone record and there are things on this recital which are unlikely to do less to all but the most hardened listeners. There is only one oddity on the record, the musically rather empty Polonaise, 'Je suis Titania'. Callas negotiates the fioriture well up to a point but the tone seems blanched and pinched; this item alone gave me diminished pleasure. The rest is glorious. Callas' Juliet, like her Gilda, is a remarkable study in a particularly dedicated kind of innocence; the top is raw in the climax of the Waltz Song but the whole thing is spellbindingly done, taking us closer to Shakespeare's original than Gounod's music really deserves. The crepuscular beauty of 'Pleurez, mes yeux', the opening words of the lament of the grieving Chimène in Massenet's *Le Cid*, is outshone only by the vigour of Callas' attacks and pleas elsewhere. Callas is riveting in both roles, showing no more condescension to Charpentier's Louise than she would to Puccini's Mimi. The last of the Delilah items is new to the catalogues .It's the duet which our grandmothers knew as 'Softly awakes my heart.' Callas is glorious and, as there is no Samson on this recording, it is left to us at the appropriate moment to touch in with gratitude and affection the adoring asides. Records like this change people's lives."[4] Mr Osborne was equally enthusiastic over the CD release in 1988, though less than happy about the inclusion of five items from her second French recital when she was in poor physical and vocal health: "The sentiments of Carmen's Habanera may have been anathema to Callas but the performance is extraordinarily charismatic, as is her recreation of the other great human archetypes revealed here – Orfeo, Alceste, Delilah, Chimene and Juliette."[5]

* * *

CALLAS À PARIS

SAX2503

The second French recital did not maintain this excellent impression. As Andrew Porter summed up in his **Gramophone** review: "It is something very special. I would not want to be without it. But all the same, from Callas I expected something more. There are no revelations – nothing quite so wonderful as many things on her previous record." He finds much that is wrong with Pretre's accompaniments throughout. In Gluck's magnificent aria 'O malheureuse Ifigenia', Callas' performance has "grandeur and style" but the words are tamely pronounced and the Berlioz finds Callas only at half strength, not merely in voice but also in interpretation." Better are the items by Massenet, in particular Charlotte's Air des Lettres in which she "becomes again Callas at full strength, 'I should destroy them ... I cannot!' The way Callas utters 'Je ne puis!' reassures us that she still has it in her to be not merely the brittle, glamorous, expensive (and still bewitching) star of a television spot, but a serious hard-working interpreter concerned only to make the composer's music as eloquent as possible. In this air the feeling for timbre and weight and the shape of a phrase are memorable, as are the distinction between the thoughts uttered aloud and the phrases read from Werther's letters, and the moments when she looks up, pensively, repeating a line just read. All the same, the Callas of a few years ago would, I feel, have been more stirring at the 'avec expression' passage 'Non, Werther, dans leur souvenir ...' As Manon in 'Je marche sur tous les chemins' she sounds glittering, elegant, young, proud and superb. This is very successful, even without a real 'eclat de rire' to close it. 'Adieu, notre petite table' I find somehow indeterminate in tone, a little lacking in character. Bizet's 'Comme autrefois' suffers again from Pretre's unsettled tempi. Callas' treatment of the grace notes is excellently graceful, but anyone who loves sweet, gentle, limpid tones in this air will not readily accept these dark, passionate sounds. Except, of course, that Callas at her best can make one accept almost anything she chooses to do." About the Gounod, he is again equivocal: "Yes, it is good, and sensitively and intelligently phrased and better voiced than I had dared to hoped; and yet from Callas I had expected something more."[6]

Harold Rosenthal's response in Opera was similar, rather more positive, amazed at the singer's versatility in a sphere virtually new to her: "The voice is under better control than for many a day but one has the feeling especially in the Gluck and Berlioz that this steadiness has been achieved by so conscious an effort that the dramatic intensity that one always associated with the singer has suffered as a consequence. Even so, I would rather hear these versions of the several arias than most others. The old Callas comes to the fore in Charlotte's letter scene from 'Werther' - this is a role surely made for her, and Manon's 'Je marche sur tous les chemins' runs it a pretty close second. In both the Gounod and the Bizet arias, which are beautifully phrased and most elegantly sung, one is rather too conscious of the artistry - perhaps the attempt to make a voice that is really sensuous sound girlish and virginal defeated her. Yet again, the performances themselves are models of style."[7]

Reviewing five items from this recital issued on CD in February 1988, Richard Osborne found [a "very fine 'Adieu'" apart] Callas' voice "strained and bleached; the texts hacked about and the orchestral playing and microphone placing, awkwardly close, leaving much to be desired."[8]

* * *

MOZART, BEETHOVEN, WEBER ARIAS

The Mozart, Beethoven, Weber recital which followed a year later compounded many of the faults above and in addition consisted of music not associated with her great gifts. Edward Greenfield who reviewed the disc in **Gramophone** described the voice as in excitingly fresh condition but proceeds with considerable justification to compare the Mozart items unfavourably with Joan Sutherland and Elisabeth Schwarzkopf. (Though Richard Law

SAX2540

[**Opera** 1987] considers Callas' 'tragic grandeur' in 'Or sai chi l'onore' surpasses the famous record of Frida Leider.) None of the three roles – the Countess, Donna Anna, Donna Elvira – is entirely convincing. The point is made that it is less the voice that fails than the prepared interpretation, obviously very rare in Callas. But her well known disinclination for Mozart's music might well account for that. Weber's 'Ocean, thou mighty monster' is hardly a natural choice either. It is Beethoven's epic 'Ah! Perfido' that, as Greenfield reports, is in some ways the most successful item on the disc: "Here the flashing eyes are completely in character. It is a comparatively early Beethoven piece and its reliance on old eighteenth-century conventions suits Callas in the opening recitative where she gives a new depth to ' Voglio morir per lui'. But the aria itself is comparatively sluggish in rhythm, very much lacking a sense of eighteenth-century style and with some ungainly top notes." He concludes by expressing the hope that his reservations "will not mask the essential truth that this is an exciting Callas disc to fire and excite admirers. Where a year ago one might have thought Callas' wonderful recording career was at an end, this gives wonderful promise for the future."[9] As this was certainly Callas' least successful recording, he cannot but be right.

Philip Hope-Wallace, having given way to Greenfield above, was back for Harold Rosenthal (in Opera): "This disc needs approaching with care and a good deal of readiness to forgive out-of-tune or squally notes for the sake of the interpretation (if one can really separate the two factors). The Weber, sung quite properly in English, is sung in rather unattractive English ... my contention that if ever Callas lost her voice she would still be a great *conductor* is borne out by the sheer handling of 'Ah, perfido' which bespeaks the great artist in every phrase. Donna Anna's 'Or sai chi l'onore' has great presence but 'Non mi dir' is an awful struggle and indeed none of these Mozart selections is recommended for people who like at least a semblance of poise in the singing of such music".[10]

Only 'Ah! perfido' has received any subsequent attention, first when it was coupled in 1991 with Medea on CD, the clarity of which J. B. Steane found "positively cruel, exposing wear on the voice with all the ruthlessness of a light shone into an ageing face; still, an apt choice for a fill-up and an expressive, valiant performance."[11] Two years later, he found it again on the Rarities CD, "a forgotten corner of Callas' repertoire."[12]

★ ★ ★

VERDI ARIAS

SAX2550

And indeed the next recital, Verdi arias from *Otello*, *Aroldo*, *Don Carlos*, exactly prove the point because Andrew Porter in **Gramophone** found it "wonderful. Callas gives a rapt, intent performance of the Willow Song. Even though there is no Emilia, she recreates the scene before us: bewilderment, love, foreboding, melancholy and passion are all there. Verdi's music is brought to life as by no other artist. Her voice is in fine state: very beautiful, and drawing a full glorious line in the 'Cantiamo' phrases. There is one particularly magical moment in the Ave Maria – the move to the first 'prega' after the monotoned introduction, the portamento on the second syllable of the word, and the gentle, fragrant tone in which it is sung. There are some unsteady notes. It is a great performance. The earlier prayer from *Aroldo* is in interesting contrast and shows off excitingly Callas' big dramatic chest voice. In the full-scale scena ed aria from the same opera, it is hard to avoid comparison with a roughly comparable number from *Attila* which Joan Sutherland recorded recently. The vivid pronunciation of the words, the burning emotion conveyed by tone-colour, and the powerful use and eloquent sense of rhythm, are all memorable. So is the fearless quality of Callas' singing; high notes ring out in full tone, several of them perfectly steady under pressure. The aria is a fine piece, with very interesting scoring in the accompaniment to its beautifully balanced phrases; and scorn and anger flashing out in the cabaletta. The new Callas is a happier and more confident artist than the one of the 'careful' years. This Verdi, at any rate in the items so far mentioned, is a triumphant success. But even though 'O don fatale' is exciting, very exciting, here one can start weighing pros and cons and going through all the familiar Callas arguments again. And for Elisabetta's gentle romanza of farewell, I feel that Callas adopts too big and dramatic a tone; and the heavy climaxes are, to my ears, somewhat painful."[13]

Philip Hope-Wallace, writing again for Opera, is also impressed: "One can scarcely imagine the name 'Barbara' being more hauntingly sung in the opening of the Willow Song and throughout the scene [complete except for Emilia, which seems an odd omission] Callas brings to the music a sustained and poignant dramatic awareness, with particularly beautiful and musicianly progressions in the prayer. To my ear the arch of the 'Cantiamo' sounds as if it had been doctored [i.e. unwobbled] but this may well be an illusion. What is certain is that the A flat before the last Amen is not the steadily glowing, perfectly poised note that I at least really do demand of the singer in this wonderful piece. Yet the performance is unforgettable. The big scena from 'Aroldo' is thrilling and a pure gain to the catalogues. Eboli's aria, again, is done with such musicianly art that it makes many singers of the famous piece sound merely luscious and bovine, but the Queen's consolation to her lady-in-waiting is more uneven."[14]

Desmond Shawe-Taylor, so critical of the diva in the early years of her recording career is, if anything, even more enthusiastic: "The entire first part of the last act of *Otello* is subtle, poetic and intensely atmospheric. How lovely are the real echo effects in Callas' repeated 'Salce' though I can't agree (with Andrew Porter) that the F sharps on 'Cantiamo' are quite happy, for they sound breathy and unsteady to me. Nevertheless, this is one of the most haunting accounts of the music to have appeared on record. The two scenes from *Aroldo* show Callas' dramatic style at its most vivid. In Eboli's 'O don fatale', her rapid, impulsive opening riveted my attention and she is very striking in the slow central section, failing only in the powerful concluding declamatory passages above the stave. In the Queen's farewell to her dismissed companion, Callas catches the elegiac tone to perfection, but I'm worried by the soft final sustained notes of the aria which sound like slow trills. In all, this is one of the richest and most rewarding recital discs we have had from Callas; to listen to her after most other sopranos is like taking a brilliantly responsive Upper Sixth after a gruelling spell with the inky Lower Fourth."[15]

In 1986 when the recital appeared on CD, Richard Osborne was uncharacteristically dismissive. Maybe it compared too unfavourably with the superior 1958 recital, or contained too many less satisfactory performances from her late career. He found the disc only "memorable for Callas' superb account of Desdemona's Act IV vigil. Elsewhere she is often out of voice or out of character" – an astonishingly different assessment from Shawe-Taylor's [and, incidentally, my own] thoughts on the subject. He adds: "It is touching to hear what she could achieve in 1969 in the two items from *Il corsaro*, and there is plenty of dramatic thrust in the 1964 *Trovatore* scene."[16]

* * *

CARMEN

It would be another eight years before his colleague Andrew Porter welcomed another recital made up of unpublished recordings from the Sixties. Meanwhile Callas brought her recording career to an end (the second *Tosca* apart) with *Carmen*. It was a concession to EMI who had nurtured her career so faithfully (again, omissions apart) and also to the public who craved to see her Carmen on the stage. But if she had performed any mezzo role, it would probably have been Charlotte in *Werther*; she did not approve of Carmen.

And what a concession it was! Philip Hope-Wallace, often so critical of her earlier recordings, was transported, first by Prêtre's handling of the score, the supporting cast, in particular Gedda as Don José, but most of all by "Herself. Carmen is Callas, every note imprinted with her individual stamp. You may find it too intrusive but ignore it you cannot. Let me touch on a few points of disagreement before going overboard. She strikes me at times as inclined to overact the part: the card scene is a case in point where one can't see the wood for the trees or to put it differently, she does so much with each syllable, each phrase, each shimmer of meaning that somehow the existential tug at the heart strings is not exerted. Then it is no use pretending that her French, though wonderfully convincing, is as impeccably French as (say) Andrea Guiot's. Unquestionably some of the very few high notes either go sharp or squally, and with upward portamento especially, there is an occasional sudden access of plumminess, or whatever. But, when these things are said, how very little do they matter beside the extraordinary ripeness and vividness of the characterisation, the sheer force of personality exhaled like a genii rising from a lamp and brooding over the whole room – from the very first syllable … Her musicianship is scrupulous (like Gedda's). Every tiniest detail in the part has (one feels) been examined and mined for musical and dramatic effect; Mme Callas, if she can't always open up with thrilling effect, always contrives something that sounds dead right, and where sarcasm is wanted, or real rage,

Nicolai Gedda [Don Jose], Georges Pretre [conductor], Michel Glotz [producer] and Maria Callas [Carmen] like what they hear in the Salle Wagram, Paris in July 1964

her 'acting' with the voice just makes Carmens like Rise Stevens or Leontyne Price sound babyish. Curiously enough though, where Callas actually drops into speech, she seems to lose her magic. As you will perceive, I'm fairly under the spell myself: the tessitura of the part and the present timbre of Callas' voice now seem perfectly matched. She is entirely inside the musical portrait and never at odds with it (as for my taste she has been, however excitingly, at odds with heroines who took her up to those wildly perilous, tottering top notes). Hers is a Carmen to haunt you."[17]

Harold Rosenthal was rather less captivated, preferring the classic Beecham set: "Callas has not sung *Carmen* in the opera house; but there is nothing tentative and nothing unpositive about her Carmen. It is as if she had been singing the role for years, so completely is she in the part. Vocally, it suits her well and the seductive sexy equality of her voice in the Habanera and the Act 2 duet with Don Jose, certainly helps her to make her point. In the difficult card scene she is dramatically foreboding, though in the last scene of all, she fails – and how rarely Callas does fail – to bring any new light to bear on the part: in a word, this scene is something of an anti-climax. Although I want very much to see Callas' Carmen on the stage, I would not, in the last resort, choose her Carmen on records to live with for the rest of my life, for it lacks, in the final analysis, charm – a quality that Victoria de los Angeles' miraculous performance possesses."[18]

Desmond Shawe-Taylor in his **Gramophone** Quarterly Review, comparing a current spate of Carmens, took up a middle position: "An odd fact is that neither Callas nor Leontyne Price has so far been seen in this role on stage – and no more, come to that, has de los Angeles, the star of that HMV Beecham *Carmen* which remains, in many respects, the best of all. Miss Price, whose strong, forward tone I always enjoy, does from time to time sound like a novice in the part, whereas no one would ever suspect, on the evidence of these records, that Maria Callas was a newcomer to Bizet's score. Her grasp of character and mastery of inflection is most striking; her supple rhythm in the Habanera and Seguidilla enchanting, her final scene almost painfully vivid. The contrast between the two protagonists comes out sharply at the point where Carmen mocks Don Jose's anxieties about missing his roll-call; here Price adopts an embarrassingly infantile manner, while Callas flashes and sparkles with dangerous wit. Of course, she has corresponding vocal drawbacks from which Price is free. The middle of Callas' voice has become weak and cloudy, and there are disconcerting moments when in the process of moving up from a relatively strong chest register, she is obliged to 'turn down the volume', so to speak, suddenly and drastically when no such effect is required by the musical phrase. She finds it hard, too, to make the open French 'a' sound in this part of the voice – an embarrassment in music which abounds in 'la-la' passages. For instance, the little tune which Carmen impudently hums instead of replying to Zuniga's questions in Act I becomes suddenly muted and ineffective as Callas carries her voice up from the loud low E with which each phrase begins. The scene in which Carmen dances for Don Jose offers a fascinating glimpse into these peculiarities of Callas' vocal methods and present vocal condition. The first eight bars offer some of the loveliest, smoothest, best open singing she has ever given us, with a rhythm and vocal allure that are absolutely captivating. Then, as she needs to increase the volume in a somewhat higher register (when the tune moves to the dominant) she is at once obliged to darken and muffle the tone so that the open 'a' sound vanishes. Such little problems face her throughout the score, and she shows astonishing resource in coping with them. Nevertheless, one is aware of the element of contrivance – a quality entirely foreign to the notion of Carmen's character."[19]

When the recording has issued on CD, Richard Osborne was captivated as was Philip Hope-Wallace 20 years previously: "No singer since Supervia has so obviously appropriated the role of Carmen on the gramophone and made her own. Callas and her excellent supporting cast and conductor mine the opera for meaning bringing it close to its roots; but it is with Bizet's text and some of the old grand-opera accretions clinging to it which more recent recordings of *Carmen* have tended to strip away. At this period of her life and career, the role of Carmen was entirely right for Callas. The result is a characterisation of great force and complexity. Callas as Carmen is an exceptionally dangerous creature: dangerous in the familiar sense of physically threatening and in the much older sense of someone exuding intense sexual allure. Oddly, Callas, who in this edition has virtually nothing to speak, is no great shakes as a diseuse; yet no singer of the role in recent times better illustrates how, in *Carmen*, song is a physical and psychological necessity, dialogue and recitative turning into song which itself always retains, in Carmen's case, its kinship with the spoken word. Listen to Callas prefacing the Habanera, and then listen to the Habanera itself; or to the end of the Seguidilla; or to the snarl in the voice at the close of the derisive 'Non, tu ne m'aimes pas énivrante'. As Philip Hope-Wallace noted, you don't have to drink the whole bottle to catch the flavour of this performance, one sip is enough. True, there are some murky and insecure notes here and there, and there are some coverings of tone; but the overall effect is never less than riveting: like Shakespeare's Cleopatra 'the vilest things become themselves in her', even her defects have their point and charge."[20]

When the uneconomical three CD set was reduced to two, six years later, J. B. Steane was given the opportunity to give his view: "This is one of those recordings that never stay 'the same' from one playing to the next. There is always something new or something not quite as one had remembered it. Sometimes it seems that Callas almost grotesquely caricatures the memory: the 'yoddle' across from chest register into the middle voice seemed this time more pronounced than ever. Often it is the underplaying that is freshly impressive. She has a magically quiet, seemingly innocent way of questioning José's intentions and her delivery of 'Je suis amoureuse' is deliciously ambiguous, not a downright lie, but as though in inverted commas, the experimental attitude of the moment."[21] For the 25th anniversary issue he adds: "Her Carmen, of course, is controversial. It goes against the current trend, which is rather to tame her into a kind of heightened normality. Callas' Carmen is utterly self-absorbed until her little solo to Escamillo in the last scene; and there is both charm and ferocity in her. Yet, strong as is the memory, when you go back to listen what is most remarkable is the restraint. It is a fascinating performance, and of course the low tessitura frees her (and us) from the affliction of the high notes, which by this time (1964) had become more of a trial than ever."[22] And Michael Tanner: "Callas never sang Carmen on the stage – 'Not with these legs,' she said" – (a joke to cover her antipathy to the role). "Her Carmen chews men up and spits them out. But she has a mordant humour too; and in the great 'Card Song' a bleak acceptance which is uniquely effective. The final scene with Don Jose, well sung by Nicolai Gedda, is hair-raising. Though there are weaknesses in the casting this is, I think, an indispensable version of Bizet's miraculous score."[23]

* * *

ROSSINI & DONIZETTI ARIAS

Callas' final recital at this time was devoted to arias by Donizetti and Rossini. It was, a few reservations apart, warmly welcomed by Lionel Salter whose review in **Gramophone** of the *Cenerentola* aria raised once again the possibility of Callas pursuing a mezzo career and "a vocal register where she is less beset by technical troubles and where her unrivalled powers of dramatic interpretation can have full play". But despite her complete recording of *Carmen* six months later, this of course, with her final Toscas and Normas, was not to be, and rightly so. Maria Callas was Prima Donna Assoluta, even when she could no longer go on.

SAX2564

With many items on this CD, Mr Salter found much to admire: "At first sight, these arias would not seem to offer her much more than opportunities for conventional bel canto and florid singing with characterisation reduced to a minimum: two (*Semiramide* and *Lucrezia Borgia*) are for mothers to their sons; two (*Fille du Regiment* and *Elisir d' amore*) are for young girls to their newly-enlisted lovers. Yet it is extraordinary how the whole quality and colour of Callas' voice changes as she moves from one character to another. For example, from the grand manner appropriate to the

Babylonian Queen to the passion of the spoilt Italian Duchess and thence to the simple charm of the countrywoman Adina. The *Lucrezia* aria here does not figure in the current catalogue in any alternative performance, so those interested primarily in the recorded repertoire rather than the artist (if there are any in the present case) may go for this first: though it is sung with intensity, the later fioriture tend to be sluggish and at the end of the aria Callas is distinctly sharp. There is slight sharpening, too, in the otherwise attractively sung *Elisir* aria but elsewhere intonation is not a problem. 'Selva opaca' has a sense of rapture and seriousness of purpose, and, except for a slight uncertainty about one upper note, is beautifully handled. In the *Cenerentola* aria, Callas indulges overmuch in a plummy, hollow tone in the lower register which contrasts strangely with her brighter tone 'upstairs'; but all the florid passages are accurate and fluent, and it is therefore the greatest of pities that the end should be marred by a painfully out-of-control penultimate high B. Marie's Act I romance in *Fille du Régiment* however, finds her vocally at ease; and the best performance on this disc is certainly of 'Bel raggio', where her fioriture on the word 'gioa' have a splendid abandon, and where the orchestra even more than elsewhere, gives admirable support."[24]

Harold Rosenthal was much less impressed: "This is not one of Callas' best recital discs, though it does contain some interesting things, as for example the rare aria from the prologue to *Lucrezia Borgia*, a role that should suit Callas down to the ground in the theatre. The interesting thing about all the arias on this disc is that Callas has never sung in any of the operas from which they are taken. Truth to tell, I could not really imagine her as either Cenerentola, Adina or Marie in *La Fille du Régiment*, while Mathilde in *Guillaume Tell* is rather a small role – incidentally why does Callas, usually such a stickler for authenticity and perfection, sing the *William Tell* and *Daughter of the Regiment* arias in Italian and not in the original French? In fact, it is only as Semiramis or Lucrezia Borgia that I can envisage her."[25]

Nearly twenty years later in 1981 Alan Blyth clearly agrees with Mr Salter: "What conflicting thoughts coursing through one's mind in this, one of the last of Callas' recitals, recorded in 1964, not long after her London triumph as Tosca. Only a few, very few stage appearances lay before her and these were to reveal the sad deterioration in her vocal condition all too apparent in this taxing programme. Yet, when that is said, when the occasional hardness of tone is noted, the odd, disintegrating high note is duly frowned on, who today can match the delicacy of much of the singing or the amazing variety of the characterisation? Favourites here with me are the 'Selva opaca' (but why not in French?), when Callas is so aware of Mathilde's predicament, so gently persuasive and rapturous in mood, and 'Com'e bello', which rises above all too evident technical difficulties to give us a glimpse of an ideal Donizettian style. An abundance of playful charm was not one of Callas' natural gifts so that her *Cenerentola* rondo, for all its eminence in fioriture, fails to scintillate, and the tone is too hollow. The *Semiramide* (once more in Italian) has more abandon, but one feels that an earlier Callas would have managed it more easily – here, as in the *Cenerentola*, Callas' gifts for plangency and exquisite line are at a discount. The recording, though adequate, has little feeling of atmosphere: we are definitely in the studio. But it is still Callas' gift to take us out of it at treasured moments, intermittent, but eagerly awaited, throughout this programme."[26] Five years later, he finds the CD transfers of the Donizetti arias "splendid, giving the voice a fullness and faithfulness of reproduction which LP never quite achieved. It can be argued (as John Ardoin did) that Callas wanted the charm and scintillation for the lighter heroine herein portayed but as one listens to her way with 'Com'e bello' and 'Prendi', the criticism seems misplaced, for these are elegiac pieces and Callas, in spite of faltering moments, fulfils their needs for that kind of sentiment."[27]

Chapter Nine

1972 – 1997

BELLINI-VERDI RECITAL THE LEGEND THE UNKNOWN RECORDINGS RARITIES

BELLINI-VERDI RECITAL

Maria Callas' last appearance on the operatic stage was as Tosca at the Royal Opera House, Covent Garden on 5th July 1965. She was only 41; her career had been exceptionally intensive and correspondingly short: just eighteen years. Most singers have at least thirty years before their careers are over; with Callas, her life was over. In 1947 at Verona, her bright star suddenly appeared in the operatic firmament; ten years later in 1957, it dazzled as never before at La Scala; a further ten years in 1967, the light had dimmed and the voice was silent; a final ten years, on 16th September 1977 in Paris, her heart stopped beating. Her personal suffering was acute: she lost the man she loved to another woman and when he died, she lost the will to live. The public were intermittently aware of her unhappiness, and rumours of professional consolation abounded. These included recording sessions, and in the twenty years following her death, every scrap of recorded material was made available to eager listeners. Much to the joy of Andrew Porter in **Gramophone**, the first – a Bellini/Verdi recital – was released in 1972: "A new record by Maria Callas, the first for eight years! Exciting event! Of course, rumours had reached us that in the Paris studios few years ago she had been busy. A tape or two had been sneaked out and found their way to London, whetting the appetite. And now the disc. It is a marvellous display of the personality, the art and the voice which, it is not too much to say, have left their mark on musical history, and influenced the operatic repertory of our day.

We start with Imogene's entrance aria in *Il pirata*, a key work in Bellini's new dramatic style which – both directly, and by way of Donizetti – was to lead to Verdi. Some people thought that Montserrat Caballe's handling of the opening recitative (in the complete recording) was too grand, as she swept on playing Lady Bountiful to the distressed mariners. Callas' characterisation is exactly right. There are moments in the cavatina, and especially in the cabaletta, where caution seems to temper her natural rhythmic vitality; but it is splendid

ASD2791
The diva in her magnificent Paris apartment in the Avenue Georges Mandel where her name was commemorated in December 2000

to have this companion piece to her recording of the final aria, issued in 1959. One high B wobbles rather; but there Callas is a miracle of steadiness compared to reported judgements from the past. The *Pirata* piece was recorded in 1960. The Paris recordings were between 1961 and 1964 but in fact they show the voice in more confident and more ample form, steadier, able to soar the broad phrases of the *Ballo* aria, and to negotiate delicate turns. Of course, the timbre is not always, perhaps hardly ever, conventionally beautiful; but it is expressive, eloquent, and moulded to the meaning of the phrases. This has its own kind of beauty. The romance from *Attila* is an exquisite aria and Callas captures all its warmth and delicacy of inspiration. The *Vespri* romance set into the Act IV duo is beautifully phrased, including a chromatic scale descending from C above the treble stave to F sharp in the bass, which is a little slithery but no more so than Callas' chromatic scales have always been. In Giselda's air, the voice is a little thin and strained to begin with but becomes very beautiful, I think, in the cantabile. There is a sweet, sure high D flat here. The *Ballo* Act 2 aria is powerful and affecting – even more so, I think, than in the complete recording of 1956. And in 'Numi,pieta', Callas' unerring sense of portamento demonstrates once more her rare understanding of line. I love this record: for Callas' command of line, of declamation, of rhythm, of dramatic and musical sense. Whatever she touches comes to life."[1]

Fifteen years later, these items were included as fillups on a number of recital discs when they were issued in CD format. Richard Osborne generally echoed Andrew Porter's enthusiastic response: "There is some sour tone in Giselda's aria from Act II of *I Lombardi* but Elena's 'Arrigo!ah parli' is magnificent and Callas realises the start of Act II of *Un ballo in maschera* even more powerfully here than on the complete recording, 'l'orrido campo' as much of landscape of the mind as the place in which Amelia distressingly finds herself. Callas' Aida is not to everyone's taste but one is bound to thrill to this recording of 'Ritorna vincitor', the line of 'Nume, pieta' gloriously intact despite a terrific sense of agitation with which the scene is invested. Rescigno told John Ardoin that this recording happened by accident after the break in an edgily unsuccessful recording session, during which Michel Glotz mischievously played a recording of the aria taped the previous day by Regine Crespin. So incensed was Callas by a performance that was, to her perception, so dramatically misguided, she asked if the parts were still in the studio and proceeded to make the recording in a single, blazing take. One can believe the story; the performance still rivets sense."[2] Reviewing the Pirata aria from Act I, Alan Blyth had to observe that it "starkly indicates the sharp decline in Callas' voice between 1958 and 1961 when the Mad Scene (now alongside on CD) was recorded: uncertainty and discoloration sadly mar her performance – though the artistry remains undimmed, of course."[3]

Regarded subsequently as an unsatisfactory arrangement, these 'fill-ups' reappeared in the 20th Anniversary issue on their own CD with other miscellaneous tracks hitherto unreleased.

* * *

THE LEGEND

Before this however, yet another surprise. Exactly a year after Callas died on 16th September 1977 another recital – The Legend – was released in the first glow of posthumous fame. J. B. Steane tells the story: "Rumours of late recording sessions have been fairly widespread for some years and rumour also had it that the famous voice was in wonderfully good form. Even so, I think the prospect of such recordings actually being released caused some apprehension along with the excitement. One prepared to flinch before the high and even the not-so-high notes, and to make the most of the artistry. The two arias from *Il Corsaro* require no such exercises in indulgence. Recorded in 1969, four years after Callas was last seen on the operatic stage, they suggest that the voice lost power but gained in steadiness. In the first, Medora's Romance, there are many touches that are not merely magical as 'interpretation' but also as vocal mastery. It is quite possible to compare these performances with those given

ASD3535

by Jessye Norman and Montserrat Caballé. Both of these sopranos have their rich and beautiful voices in full bloom, but in many ways Callas is preferable. Her legato is remarkably good, not pressing individual notes as Norman tends to do, and not aspirating as Caballé habitually does. And in recitative she is absolute mistress: the sighing loneliness is most beautifully caught. Then from 1955 comes an unpublished recording of the principal solos from *La sonnambula*. This is from the years of Callas' prime and, despite the characteristic limitations, they are marked throughout as the work of the great artist. The passage from Act one is often rather preferable to the performance Callas gives in the complete set. It is rather more relaxed, and certain phrases are taken with easier, fresher vocal quality. Yet on the whole the records here provide curious commentary on the observation in the sleeve-note that 'no two Callas performances were alike'. This refers to stage performances yet I'm often surprised that the vocal interpretations didn't vary more. The two recordings of 'Ah! non credea', for example, are almost identical, and so, in interpretation, are this recording of the *Ballo in maschera* aria and the one in the complete set. Still, 'The Legend' is almost by definition a thing of wonder and surmise; with its first two items – the 1969 recordings– the new issue has at least turned one legend into reality."[4] In **Opera**, Alan Blyth is not quite so happy: "Although one may admire the way Callas husbands her reduced resources and spins out a refined legato, anyone who knew the voice in its prime must weep at the shadow of its former self. As Callas had earlier recorded the two other Verdi arias, it seems a pity to have to hear her 1964 performances when the technique and tone were no longer what they were. Against that it must be said that Callas brings a shade more feeling and nuance to Amelia's prayer than she did earlier. There is a strange sense of loneliness about these late appearances in the studio, a kind of fragility that has its own appeal. In the Bellini arias, even an unsuspecting ear will learn what all the fuss was about. Here the voice has its pristine freshness and power, the line firmly held in 'Come per me sereno' and the Sleepwalking scene."[5]

[These performances are further considered in Chapter Six – La Scala recital (Bellini) and Chapter Eight -Verdi II recital]

* * *

THE UNKNOWN RECORDINGS

On the 10th anniversary of Maria's death, Richard Osborne reviewed a newly-released CD of unpublished material which "included three items from live concert performances in Athens and Amsterdam and half a dozen items retrieved from a stock of recordings – some already issued, some held in reserve, some cross edited, some abandoned – accumulated by EMI in studio sessions throughout the 1960s. Since Callas was famous for reacting to the advice of colleagues, not to mention the stimulus provided by the performances of her rivals, variant performances of single arias hold great potential interest. Her interpretations were never arbitrary; equally, nothing with Callas was a foregone conclusion. That said, it is reasonable to conclude that the best of the 1960s material has already been issued. The previously unissued 1969 recordings arias – from *I Lombardi*, *Attila* and *Vespri* – are interesting in as much as they confirmed the kind of work Callas was doing on her voice at the time, stabilising the thinning top register and rematching tones and registers lower down the scale. Odabella's romance from *Attlia* is particularly fetching but it would be idle to pretend that this remake of Elena's 'Arrigo! Ah parli' comes anywhere near the 1964 recording with its broader tempo and its generally formidable command of the 21-note-wide tessitura. Wisneski dubs the 1964 version as one of Callas' most intimate and deeply felt on record, and so it is. The Rossini items parallel those made with Rescigno in 1964. These earlier, 1961 recordings are often sweeter-toned and more limpid-sounding, though it is difficult to determine whether this is attributable to the state of the voice, interpretative intent, or Tonini's limp conducting. In the aria from *Guglielmo Tell* Callas does not erase memories of Muzio, one of her own favourite singers, and there appears to be trouble with a poltergeist in the adjoining studio. Callas' 1960 *Semiramide* is alluring but comparatively conventional by comparison with the altogether more regal, more ferocious, more desperate, more emotionally wayward woman she presents us with in the 1964 'Bel raggio'. The two performances highlight aspects of character previously explored by Rossini in *Armida*, another famous Callas assumption, and underline for us not only Callas' special affinity with Rossini's Colbran-inspired roles but also a wonderful ability to penetrate beneath the bel canto surface to the woman the subtle mechanics of the bel canto method so variously evoke. It used to be argued

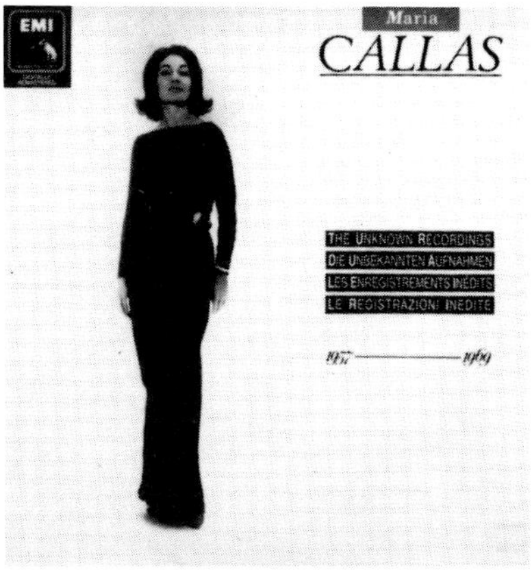

CDC 749428.2

that Callas wasted her talent on too much slight music and too many fragile heroines. In fact, not only did she show immense technical skill in handling the whole range of the Colbran/Pasta repertory – turns, appoggiaturas, trills and portamento deployed with a musicality, taste, rhythmic accuracy and dramatic flair that no one in recent times has consistently rivalled – she also interpreted the music in a way that could have led to a wider public understanding of the Rossini/Donizetti/Bellini repertoire had she and her most talented rivals given us more opportunities for comparative study of key roles than they in fact did. The extract from Rossini's *La Cenerentola* is a telling example of Callas' insight into music which critics, misunderstanding the music themselves, have often accused her of singing unsympathetically. In Rossini, Callas was said to lack lightness, charm and good humour; but she must have sensed that *La Cenerentola*, like much else written by the allegedly easy-going Rossini, is far from benign. It is a pity Callas never sang *Cenerentola* on stage where she might have printed the work's semi-serious, tragic-pathetic nature indelibly on the public imagination. In the closing scene recorded here, it is, not surprisingly, Cenerentola's reconciliation with Magnifico and the ugly sisters that haunts the imagination in her performance. Her Cenerentola has a Cordelia-like intensity whilst her fourfold repetition of 'Tutto', like Cordelia's 'No cause, no cause' or Lear's fivefold repetition of 'never' carries a burden of emotion that cauterises the terrible wounds that Magnifico's earlier treatment of her had opened up. As Teodoro Celli wrote of Callas' Medea: "She went beyond the notes, directly to the monumental character of the legend, and she handed it back with devotion and humble fidelity to the composer." Again, with *La Cenerentola*, it is the later, previously published recording which is the more imposing, but this earlier recording is cherishable for the greater beauty of the coloratura display allied to the sketch of the impersonation that was to come.

The 1959 Holland Festival performance of the *Il pirata* Mad Scene is, if anything, even more sensitive and thrilling than the 1958 studio recording. It was the concluding item of the recital and seems vocally and dramatically freer than the *Don Carlo* scene which lacks presence when compared with the admittedly more vividly recorded studio version of the same session. As for the Athens Festival *Tristan*, it is phenomenal. Like her Elisabetta, though in another style and dimension, Callas' Isolde is an essay in the triumph of will over despair. It is the blazing affirmation of a brave, desperate, vulnerable and partially overwhelming woman. It begins on the voice and if there is one inconvertible fact about Callas it is that her voice was unmistakable, instantly recognisable. To meet it head-on is still one of the most thrilling experiences opera has to offer."[6]

Alan Blyth, in **Opera**, is equally enthusiastic: "The jewel here is Callas' account of the Liebestod at an Athens recital in 1957, catching all Isolde's sense of elevated ecstasy and sublimated eroticism. From an Amsterdam concert in 1959 comes an even better version of the *Pirata* closing scene than that made in the studio with all the famous attributes of word colouring and plaintive accents; similarly 'Tu che le vanità' is more spontaneous than the previously issued version. Giselda's prayer from *Lombardi* is a precious addition to her Verdi discography, as hushed and intimate as you could wish. The arias from the Rossini operas, made in 1960 and 1961, previously unissued, surpass the 1964 remakes. The 1969 Verdi records, apart from Giselda's prayer, show the frailty of all the late Callas, also their moving quality."[7]

* * *

RARITIES

Six years later, another CD of new material – Rarities – was issued. J. B. Steane explained and analysed its contents as follows: "This is an important issue and not just another selection of items already familiar as anthology-pieces. Except for the most assiduous of Callas collectors who have made a point of seeking out everything listed in John Ardoin's 'The Callas Legacy', annotating their copy and supplementing their collection with everything that has appeared since, the material will be largely new and in many instances genuinely exciting. The rarity varies in degree. One of the items, 'Ah! perfido', was published in the usual way but comes from what tends to be a forgotten corner of Callas' repertoire. Another, the 1953 'Non mi dir' has appeared on CD previously but is relatively little-known, having started life as a test-recording in preparation for her first EMI opera, *Lucia di Lammermoor*. Most of the others are alternative, formerly rejected versions of solos which eventually appeared in the catalogue in a form originating in some other recording session. These are not alternative 'takes' but products of a different year, sometimes with a different conductor: most notable under this heading are the items conducted by Antonio Tonini, which hitherto have comprised, as Ardoin said, as 'the largest body of unreleased Callas material'. Then there is the *Aida* duet, legendary and single survivor of an aborted album with Corelli and Prêtre. And best of all are the two items from a concert at San Remo in 1954 in which the soprano sang the

CDC754437.2

Armida aria and 'Martern aller Arten' from the single Mozart opera in which she appeared on stage. These show Callas at her most brilliant and breathtaking. In Rossini, the variations involve triplets-sequences and scale-work of dazzling virtuosity: the applause that breaks in on her last note obviously comes from an audience that could not hold back a second longer. The *Seraglio* aria is, if possible, still more wonderful. In expression, the defiant spirit bears itself with dignity; technically, the control and precision are astonishing. She is on best form vocally here. In one's list of enviable occasions this concert must stand high, for Gigli was also singing in it and the only consolation for the incurably envious is that there were no duets. The *Aida* duet with Corelli, however, is another collector's item almost equally to be desired. While it is the tenor who provides the thrills, it is Callas who gives the recording its individuality as a dramatic performance: the mean, cold voice of assumed hostility at the start softens into a quiet, utterly sincere expression of longing in the phrases which introduce 'La tra foreste vergine' which she sings privately, as though to herself, momentarily forgetting the betrayal into which Aida has been so cruelly ensnared. For the rest, it is usually a matter of picking and choosing. In some ways the newly released version will be preferable, in others the one with which you compare it. In 'Ocean, thou mighty monster', for instance, she sings with more feeling for contrasts of weight and lightness in this 1962 recording, but also with grotesque (if fascinating) exhibitions of that extraordinary 'cupped' or 'muzzled' effect on some low notes and with a tortuous growth of discomfort towards the end. The 1963 re-recording brought gains and losses. Similarly, the *Trovatore* aria comes to a somewhat desperate conclusion though there have been lovely things on the way. 'O don fatale', by contrast, has little to commend it till the coda, when the exclamations 'Oh ciel! E Carlo?' suddenly flash into life. But each item, each phrase almost, has something to be said about it: the whole collection makes essential listening."[8]

A double CD of Callas Rarities was issued as part of the 20th Anniversary Callas Edition in 1997 which included all the studio items in the above CD, plus another 1953 'take' of 'Non mi dir', a mono 'take' of the 1958

Sleep-walking scene from *Macbeth*, and a hitherto unreleased 1960 recording of 'Bel raggio' from *Semiramide*. The three live items issued in 1987 were joined at the same time by ten further live performances given between 1935 and 1959 on a double CD 'Live in Concert'.

Chapter Ten

1980–1998

LIVE PERFORMANCES:
LA TRAVIATA
LUCIA DI LAMMERMOOR MACBETH
IL PIRATA ANNA BOLENA
POLIUTO IFIGENIA IN TAURIDE

COMPILATIONS:
MARIA CALLAS SINGS OPERATIC ARIAS
MARIA CALLAS &
GIUSEPPE DI STEFANO – DUETS
THE INCOMPARABLE CALLAS
THE ART OF MARIA CALLAS

LA TRAVIATA (1958)

Within a year, in 1973 EMI embarked upon an ambitious re-issue of all the Callas recordings, starting with the famous de Sabata *Tosca*. Many of these incorporated simulated stereo in an attempt to improve the often boxey sound of the Scala originals. At the tail end of these, came a complete surprise. In 1980, EMI, perhaps no longer able to live with their ignominious failure to capture Callas'Violetta in a studio recording, issued her 1958 live performance of *La Traviata* from Lisbon. J. B. Steane, of course, warmly welcomed the set and though he correctly states that Callas was none too delighted to be excluded from the 1955 EMI set because of contractual reasons (she had recorded the opera two years before with Cetra), he is surely wrong to hint that she, rather than EMI, was to blame for the continuing absence of a recording of her Violetta in her company's studio. Here is his review in full: "*La Traviata* was the opera most conspicuously and regrettably absent from the great series of recordings made by Callas for EMI. She recorded it on the Cetra label in 1953 and it seems that a clause in the contract prevented her from playing her role in another version for several years (five, in fact). Meantime, EMI had come out with their Scala *Traviata* under Serafin with di Stefano, Gobbi and Antonietta Stella. Callas was none too delighted about this and never made another commercial recording of the opera despite its importance in her repertoire. The Cetra version was poorly conducted and not well recorded and the other singers provided little pleasure and Callas herself had much more to give than appears in a generally unsatisfactory set. So the issue of this present recording

Callas' 55th performance as Violetta on 27th March, 1958 at the Teatro Sao Carlos, Lisbon, with Alfredo Kraus

of a performance given in Lisbon is a matter for some rejoicing. There is also the fact that it comes direct from the opera house so that at last we can hear, without resorting to the pirates, Callas 'live': the great singing actress of our time in her proper setting on stage.

The famous characterisation emerges vividly throughout. Even at the start, the gaiety is overshadowed; as she sings her verse of the 'Brindisi' one expression after another passes through the voice with miraculous subtlety. In the great aria all moves towards the moment of acceptance and emotional release: 'A quel'amor'. Similarly in the duet with Germont père all turns upon the single held note, the B flat eventually descending to the G and to renunciation: 'Dite alla giovine'. A frail, limp tone makes still more pitiful the passage that follows where Violetta can foresee the agony of more decisions and the ultimate outcome: 'Morrò la mia memoria' has the true, rare ring of tragic nobility. Then in the last act comes a most lovely performance of 'Addio del passato' with its ghost-voice at the modulation 'Conforto' and the heroic crescendo of 'Ah, tutto, tutto finì'. The voice itself sounds perilously frail here, and elsewhere in the opera there are notes that are unsteady and occasionally notes that are hard. But much is beautiful as pure singing and the spirit shines through all. Despite the prominence of prompter and coughs, the recording itself is admirably clear. The great portrayal is on record; that is what matters."[1]

Alan Blyth in reviewing the reissue on CD actually professes gratitude to EMI for not recording Callas' Violetta in the studio since we might have been deprived of this official record of what she sounded like in the theatre. Given EMI's later releases of live performances, this is surely very doubtful and in any case the same could be said of so many of her other complete recordings. As it is, the sound is so relatively bad as to preclude its recommendation in Radio 3's **Building a Library** in February 1998. Mr Blyth writes: "If the choice had to be made, I would go for *La traviata* as a representation of Callas' art, simply because Callas caught live is preferable to Callas recorded in the studio and because Violetta was perhaps her supreme role. The Covent Garden producer Ande Andersen has pointedly commented that whereas other sopranos make you cry in final act of *Traviata*, Callas also made you cry in the second and one hears here what he meant as Callas' Violetta comes to the stark realisation that she is going to have to give up the one and only true beloved seemingly for ever. The desperation that enters her voice at 'Non sapete' is surpassed only at the sorrow and emptiness in the lead-in to 'Dite alla giovine', then the fatalism of 'Morrò la mia memoria' which J. B. Steane, in his note that accompanies this essential CD reissue, describes as being sung with such 'fullness of heart and voice'. Then the final act is almost unbearable in its poignancy of expression: the reading of the letter so natural and its feeling of emptiness, the realisation that the doctor is lying so truthful, the sense of sheer hollowness at what is possibly the whole opera's most moving moment 'Ma se tornando...' All this and so much else suggests that Callas more than anyone in my experience understood what this role is truly about. Much of what she achieved here can be heard in embryo on the 1953 Cetra set made before she was quite such a mature artist. Those of us who heard her at Covent Garden a few months after the performance enshrined here will know that it is a true likeness of those unforgettable readings."[2]

Indeed, as one of the lucky ones, I do! That morning we were up before dawn to make sure of an orange-box. In those days, oranges meant Covent Garden and Covent Garden meant Maria Callas. After only a few hours, a numbered token secured our place in the queue and by mid-afternoon I had a 12/6d (62p, in 1958) ticket in my pocket to stand at the back of the Stalls Circle. I'd taken along my grandfather's field-glasses, and watching our beloved Maria let loose her final first act E flat, I felt as if I'd been swallowed whole. Every great performance has its special moment and that came after Violetta's horribly public humiliation at the hands of the tortured Alfredo. When Callas' soft, wounded voice stabbed the hushed auditorium, 'Alfredo, Alfredo, di questo core', I hardly dared breathe and as the curtains fell I was pushing my way out into Bow Street for air. That was 42 years ago and it could have been yesterday.

* * *

1988 – 1990

The first Callas CD compilation – MARIA CALLAS SINGS OPERATIC ARIAS – was on a budget price label [EMX2123] and good enough to command not one but two reviews in **Gramophone**. First, Richard Osborne in February 1988 warmly welcomed, and was deeply moved by, it: "The many striking things on it include five plums from the 1961 French collection (plus Manon's 'Adieu') and four striking examples of Callas' achievements in the Italian repertory. The performances themselves hardly need further notice here though it should be noted that 'Una voce poco fa' is very properly taken from the complete recording of *Il Barbiere di Siviglia* and that 'Vissi d'arte' is taken from the later of her two complete recordings of *Tosca*, unbearably touching when one recalls that at this point of her career Callas' genius was hovering on the edge of its own extinction. Sadly, there are no texts or translations with this mid-price issue. The sleeve-note tells us that at this point Tosca is desperately trying to escape the unwanted advances of the hateful Baron Scarpia; but anyone wanting to understand the true force of this performance must read the text. Forget about Scarpia; this is a woman who has given her life to art and to love and who in her hour of pain asks God why she has been brought to this pass. Only if we understand the terrible congruence of Callas' situation and Tosca's can we know why this is a performance of such fearful poignancy. EMI should be ashamed of their omission."[3]

J. B. Steane, two years later, was equally appreciative of what made Callas special: "There are moments of loose or raw tone, and then suddenly a passage where Callas the Great emerges and sends a shiver down the spine, including Dalila's 'Printemps qui commence', beautifully sung and so assured in its restraint, its occasional thrilling portamento, its slimlined voice that has no interest in the sultry, cloying ways of the conventional vamp."[4]

* * *

CDM769543.2

The second compilation – MARIA CALLAS & GIUSEPPE DI STEFANO – DUETS – followed hard upon: a collection of duets with di Stefano, culled from the complete recordings about which J. B. Steane said he could "write much in praise of Callas' part in them. As ever, the first sound of her voice brings a thrill of recognition – not simply of the sound but of the art and soul within it. We sample her Gilda in *Rigoletto* and Mimi in *La bohème,* both special voice creations: not disguises which might fall off in an accident, but through-and-through identities. Di Stefano is best suited in the Puccini excerpts, least well in the Bellini (*I puritani*), but one must always be grateful for his responsiveness, never inert or merely nominal. Wanted now is a similar disc in which we can hear Callas with a partner who most fully matched her, Tito Gobbi."[5]

But this was not to be. The truth is that Gobbi's much-vaunted partnership with Callas was in fact a gramophone invention – seven complete recordings in the studio but only three operas on the stage (*La traviata* in Sao Paulo and Chicago, *Il Barbiere di Siviglia* at the Scala and *Tosca* in Paris, London and New York). This is in somewhat marked contrast to di Stefano who partnered her in ten complete recordings and nine operas on stage (*I puritani* in Mexico City and Chicago, *La traviata* in Sao Paulo, Mexico City and La Scala, *Lucia di Lammermoor* in Mexico City, Florence, Genoa, La Scala, Chicago, Berlin and Vienna, *Rigoletto* and *Tosca* in Mexico City, *Un ballo in maschera* and *La gioconda* at La Scala, *Mefistofele* in the Verona Arena and *Madama Butterfly* in Chicago). Gobbi was the greater artist, unquestionably, but di Stefano the finer colleague.

★ ★ ★

CDM 763182.2

Eighteen months later came two mid-price compilations – THE INCOMPARABLE CALLAS, and THE ART OF MARIA CALLAS (a 257 minute anthology on four CDs). Originally released at full price on the 10th anniversary of Callas' death, the single disc gave Alan Blyth much pleasure: "For me, the incomparable Callas is the one to be heard in her absolute prime on the *I puritani* set that was the period of the early and mid 1950s. Around 1960, the marked decline began and as most of these extracts from complete sets and recitals are from after that date, I would not consider this the most convincing representation of her art. Having said that, I would have to add, even though the voice is no longer as luminous or reliable as it once was, the artistry is not merely undimmed but often increased; that can be heard in her singing of both 'Casta diva' and 'Regnava nel silenzio' from her second *Norma* and *Lucia* which surpasses the earlier sets in detail of phrasing and colour. Then 'Ernani, involami' and 'Suicidio!' were made just early enough to capture the singer still at her very best. She always claimed that the last act of her second *La gioconda* was one of her most notable achievements, and this solo, climax of the much underrated opera, is almost frighteningly immediate in its exposure of the heroine's terrible predicament. To move from these to the later 'Ritorna vincitor' and 'Vissi d'arte' is to realise just how the voice had deteriorated yet there is something in the depth and imagination of the readings to compensate for the frailty of the singing. Of the French items, Callas is heard in the extreme opposites of coloratura and mezzo arias. In the former, the familiar insights and delicacy are there but the tone often sounds worn and/or edgy. The first of the *Carmen* extracts shows a somewhat snarling, unsmiling gypsy, but the Card scene is mesmerically fatalistic. Most persuasive are Orpheus' lament and Dalila's famous aria, unissued at the time it was made but recorded at the same session as the Gluck. Max Loppert has written of Callas' 'J'ai perdu' that 'her tone was raw and thin, even in middle and lower register but how searingly meaningful, how cogent and passionate her union of words and music.' That 'union' is heard even more arresting in 'Mon coeur s'ouvre', where she brings to the familiar music an appropriately sensual tone and manner. In these two pieces Callas is indeed 'incomparable'."[6]

Reviewing both mid-price issues, J. B. Steane was not uncritical: "Among those who approach the altar there will no doubt be both believers and sceptics, but the majority will be ordinary visitors to the shrine, always hoping for revelation but prepared simply to get as much as they can from what the experts proclaim a masterpiece, and to feel as they pass on that perhaps something has eluded them for they can't help noticing the smudges, the flakes and flaws. Certainly it would be unfortunate if the experience were to start [as mine did] with the first tracks of 'The Incomparable Callas'. Incomparable she was indeed, and especially incomparable was her Norma; but just about the last place to look to is her 'Casta diva', particularly in the second recording of the opera. All that is 'incomparable' here are the chromatic scales; plenty of sopranos have sung the aria better. Again, if the Fountain scene in *Lucia* is to be selected, the first rather than the second recording has the voice in something like good condition, whereas in the second we flinch, almost involuntarily before the high notes. Then the *Ernani* aria, and more flinching, with unlovely tone in the cadenza and a horrid B flat at the end. But of course the truly incomparable Callas is not to be found - or only incidentally – in such arias: her greatness lay in something else and it suddenly breaks through into the light of day with 'Ritorna vincitor', which is not so much an aria as a dramatic monologue. Here she is magnificent in intensity, unfailing in the appreciation of changing moods and the ability to seize the crucial moment. From then on there is much to relish, much that is simply unmissable, even in those later recordings when the soprano tone has worn badly, beauty remaining only in the mezzo range."

With the big four-disc set [CMS763244.2], he was generally much happier: "The programme has been exceptionally well thought out by Jacques Bourgeois, and forms a balanced triptych with the 'tragic' and the 'verismo' heroines on each side of the 'romantic' heroines. This stands a much better chance of capturing 'the incomparable Callas' because it includes whole scenes rather than simply arias. Thus, Norma is represented not by 'Casta diva' but by the formidable phrases of 'In mio man alfin tu sei' going through to the end of the opera. Lady Macbeth is there in the complete Sleep-walking scene, Tosca in the Love Duet (first version) and Violetta is live from Lisbon." At this point, J. B. Steane started to pick holes in EMI's presentation of the discs, with its muddle over recording and publication dates. "But as Richard Osborne once said: 'Records like this change people's lives.' That is the way with shrines and (despite some criticism) these new issues contribute handsomely to the upkeep."[7]

* * *

LUCIA DI LAMMERMOOR (1955)

The success of the Lisbon *Traviata* release must have encouraged EMI to issue more recordings of famous live performances. This they did in the early 'Nineties following a further release of all the studio recordings in digitally re-mastered sound on both LP and CD between 1985 and 1991. This breakthrough was initiated with the CD issue of two legendary performances – the Berlin/Karajan *Lucia di Lammermoor* of 29th September 1955 (my 19th birthday) and (would you believe it?) another *Traviata* – the epoch-making production earlier that year on the 28th May at La Scala, conducted by Giulini and directed by Visconti. *Lucia* was first reviewed in **Gramophone** by Alan Blyth in 1978 when it appeared on LP on the Cetra Opera Live label: "By common consent, this is about the best performance of Callas' *Lucia* recorded live or in the studio. Karajan had performed the work with her at La Scala a year earlier; here they seem to have perfected the partnership. Callas presents a more fragile, vulnerable, perhaps more orthodox portrayal than in her two EMI sets. The tone is more forward, lighter, but the characterisation no less vivid. To support her, Karajan provides vivid accompaniment, and throughout reveals Donizetti's work as something of a masterpiece; he ideally fuses music and drama, and is alternately fiery and delicate. Almost needless to say, he extracts superb playing from the Berlin orchestra. To make our cup overflow even further, there is di Stefano as Edgardo at the very peak of his form, phrasing his music with even greater attention to the text than the 1953 studio recording, while Panerai provides just the kind of high-baritone dash this role needs, his tone fierce and vibrant. I could enthuse much more extensively about the set but enough has already been written here and elsewhere about Callas' Lucia; suffice to say, it is here refined through the touch of a great conductor and fired by the sense of a real occasion. Of all Callas' live performances, I (like John Ardoin) might well choose this one to take to a desert island."[8]

A Night to Remember – 29th September, 1955, at the Stadtische Oper, Berlin after the performance of *Lucia* conducted by Herbert von Karajan

Fifteen years later for the EMI CD release, Richard Osborne (Karajan's biographer) wrote in **Gramophone**: "For many years this live performance was one of the most prized of all unauthorised sets, offering those of us who weren't there a chance to sample a sensation and discover why some normally robust critics were robbed of sleep for a week by the experience. EMI have now the rights to this recording and in many respects it is a set that can lay claim to being the most representative – the most vivid and searching – of all extant recordings of Callas in this, one of her most famous roles. The fact that the performance is live, rather than studio-bound is crucial in a single key respect. Callas is herself transformed by the experience. In the very act of playing Lucia on the stage, she completely becomes her in mind and spirit. And she does this in a way that was never quite the case in her two EMI recordings, either the earlier and better of the two, the 1953 Florence version or the perceptibly over-the-hill 1959 London recording. The live version brings with it some technical limitations which I mention below but it is not without its advantages, not least in the crucial matter of perspective. In this Berlin recording, Callas herself is often more naturally 'placed' than is the case in the 1953 Florence set, where the close microphoning favoured by EMI's Italian production team tends to rob the singing of mystery and allure. It must be said that the engineers of 'Sender Freies Berlin' whose tapes are here digitally mastered by EMI, were enormously helped in all this by Karajan's production. Franco Zeffirelli recalls: 'He arranged everything around her. She did the Mad Scene with a follow-spot, like a ballerina, against black. Nothing else. He let her be music, absolute music.' It was, Zeffirelli, argued the only way to produce Callas whose musical command and command of gesture obviated all need for fabricated play-acting. Callas' was not a Lucia that needed to flutter about the stage like a demented dove. Musically and dramatically, the relationship between Callas and Karajan was symbiotic. As a result, Callas' portrayal of Lucia is here deeper than ever it was. In this performance the depth of her love for Edgardo, and her trust in him, are so overwhelming that when she is shown the fabricated letter of betrayal the shock is monstrous. We hear this not only in her renunciation of the words 'Me infelice!' but in the Larghetto that follows where she seems already to have passed beyond this world. The Mad Scene is not so much presaged at this moment; spiritually, this is just where it begins. In the Mad scene itself, the lines are longer than in the Florence recording, the phrasing subtler, the gradations of tone more unerringly placed. And the voice is in generally excellent shape. Reviewing the performance in **Opera** in December 1955, Desmond Shawe-Taylor wrote: 'I dare say she will never sing better than she does now; there is Greek resin in her voice which will never be quite strained away; she will never charm with the full round ductile tone of Muzio, Raisa or Ponselle. But she has sudden flights, dramatic outbursts of rocketing, virtuosity of which even those more richly endowed singers were hardly capable.' The opening scene by the fountain, in fact, is the grain in Callas' tone – the Greek resin – that helps give the performance its disturbing, visionary power; more Graham Sutherland than Joan. As a study of Lucia herself this performance is well-nigh unsurpassable. It is the Lucia of a lifetime."[9]

Richard Fairman in **Opera** totally agreed: "The recording of *Lucia* was always of better quality than its Traviata counterpart and the new transfer is good enough to be acceptable to the general listener. Although Callas and Karajan performed the opera to acclaim at La Scala, it was the Berlin performances a year later that have done most to make their collaboration familiar through this live recording. The set makes a useful corollary to EMI's two studio recordings, not least because it shows without a shadow of doubt that Callas in the opera house could achieve the same remarkable vocal standards, often heightened still further in rhythmic precision and energy, that she managed in the studio – unlike some later purveyors of the role."[10] In 1997, with the 20th Anniversary reissues, J. B. Steane summarised the whole Callas/Lucia industry:' "The role which her performances most extended in the public perception was probably Lucia di Lammermoor. We never heard her in the part in Britain, so that it was in the Zeffirelli production for Sutherland that the opera came to new life on stage for us. But Callas' first recording had prepared the ground, and, in those houses which were lucky enough to hear her, audiences felt themselves present at a revelation. That was nowhere more markedly so than in Berlin, where with the Scala company under Karajan she gave performances that were rapturously received, as we can hear in the recording made live on the first night. Everything works together for good here. Karajan brings out the richly imaginative quality of the orchestral score, di Stefano rises sometimes as one inspired, earning an ovation in the final scene, and Callas is at the height of her powers. Of the two studio recordings, the second, made in 1959, is dispensable (the worn high notes are more of a trial here and the promise of some distinguished lyric singing by Tagliavini's presence as Edgardo was not borne out). The 1953 version with di Stefano and Gobbi (both are conducted by Serafin) is much finer, and taking into account the matter of recorded sound (for the Berlin performance is subject to the hazards of unplanned live recording) this may be the safest choice. But for a great opera house occasion – and there should certainly be an example of that in any Callas collection – the Lucia in Berlin is unrivalled. Ardoin goes so far as to say, 'if I could own but a single Callas set, it would be this one.'"[11] This interesting reflection nearly 50 years after Callas' first Lucia burst upon the scene would not, I think, be acceptable to Andrew Porter whose 1960 review found the second Lucia anything but dispensable!

* * *

LA TRAVIATA (1955)

The 1955 Scala *Traviata* which was issued alongside had also been previously reviewed by Alan Blyth in **Gramophone** when it appeared on a Cetra LP set: "However much we may miss an EMI studio *Traviata* with Callas, it could hardly have equalled the dramatic truth and power of the Scala interpretation so carefully prepared by Giulini and Visconti, and given added inspiration by the presence of an audience. This is a performance of Verdi's work to set quite apart from all others, a realisation I never expect to hear equalled. Here, in very reasonable sound, at least until the last two scenes, the full force of the achievement can be experienced. Adjectives fail me in describing Callas' account of Violetta's role: it is so inevitably right from start to finish that to dissect it would be unfair. Practically every aspect of the part, technical and emotional, is fulfilled in a single overwhelming interpretation. She is wonderfully supported by di Stefano in fresh vibrant voice (though he is not always obedient to Verdi's dynamic markings), rather less so by Bastianini's honest but monochrome Germont père. The Scala Orchestra is at its most sensitive under Giulini, who is attentive to detail while shaping the music in long, lyrical lines. His tempi are always judicious, always yielding to show the respect he has since stated he held for Callas' art and his own complete involvement in the whole production. The usual theatre cuts are made – no matter: the set is *hors concours* and should be in any respectable opera collection."[12]

On the EMI CD, the set was likewise ecstatically welcomed in **Gramophone** by J. B. Steane: "Possibly the most famous production of *La traviata* since its premiere proved almost as controversial as its ill-fated original. In dispute were Visconti's updating of setting and costumes to the 1880's, the prominence of his name on the hoardings, the conductor speeds, the soprano's voice and the tenor's general exasperation. For Callas it was the culmination of all artistic endeavour, to work on the great role in the great house and in such enriching detail with the aristocracy of Italy's theatrical and musical world as represented by Visconti and Giulini. It was the year of fulfilment. Her voice and art enjoyed a brief period of equilibrium, and there still tingled a sense of discovery, of widening prospects and changing perspectives. The production survives the controversy of its day with remarkable serenity to re-emerge quite simply as a performance of rare depth and beauty. Although it is still mildly astonishing that the baritone, Ettore Bastianini, could have been on stage with Callas for twenty minutes without something touching his art into a different kind of life, and, almost equally that Callas could have played her own part so movingly with so little coming back from her colleague. And yet she does. Nothing could carry more sure and touching conviction than her 'Oh come dolce' and rarely can the remark have had less to prompt it. There are marvels in this scene. 'Non sapete' struggles against fate like a caged bird. The desolate acknowledgement, 'E ver', just escapes from her lips, and the despairing 'Morrò' has an annihilating force that should have sunk father Germont and his middle-class morality into the ground. The final act is greatness

Curtain call for "an artistic landmark" – Visconti's *La traviata* at La Scala on 28th May 1955 – with Ettore Bastianini, Carlo Maria Giulini, Maria Callas and Giuseppe di Stefano

itself, and indeed no part, and hardly any phrase, of Callas' performance throughout the opera fails to provoke and deserve special comment. At one point the Milanese audience makes its own comment on the way it knows best by applauding while the music and action still continue. This is after the outburst of 'Amami, Alfredo' sung with such blazing sincerity that Alfredo's reaction to the letter five minutes later seems not merely unperceptive but moronic. Callas' intensity here has powerful support from Giulini, who builds the orchestral crescendos with overwhelming passion." Mr Steane concludes, having declared a very marginal preference for the Lisbon set: "Even so, somewhere at the heart of this performance from La Scala, there glows a warmer, fuller life of voice and spirit. I find more love in the memory of it even though the other version commands in many ways greater admiration and provides enjoyment with fewer checks and limitations."[13]

We get a rather different view from Richard Fairman in **Opera**: "The Scala *Traviata* is especially welcome even if it does still sometimes sound as if it was taped from the prompt box or by someone hanging Mapleson-like from the flies. The story of how Callas, Giulini and Visconti rehearsed this production for months on end – much to di Stefano's chagrin – is well-known, its truthfulness borne out here by the astonishing unanimity with which every detail of the conception has been realised. Perhaps Callas' Lisbon performance of the opera catches her fine tuning of the role of Violetta to an extra degree; but that production did not have the soprano working in a team of anything like the same calibre. The difference wrought by Giulini really does show in the pacing of scenes, in the heart-rending climaxes that well up at the close of 'Dite alla giovine' or 'Amami, Alfredo', and ultimately in the final ensemble, where colour and phrasing in voice and orchestra and fuse into a single musical line. This is what turning music into drama is all about. Di Stefano, despite the impatience he may have felt with his colleagues or even possibly because of it, makes an ardent Alfredo, who explodes into a fit of near manic rage during the showdown at Flora's party; Bastianini is a strong Germont père. No other *Traviata* on disc can touch this as a thrilling occasion."[14]

For the 20th Anniversary release, summarising *Traviata* with Callas as he did with *Lucia*, J. B. Steane finds it less successful sonically: "On the whole, the less likely-looking Lisbon performance is far more satisfying than the Scala, which has thrilling moments such as the great cry of 'Amami, Alfredo' in Act 2 when almost for the first time Giulini seems to have become really involved. The conductor at Lisbon, Franco Ghione, is more sensitively in charge throughout, and Callas herself gives a more complete performance even though some of the singing is perilous indeed. The studio recording for Fonitcetra (1953) is hampered by the indifferent conducting and work of the other singers. But Callas'Violetta is still the most memorable and in one version or other it must be had: I would recommend the Lisbon, in spite of vocal frailties and the incidental distraction of noises from on stage and off."[15] Michael Tanner at the same time thought it "a tragedy that we don't have a recording in very good sound. The live performance from Lisbon in 1958 had a prompter who ought to be listed as a cast member; but Callas is simply incomparable. If you don't want your opinions of any other performer to be spoilt, don't listen to the set because Callas will surely founder your allegiance."[16]

★ ★ ★

MACBETH

Obviously encouraged by the success of three live issues, EMI released a further five between 1994 and 1997 – *Macbeth*, *Il pirata*, *Anna Bolena*, *Poliuto* and *Ifigenia in Tauride*. Callas had recorded items from all these except *Poliuto*, some memorably. But nevertheless, the lack of complete studio recordings, as time passed and her greatness grew, necessitated a representative live performance on disc. In this however there are always problems. Of the five sets issued, two (*Anna Bolena* and *Poliuto*) are technically good enough to be included in **G.C.G.CD G.2000**. Unfortunately, the relatively poor sound of *Macbeth* meant that the set could be recommended to Callas collectors only, in a 1999 Radio3 **Building a Library** programme. Alan Blyth reviewing the performance on a Cetra LP set in 1978 wrote: "Callas effectively puts in perspective the Verrett and Cossotto readings and convinces me beyond a doubt that the role should be cast with a soprano – and one of exactly Callas' mettlesome quality. In 1952, she was still a large lady, but as photos of the Ebert production at La Scala show, she already used her face and body to convey character, and the vocal performance is penetrating in its perspicacity of utterance and in Callas' clever differentiation between Lady Macbeth's external and internal thoughts, also in the way she understands Verdi's development from the rudimentary early composer of 'Vieni t'afretta' to the subtle, disturbed writing of 'La luce langue', rising from the veiled half-voice at the start to full voicing of the final section as Lady Macbeth imagines her triumph. Her variation between the two verses of the Brindisi is further evidence of the thought behind her revealing interpretation. So is articulation of the Sleepwalking scene, but this is partially vitiated by de Sabata's ludicrously fast and light treatment of the scene." Richard Osborne, on welcoming the EMI CD issue, found the sound of the performance seriously flawed, though not insurmountably: "As always the ear adjusts. Once past the opening scenes, it is possible increasingly to discount the vagaries of vocal and instrumental balance. The ear adjusts even to the troublesome shadows thrown over the performance by an unusual amount of pre- and post- echo. If there is a real frustration, it comes in a short section of the sleepwalking scene when the sound is fogged by what seems like indifferent radio reception. It has often been said that the Callas/Gobbi studio version of *Macbeth* was one of the century's great unmade recordings. Unlike Gobbi, La Scala's Macbeth, Enzo Mascherini is barely adequate. (Lady Macbeth's 'Leave all the rest to me' seems at the time like a production note, an injunction from Callas herself as well as from the character she is playing.) That said, the portrait gathers power as the drama unfolds. The other key collaborator in the Scala production is the conductor Victor de Sabata. Much of his conducting is superb. In particular, there is the way scenes build, taking on weight and fire at nodel points. He makes cuts in the score but they are usually strategic cuts. (The pacing of the banquet scene is effectively tightened by a one-verse-only start to Lady Macbeth's drinking song.) It is also marvellous to have the Act Three ballet music, to which Verdi attached considerable importance, included in so purposeful a reading. There are, however, miscalculations. There is a curiously muzzy, unfocused feel about the crucial hushed colloquy after the murder. Worse, there is the very rapid speed adopted by de Sabata and Callas in the Sleepwalking scene. True, the tempo is only marginally quicker than the printed metronome, but the metronome mark itself is clearly too fast. The result is a mere sketch, a fleeting impression of the scene. This in turn means there is no real moment of catharsis in the opera's (otherwise perilously banal) denouement. Callas's later studio recording of the Sleepwalking scene, conducted by Rescigno and produced by Walter Legge is much to be preferred. This unforgettable account of that scene is the recital disc's one claim to indispensability. In the other two scenes, the 1952 live performance is much to be preferred. In the first place, there is the commanding sweep of the whole – Callas' Lady Macbeth determining everything from her first moments, where majesty and brooding power are attended by a viper's power to strike and wound, through to the traumas of the Banquet scene where Lady Macbeth is both the dauntless hostess and urgently confiding psychotherapist. And then there are the telling details. Above all, they come in Act II in a supreme account of 'La luce langue' which far outshines what Callas was later to give us, out of

Callas as Macbeth's "fiend-like queen" opens the 1952 Scala season

context, on the Rescigno disc. The text of 'La luce langue' is more or less Verdi's own, closely based on words Macbeth utters in the original play. The music is also new; it dates from the 1865 revision. Here, indeed, we have Callas at her greatest. 'An eagle among chickens' is how Julian Budden describes the revised scene, sitting, as it does, in the midst of the 1847 original. On this recording Callas, too, is an eagle among chickens."[18]

Charles Osborne was also impressed, as he explains in **Opera**: "This *Macbeth* shows Callas in something close to her prime and in a role which suited her to perfection. It is a role which surprisingly she never recorded in the studio. Commenting on a proposed performer for Lady Macbeth, Verdi wrote that the singer's voice should be "hard, stifled and dark". The latter-day Callas would no doubt have seemed ideal to him, but he would also have appreciated her superb vocal acting at the time when her voice still retained a steely beauty as well as exhibiting a thrilling dramatic intensity. On this Scala first night, phrase after phrase is meaningfully and convincingly articulated, and her performance of the Sleepwalking scene is magnificent. It is hard to believe that Callas was singing the role for the first time. After five performances at La Scala she never sang it again."[19]

⋆ ⋆ ⋆

IL PIRATA

J. B. Steane could not entirely overlook technical flaws in *Il pirata* despite the splendour of Callas' assumption: "We already know Callas' way with some of the principal solos, but of course what Callas had most characteristically to offer was quite likely not to be found in those so much as in some turning-points in the drama or some apparently incidental phrase of recitative, and so it proves here. Another of her qualities was to inspire an audience with the sense of a great occasion and to key-up a sympathetic conductor into the production of something to match her own intensity and the public's expectations. Rescigno rises marvellously well to the occasion at the start. This, with its storm at sea witnessed from the shore, inevitably calls to mind (as Andrew Porter has observed) the opening of *Otello*; but just how close Verdi came to making direct quotation at the point where the ship is seen to strike the rocks becomes patent in this taut, hard-driven performance of Rescigno's. As for the audience, once Callas herself has arrived excitement seems almost frenetic. Great waves of applause rise out of what, objectively assessed, is often remarkably little. The big solos of the first scene have their merits, to be sure, but what seems to galvanise the audience as though with an assurance that this is 'the goods' is the culminating D, a raw uneven sound, arrived at with peril and sustained with endurance. This tends to be the pattern throughout. In quiet passages, especially where there is no Callas, the coughing testifies to the ravages of the New York winter; when soprano and tenor hurl themselves full voice at a top C pandemonium breaks loose as at the winning goal in a football match. The occasion was certainly a special one. This was the high season of Callas-mania, and phobia too, for she had recently broken with the Rome Opera and La Scala and more relevant to New Yorkers, the Metropolitan. So this appearance with the American Opera Society in a concert performance at Carnegie Hall was the Big Event. Its magnitude was hardly reflected by the tenor and baritone at her side. Callas herself achieves a kind of fitful greatness. At first it is evident, not so much in the *Norma*-like 'Sorgete', as in the anxiety expressed by tone-colour and accentuation in ' Lo sognai ferito'. Then in Act II, there is her verse in the duet with Gualtiero, an object-lesson in the delicacy and restraint beneath which the fire burns steadily. The finale is vividly done."[20]

Callas as Imogene in a concert performance of Bellini's *Il pirata* at the Carnegie Hall, New York on 29th January, 1959

Charles Osborne, more grudging in **Opera** than for *Macbeth* writes: This recording was made when the soprano's best years were already behind her. Reviewing the event in Opera, Jeremy Noble said that Callas' 'first note might have been emitted by a Hudson tug-boat but that she improves steadily throughout the opera.' These discs bear him out. That first sustained note introduces simultaneously both the hoot and the wobble for which Callas became as renowned as for her dramatic intensity, but once one accepts the fact that this is not going to be an evening of bel canto, one can derive great pleasure from the soprano's intuitive intelligence and forceful presence. She is impressive, if still occasionally squally, in the duet 'Tu m'apristi' with Ernesto and especially moving in its larghetto section 'Ah! lo sento'. The Carnegie Hall audience contributes coughs and screams of frenzied appreciation in equal measure, and responds excitedly to Callas' final cabaletta. Musically uneven and dramatically unsatisfactory though it is, *Il pirata* still contains enough of Bellini at his best to deserve its reacquired place in the repertory. And this performance will certainly not disappoint hard-core Callas fans."[21]

* * *

ANNA BOLENA

For some, Callas gave her very greatest performances as *Anna Bolena*. It was the fourth of her five colaborations with Visconti; the conductor Gianandrea Gavazzeni said it was his finest night in the theatre. Alan Blyth conveyed his excitement in 1978 when he reviewed the LP set on Cetra Opera Live: "This is a great performance of a great opera and another indispensable part of the Callas legacy. By the universal consent of contemporary listeners – and I wish I had been among them – 1957, and this performance in particular, formed the peak of the diva's career. Under the spell of Visconti's inspired direction and in the handsome Benois sets, Callas brought to the role of the forlorn yet dignified, remorseful yet fiery Anne Boleyn all that she had learnt from her previous essays in the Bellini and Donizetti repertoires. Her command of colour, temperament and verbal nuance seem here to reach their zenith and she identifies with the tragedy of the wronged, unhappy queen. She gives as much attention to a little aside such as 'Ah! non tradirmi, o core', where she says to herself that her heart mustn't betray to Henry her former lover Percy when he unexpectedly returns to court, as she does to the tender musings of her opening cavatina, where in a gentle, cupped half-voice she recalls the ashes of her first love. She finds just the right appealing timbre for the start of the finely wrought sextet, 'In quegli guardi', a Donizettian cantilena of refined expression, and in contrast she exclaims 'Guidici! Anna' with the vehement force of surprise at the King's revelation of his purpose. In the final scene, the

Callas as Donizetti's ill-fated Anna Bolena [La Scala, 14th April, 1957]

famous cavatina 'Al dolce guidami', elegiacally, sensuously phrased in a way singular to Callas, is crowned by an imperious 'Coppia iniqua' as Anne goes to her death. The whole scene is the answer to those who think Callas could never sing with sustained beauty. It represents the very best of Callas and, in this case, the very best of Donizetti."[22]

Certainly J. B. Steane confirms this in his **Gramophone** review of the EMI CD: "In the Scala *Anna Bolena*, Callas gives one of her finest performances. The first impression is essentially a vocal one, in the sense of the sheer beauty of sound, for recording reveals it to be so much better focused than Simionato's. Then, in the first solo 'Come innocente', she is so clean in the cut of the voice and the style of its usage, delicate in her fioriture, often exquisite in her shading, that anyone ignorant of the Callas legend would know immediately that this is an artist of patrician status. There are marvellous incidental moments, and magnificent crescendos, culminating in the Tower scene." He is much less impressed with the supporting cast but finds that "the great ensembles still prove worthy of the event and a recording which is clear without harshness or other distortion conveys the special quality of this memorable evening at the opera with remarkable vividness and fidelity."[23]

Recommended in **G.C.G.CD G.2000**, he adds that "for those who insist on a modern recording, there is an imaginatively conducted 1994 performance on Nightingale Classics by Elio Boncompagni with Edita Gruberova in the title role. But this Callas/Gavazzeni set is in a different class altogether."[24]

★ ★ ★

POLIUTO

The fourth live release, *Poliuto*, owes its place in the Callas history, as J. B. Steane says, "less to the importance of this new role in her repertory than to the triumph of her return to the house she had left in high dudgeon in 1958. The part of Paolina in this Roman tragedy is restricted in opportunities and leaves the centre of the stage to the tenor. In other ways it suits Callas remarkably well, the Second Act in particular involving the heroine in grievous emotional stress with music that here runs deep enough to give it validity. In the first scene of that act she has a duet with the baritone in which her solo has a tendency she knew so well to depend on the right, instinctively judicious use of portamento. Later, in the Temple scene, her every utterance has its

In safe hands – Callas as Paolina and Franco Corelli as Donizetti's *Poliuto* at La Scala [7th December, 1960]

beauty or intensity, or both, and the whole company rises with her to the inspired climax of Donizetti's score. As Poliuto, Corelli is stupendous. It is not just the ring and range of voice that impress, but a genuinely responsive art. It is for his part in the opera, quite as much as for Callas', that the recording will be valued,"[25] warranting a **G.C.G.CD G.2000** recommendation: "The sound is clear and faithful to the timbre of the voices which are slightly favoured in the balance at the expense of the orchestra. With it comes unforgettable testimony to what was clearly a great night at La Scala. In addition to Callas' and Corelli's achievements noted above, there is a big part for the chorus which sings with fine Italian sonority. Nicola Zaccaria, La Scala's leading basso cantabile, has not quite the sumptuous quality of his predecessors, Pasero and Pinza, but is still in their tradition. Ettore Bastianini is rapturously received and, though wanting polish and variety of expression, uses his firm and resonant voice to exciting effect. The tenor comprimario, Piero de Palma, cuts a by no means inadequate vocal figure by the side of Corelli."[26]

★ ★ ★

IFIGENIA IN TAURIDE

The most recent live Callas EMI CD release – the 1957 Scala performance of Gluck's *Ifigenia in Tauride* – was not reviewed in **Gramophone**. Callas fatigue? But Alan Blyth had good things to say about it in 1978 when the performance appeared on a Cetra Opera Live LP set: "Much of the recitative is, as ever, memorably declaimed,particularly the call to heaven in Act 3. Then, just a little after, 'O malheureuse Iphigenie' strikes to the heart, the tone superbly supple, the words grandly uttered in great sculpted phrases – a plaint from the soul. This is the opera's centrepiece, and Callas realises it. The whole scene where Orestes should be sacrificed, especially the altar aria, 'Je t'implore', are as urgent as the defiance of Thoas is thrilling. The supporting cast is not adequate. Albanese is painfully unsure of himself. Dino Dondi simply heads for cover whenever a top F or F sharp hoves into view and sings lower, unauthorised alternatives thereby depriving Orestes' part of its anguish."[27]

Twenty years on, he reviews the CD issue for **Opera**, and time, as it did for JB Steane elsewhere in these pages, has clearly mellowed his views: "There is much to admire in Dondi's sincere well-sung Oreste, and in Albanese's effusive Pylades." And of Callas he is, as ever, in awe: "At last this most neglected of Callas' performances at La Scala comes to us in carefully refurbished sound, acceptable enough now to reassess the diva's performance of the classic heroine as unerringly depicted by Gluck. The production was the last in which Callas co-operated with Visconti, and photos have long shown just how impressive it must have looked, how dignified and moving Callas must have appeared in her fine costume and headwear. Her first entry, a coup de theatre on Gluck's part, found a short-sighted Callas running up and down a huge staircase trailing

25 yards of cloak apparently to electrifying effect while Visconti died a thousand deaths, and her account of this aria itself is searing. But her whole interpretation is filled with the tone and feeling to encompass the chaste dignity and inner eloquence of Ifigenia's utterances, nowhere more so than in the recitative when she learns from Oreste's own mouth of his supposed death and heart-rendingly sings 'Sommi Dei!' as only she can sing it. Just as moving is the

La Divina as Gluck's Ifigenia in Tauride [La Scala, 1st June 1957]

moment when she senses something familiar in Oreste's tones and says 'Mi fa la vista lor terribile tristezza'. When she at last recognises her lost brother, only Callas can invest with so many overtones of meaning in a single exclamation as she does in the word 'Fratello'. Which is not to say that the arias are disappointing: each is filled with passion, vibrant tone so different from what is considered authentic in singing Gluck today, but none the worse for that. Sanzogno displays a close affinity with the mood of the piece, playing it with suitable urgency and elan, given a large 19th century orchestra. At mid-price this is a worthwhile investment, not only for Callas aficionados but also for those who already have Gardiner's fine period-instrument set and want to hear a valid alternative."[28]

EPILOGUE – A CALLAS RETROSPECTIVE

As Richard Osborne wrote in the September 1987 issue of **Gramophone** to welcome a major release on the 10th anniversary of the her death, "the truth about Callas the artist rests with her extraordinarily extensive recorded legacy."[1] Christopher Pollard, in his Editorial the same month, was very properly supportive: "Thanks to Compact Disc, Callas' powers as an interpretative artist can now reach an even wider and, one hopes, younger audience. Given the enormous advances in the field of digital remastering and audio refurbishment, opera recordings made two or even three decades ago are now achieving a lease of life that, in terms of sound quality alone, allows them to stand up in comparison with the most recent recordings. Add to that the profound interpretative insights offered by singers whose careers developed at a more restrained tempo without the help of jet-aircraft, and the record buyer is in the pleasant position of being able to choose a recording from a much wider time span than ever before without having to worry unduly about the limitation of recorded quality. Artistic integrity backed by technical prowess has shown that age need not wither the 'infinite variety' of the great interpreters of yesterday and the way is now open for a critical revaluation of other masters of their art. And when the artist in question is of the calibre of Callas, it is a unique and rewarding experience indeed."[2]

Not everyone, of course, would agree with Mr Pollard that 'in terms of quality sound alone' Callas' recordings on CD 'achieve a new lease of life'. EMI, in each of its reissues, have continually adapted their sound, as Robert E. Seletsky states in a recent survey of her recordings in **The Opera Quarterly**, to the "perceived preferences of the record-buying public, consolidating matters of balance, colour and even pitch; sonically and (even) cosmetically one generation is easily distinguishable from another." The original LP covers of La Scala, the exterior on the lower half against black background, the interior on the upper half against coloured backgrounds, show in largest letters Teatro alla Scala, alongside composer, title and conductor, with the cast in small type, aping the traditional boards outside the opera house itself. The first reissue changed all this with Christian Steiner's colour photographs of Callas, giving similar lettering to composer, work, diva and conductor – the Scala insignia and supporting cast reduced in size, a clear tribute to Callas' increasing stature. But, as Seletsky says, "given her genuine and routinely reaffirmed reverence for the composers of the works she performed, Callas would have doubtless objected to the dominance of her name in ever-bolder face capitals on the slip-cases and jewel-case liners[for the 1997 issue] while their names are rendered in tiny print." Moreover, Steiner's elegant photographs on black backgrounds have simply been transferred in monochrone and some period photographs mislead potential buyers into false expectations – as in the 1953 *Tosca* with Zeffirelli's 1964 costume, the 1959 *Gioconda* with the larger 1952 image, and so on.

Irritating as Seletsky finds these, it is predictably the sonic failings that exercise him the more. Indeed the "extraordinarily intimate, human sound" of the voices which Walter Legge produced on the original LPs he now finds "recessed, thin, harsh, or tight, lacking colour, warmth and humanity."This is the scathing view of an audio specialist which would probably escape the notice of most domestic listeners, though many such are known to prefer the extra warmth, richness and depth of LP. But that is to presume the pristine condition of grooves and needle, which never match the enduring excellence of CD and laser. As we have seen, many of the earliest reviewers complained of LP distortion which the clarity of CD has dispatched for ever. Conversely though – in Seletsky's words – "all efforts geared towards 'improving' the original period sound on LP are invariably unsuccessful; recordings from Callas' great years cannot be forced to meet current sonic expectations without erosion of genuine, original vocal characteristics. It is (certainly) a tribute to Maria Callas that her unmistakable voice and incomparable musicianship always emerge triumphant."[3]

So much so, that this legendary singer has established a standard to which other artists can not only aspire but listen, learn and marvel. As we have seen, of the 28 CD sets currently available featuring roles which Callas sang between 1952 and 1964, over half are recommended in the CLASSICAL GOOD CD GUIDE 2000, published by Gramophone as the new millennium dawns. This surely is an astonishing achievement, quite unprecedented and one which vividly demonstrates the extraordinary appeal of the diva's artistry. 23 titles featured in '2000' carry a recommendation, 15 of which go to Callas; of her contemporaries, only Victoria de los Angeles remains, with 4; Mirella Freni has 3; Caballé and Sutherland 2; and a host of others one each.

To navigate this is veritable minefield, let us resume the chronology of the legacy from where it started in 1953. First was I PURITANI which currently has five available recordings – Sutherland (2), Gruberova, Sills and Callas. None, strangely perhaps, receives a recommendation; Bellini in '2000' is left to *Norma* and *La sonnambula*. This is a pity. Alan Blyth felt *Puritani* epitomised Callas' art as well as anything she ever did. But the recording, now with greater limpidity,

1955 – LP

1978 – LP 1987 – CD

1997 - CD

spaciousness and instrumental detail than its predecessors, was marred by the traditional cuts of the period and perhaps the supporting cast was too far from the ideal. The latest sound of the now legendary de Sabata TOSCA which followed has spaciousness, exuding a certain excitement not unlike some of the later LP versions and is, unsurprisingly, one of four recommendations. The unexpected inclusion from among 25 others available is, I think, the Philips recording with Caballe, Carerras and Wixell under Colin Davis, less powerful than Karajan's with Leontyne Price, di Stefano and Taddei. But the 1953 Scala set remains one of the glories of the last century and was voted its 4th greatest recording in a Gramophone poll. The sensation caused by Callas' 1953 LUCIA was overtaken only by her own re-recording in 1959. Of the eight *Lucias* currently available, Studer with Domingo comes nearest. However, the old magician Serafin sees La Divina safely home. The relative merits of the three available Callas recordings will never be ageed upon, though I personally have no quarrel with the '2000' recommendation.

CAVALLERIA RUSTICANA, and I PAGLIACCI linked with it a year later, join Karajan's powerful rendering as top recommendations. The 1953 sound of *Cavalleria* in particular weighs against it but the unbridled conviction of the performance carries all before. Moreover, the 1997 two CD version of the

Cav/Pag set permits each opera to occupy a single disc without breaks. NORMA very much follows in *Lucia's* footsteps. Callas' second recording, which initially so clearly divided opinion, comes through 40 years later sweeter than the 1987 CD issue and, achieving a lovely transparency recalling the virtues of good LPs, gains the only recommendation in the face of five current rivals – an apt tribute to one of the great assumptions of the century, worthily set in rich sumptuous sound and with strong supporting cast. But the first epic recording six years previously is only a nose behind. Callas' FORZA was the first complete recording of the work. Containing many wonderful things but (along with poor support) not quite enough to keep it in the front rank alongside Arroyo and Gorchakova and overtaken too by a 1943 recording with Stella Roman, under Bruno Walter. Callas' 'incomparable' Fiorilla in the now classic IL TURCO IN ITALIA gets a mention but is otherwise superseded by Bartoli's 'fine modern alternative' on Decca. Of the eight Callas sets passed over in '2000', the obvious omission must surely be MADAMA BUTTERFLY. Eloquent, even desperate, tributes are paid to this recording in earlier pages. However, with over 20 recordings available, the competition is very hot: Scotto is preferred in the classic Barbirolli set, and Freni is superbly supported by Pavarotti and Ludwig under Karajan. But can we really live without Callas' searing performance?

Sixteen AIDAs are currently available on CD, including Tebaldi, Leontyne Price, Milanov and Nilsson but it is Callas' assumption of 'total understanding and conviction' that wins the joint recommendation with Caballe, which, under Muti with Domingo, Cossotto and Cappuccilli and with the benefit of superior sound, is unbeatable. However, although Callas' recording with Tucker, Barbieri and Gobbi under Serafin cannot compare sonically, the brilliance of the creations they conjure up remain undimmed. Of the early favourites, Milanov and Tebaldi, there is no sign. It is a pity though that in the interests of economy the set, like *Carmen* previously, is now on 2 CDs thereby necessitating a jarring new break in the middle of Act II scene 2. [Conversely, the unnecessary splits hitherto in *Turco*, *Sonnambula*, *Turandot*, *Manon Lescaut* and *Medea* have been eliminated.] Another Verdi recording to receive top recommendation is RIGOLETTO, the Callas set having continued to hold sway over many other attractive comers (currently 20 in the catalogue) for 45 years since its release. Carped at then by the big guns, its inherent excitement and greatness ensure its lasting appeal. Callas' Amina was one of the great roles created in collaboration with Visconti at La Scala and although the studio recording of LA SONNAMBULA under Votto did not quite match a number of her magical live performances, it is still a top recommendation (also with Sutherland's first recording) displaying much beauty of voice and spirit.

Two further Verdi recordings from 1956 are highly recommended. 'An unbeatable line up' – Callas, di Stefano, Gobbi – catch the true spirit of UN BALLO IN MASCHERA as no other, under Votto's unerring direction. After an indifferent welcome, this shares the honours with Abbado and his team led by Ricciarelli, also from La Scala. Callas' IL TROVATORE under Karajan is even better. Leonora, one of her first and finest Verdi roles on stage, is given a superbly intense, marvellously paced reading, 'D'amor sull'ali rosee' a thing to marvel at. James Levine with Aprile Millo is the recommended runner-up. Callas' sub-standard Cetra recording of LA TRAVIATA (supporting cast and conductor) precluded (in favour of Stella) her participation in the 'necessary' EMI recording at the time. The sound of both live performances in Lisbon and La Scala – subsequently issued by EMI – is sadly not good enough to recommend the greatest Violetta of the century. Honours therefore go to the admirable Cotrubas.

Rosina in BARBIERE was Callas' only failure at La Scala and she very happily put the matter right with a scintillating recording in London's Kingsway Hall. But it was not quite good enough to challenge the editor of Gramophone's choice of Sonia Ganassi's recording on Naxos, or Baltsa or de los Angeles (1962). The celebrated Spanish soprano, who alone of Callas' contemporaries remains in sight, was also the top recommendation for LA BOHEME along with Freni (and Cynthia Hayman in English). It has already been seen that Callas' Mimi was a miracle of characterisation but in the last resort she lacked in Votto the support afforded by Beecham and Karajan. The following year that was supplied by Serafin, conducting the same composer's TURANDOT and securing Callas' place alongside Sutherland's top recommendation. A much-sung early role (too much perhaps), Callas was the perfect flashing-eyed Princess.

The Cetra LA GIOCONDA, tardily released in the UK, good as it was, gave way to Callas' stereo re-recording on EMI, a magnificent assumption and the only recommendation amongst four other stellar names currently available – Caballe, Cerquetti, Milanov and Tebaldi. Callas made MEDEA, unsuccessfully attempted by Gwynneth Jones and Phyllis Treigle, very much her own. '2000' do not recommend the opera for some reason despite the 1997 issue's new focus and energy. The EMI recording was by no means Callas' best performance of the work but to pass over it would seem perverse. Callas in MANON LESCAUT, needlessly held up for two years because of the diva's doubts, is at every moment of the work 'a great artist of the gramophone' and here, with di Stefano's passionate des Grieux, we have a classic set, admired particularly for its supreme account of the death scene, preferred from out of 10 rivals, alongside Freni and Pavarotti under James Levine. Four recordings of CARMEN are recommended in '2000', none of which is Callas'. Her performance was a much-heralded affair, much liked, but neither the voice nor style (or conductor) were quite good enough in the face of over 20 rivals.

The live *Traviata* issued in 1981 led to further releases of other famous Callas roles performed on stage but missed in the studio. Of these, two – ANNA BOLENA and POLIUTO – have good enough sound to be recommended over their studio rivals, Gruberova, Sills, Souliotis and Sutherland. Visconti's Scala production of *Bolena* was one of the great Callas manifestations. *Poliuto* was less celebrated, marking the diva's cautious return to her operatic home in 1960 but with Corelli's support it was a memorable one. Another two – MACBETH and IL PIRATA – both containing great Callas roles have to be passed over because the sound remains obstinately unacceptable. The most recent release (September 98) of Gluck's IFIGENIA IN TAURIDE has been neither reviewed nor listed to date in Gramophone publications, though much praised in Opera.

Of the numerous recitals, one only appears in '2000' – Maria Callas Rarities, a miscellaneous collection of rare studio takes, and live items of unique value and interest. However, the omission of her three greatest CD recitals in particular – Lyric and Coloratura Arias, Mad Scenes, and Verdi I – is not easy to accept. But Callas' recorded legacy is generous enough to absorb a few missing highlights. Indeed it is difficult to find another singer whose recorded art has survived the passage of time so completely. Many of her recordings – *Ballo, Gioconda, Lucia, Manon Lescaut, Norma, Rigoletto, Sonnambula, Tosca, Trovatore* – remain the standard by which others are judged. Critics in her own time – in particular, Philip Hope-Wallace and Harold Rosenthal – judged her art as it broke upon the scene in the context of what had gone before. Others, like Alan Blyth, Richard Osborne and J. B. Steane, compare it with what has come since. It must be clear from these pages that the former were harder to please than the latter; that to them, Callas was a post-war phenomenon who at times fell short of their pre-war icons. Now, 50 years on, those have rather slipped from view, whilst Callas' star shines brighter than ever.

DRAMATIS PERSONAE

Alan Blyth [b. 1927] has been one of the most assiduous and admiring of Callas' critics during the last thirty years. He welcomed for *Gramophone* the very first Scala reissue – *Tosca* – in March 1973 and was quick to recognise Callas' pre-eminence in the famous recording, the first to do so, she having previously given way to Tebaldi, de Sabata and Gobbi. Thereafter, he reviewed almost every Callas reissue, first on LP and then on CD, the last to date being *Traviata* and *Gioconda* on Warner Fonit Cetra in March 2000. He is particularly fond of the 1953 *Puritani*: "It epitomises Callas' art as well as anything she ever did."

Hilary Finch [b. 1951] has been active in the arts during the last 20 years. Her critical analyses on Radio 3's *Building a Library* have twice delighted Maria's admirers when Ms Finch recommended her Amelia above all others and on another occasion quickly sidelined other *Normas* and spent the major part of the programme choosing between Callas' 1954 and 1960 recordings. Sadly, the live recording of her famous 1952 Lady Macbeth from La Scala came up in sound too poor for Ms Finch to recommend.

Jack Freestone [b. 1910] reviewed the Cetra *Puritani* 78 [released on the Parlophone label] for *Gramophone* and, though unlike Lord Harewood at *Opera* he had not yet seen a Callas performance, he knew the voice on the disc was very special. His favourable impression was unforgettably confirmed at the diva's Covent Garden debut as Norma later that year.

Noel Goodwin [b. 1927] is one of a large number of young writers and critics to emerge after the war. He has published many books, on ballet in particular. His occasional forays into the Callas legacy for *Opera* are enjoyably terse and that on *Madama Butterfly* would suggest that he rather shares Princess Margaret's well-known view of opera in general.

Edward Greenfield [b. 1928], whose knowledge is legion, is a leading critic of the day particularly on recorded music. Not being an out-and-out Callas man, he confined himself for *Gramophone* to four of the singer's Puccini recordings and much liked what he heard. Three were outright winners and one – *Boheme* – was squeezed out by a whisker.

Lord Harewood [b. 1923] founded the *Opera* magazine in 1950 which gave him the pleasure of reviewing Callas' two Cetra 78s when they appeared on the Parlophone label in the UK. As we all know, the *Puritani* disc changed just about everybody's life and Lord Harewood was under no illusions in his ecstatic review. He first heard Maria in her 1947 *Gioconda* debut in Verona and four years later in Florence in *Vespri* which swept her into the Scala. He was instrumental in bringing Callas to Covent Garden the following year for her triumphant debut as Norma.

Philip Hope-Wallace [1911 – 1979] was the chief opera critic of *Gramophone* for all but the very beginning of Callas' active recording career. Thus, he reviewed the vast majority of her recordings as they first appeared and, together with Harold Rosenthal in *Opera*, established a powerful response to Callas' art, on record at least. Both gentlemen were brought up on the famous names of the pre-war era when a beautiful voice was almost enough and both certainly did not warm to some of the unorthodox sounds from the new Greek diva. In his first review (*Cavalleria rusticana*) he described a number of her notes as "overloaded, ill-placed or pinched, with an unpredictable and hooty quality." [This is the recording that achieves a recommendation 46 years later.] Twelve years on, however, he was completely won over by her "extraordinarily ripe and vivid Carmen" in his penultimate review [he was much less happy about the *Tosca* remake]. Thus he was part of the gradual acceptance of what Callas was about but had to leave its completion to others after her death.

Dyneley Hussey [1893 – 1972] a distinguished music critic, ran a monthly article in *Musical Times* on the new flood of LP recordings as they were released. His remarks were inevitably brief, somewhat trenchant and contained some delightful contemporary reflections. For example, of the 1953 *Puritani*: "The gramophone-performance soon becomes tedious.... too much of it proceeds in a hum-drum sort of way and it all sounds very much alike." But he soon capitulated to Norma [magnificent], the *Forza* Leonora [superb] and was utterly bewitched by the time he reached Medea and the early recitals.

Max Loppert [b. 1946] was mesmerised by three Callas Puccini recordings he reviewed for *Opera* in the 80's when he was chief music critic of the *Financial Times.*

William Mann [1924 – 1989], distinguished music critic of *The Times* from 1948 to 1982, wrote but one Callas review – *Manon Lescaut* in 1959 – in the journals quoted in these pages, when he eloquently described her as "a great artist of the gramophone who transforms a wooden box it into an experience."

Rodney Milnes [b. 1936] was editor of *Opera* from 1986 to 1999 during which time he displayed his strong and colourful views in print and over the air. He would despatch those of us who love *Andrea Chenier* and its ilk to a mad-house and Callas' Nedda to a cattery. Twenty years after Callas' first *Lucia* took the operatic world by storm, he found the edition insufferable. But after reviewing over half-a-dozen more LP reissues in the 'Seventies, he parted on very agreeable terms.

Michael Oliver [b. 1937], a writer and broadcaster, contributed a masterly *Building a Library* programme on *Manon Lescaut* in 1994 when he spoke eloquently of Callas' touching portrayal of Puccini's heroine. He was equally impressed by her "incomparable" Mimi.

Charles Osborne [b. 1927] is a prolific author on opera, Verdi and Wagner in particular. But, sadly, he is no admirer of Maria Callas.

Richard Osborne [b. 1943] reviewed two of Callas' earliest reissues in the 70's, the Cetra *Traviata* and the EMI *Cav* and *Pag*. These showed an immediate appreciation of her art, echoed on many other occasions in *Gramophone* with an unusual warmth towards and understanding of Callas' personal and professional tragedy.

Professor Roger Parker [b. 1951] is included here on the strength of his *Building a Library* analysis of Verdi's *Forza* when he betrayed a regrettably equivocal view of Callas' Leonora.

Andrew Porter [b. 1928] first reviewed Callas recordings in 1957 when he was music critic of the *Financial Times*. He was the only one of the new young wave of post-war critics to break into the older establishment. He was, therefore, almost inevitably the first critic to fully understand what Callas was about, that a beautiful voice was indeed not enough. This was particularly noticeable during that testing time around 1960 when the singer's vocal difficulties caused many a critical headache. Mr Porter, almost alone, merely smiled at her heightened art and he was, of course, in large measure, absolutely right.

Alec Robertson [1892 – 1982] doyen of music critics when he first came across Maria Callas at the tail end of his career. Steeped in a church music training and a lifetime of earlier pre-war standards and taste, he was unlikely to respond to Callas' unorthodox style and his review of her performance in the famous de Sabata *Tosca* was very wide of the mark. But he admired her Lucia, saw greatness in her Butterfly and raved over her Medea.

Harold Rosenthal [1917 – 1987] was the man of opera *par excellence* during the Callas era. As editor of *Opera* for 33 years, he reviewed every one of her 36 recordings except three at the very end of her career ["discretion the better part ....?"] Alone of the 'first generation' critics, the onset of the reissues afforded Mr Rosenthal the opportunity of reassessing ten of Callas' recordings, generally to the singer's advantage. For like his fairly near contemporaries Philip Hope-Wallace and Desmond Shawe-Taylor, he had initially shared their allegiance to stellar names with beautiful voices and occasionally allowed the technical faults of Callas' recordings to blind him to the essential dramatic and musical truth of her interpretations. Of her supreme artistry, though, he was never in doubt and he revered her accordingly.

Lionel Salter [1914 - 2000] was a distinguished broadcaster and made a brief and appreciative sortie into two of Callas' later recital discs.

Jeremy Sams [b. 1957] is an immensely talented man of the arts but he adopted a depressingly flippant attitude towards the recording artists in two *Building a Library* programmes I heard on *Turandot* and *Boheme*.

Desmond Shawe-Taylor [1907 – 1995] ran a highly regarded Quarterly Review in *Gramophone* which allowed him the luxury of reflecting at length and in detail on the merits and demerits of the human voice. He probably had more of a problem with Maria Callas' than any other, as these pages have testified. But even with him, she triumphed: "A brilliantly responsive Upper Sixth former," he called her in his review of her second Verdi arias disc, "to most other sopranos' inky Lower Fourth."

John B. Steane [b. 1928] has, with Alan Blyth, taken the lion's share of Callas' reviews in the last 30 years since his first foray with the *Barber* and the Cetra *Gioconda* in December 1974: he was much impressed. His knowledge of singers is legendary and has probably led him to be less dogmatic about Callas' interpretations than most. He relished *Gramophone*'s invitation in 1997 to overview the 20th Anniversary edition and left his readers to choose the glories of one set over another. Doubtless, he loved them all!

★ ★ ★

Maria Callas

[b. 2nd December 1923 in New York; d. 16th September 1977 in Paris]

DISCOGRAPHY

BELLINI

Norma
with Ebe Stignani, Mario Filippeschi, Nicola Rossi-Lemeni
Orchestra and Chorus of La Scala, Milan, conducted by Tullio Serafin
EMI CDS 556271.2 [3CDs] (r. 1954)

Norma
with Christa Ludwig, Franco Corelli, Nicola Zaccaria
Orchestra and Chorus of La Scala, Milan, conducted by Serafin
EMI CMS 566428.2 [3CDs] (r. 1960)

Il pirata
with Pier Miranda Ferraro, Constantino Ego
Orchestra and Chorus of the American Opera Society, conducted by Nicola Rescigno (live 27.01.1959)
EMI CMS 566432.2 [2CDs]

I puritani
with Giuseppe di Stefano, Rolando Panerai, Rossi-Lemeni
Orchestra and Chorus of La Scala Milan, conducted by Serafin
EMI CDS 556275.2 [2CDs]

La Sonnambula
with Eugenia Ratti, Fiorenza Cossotto. Nicola Monti, Zaccaria,
Orchestra and Chorus of La Scala, Milan, conducted by Antonino Votto
EMI CDS 556278.2 [2CDs]

BIZET

Carmen
with Andrea Guiot, Nicolai Gedda, Robert Massard
Orchestre du Theatre National de l'Opera de Paris/ Choeurs Rene Duclos, conducted by Georges Pretre
EMI CDS 556281.2 [2CDs]

CHERUBINI

Medea
with Renata Scotto, Miriam Pirazzini, Mirto Picchi, Giuseppe Modesti
Orchestra and Chorus of La Scala, Milan, conducted by Serafin
EMI CMS 566435.2 [2CDs]

DONIZETTI

Anna Bolena
with Giulietta Simionato, Gianni Raimondi, Rossi-Lemeni
Orchestra and Chorus of La Scala, Milan, conducted by Gianandrea Gavazzeni (live 14.04.1957)
EMI CMS 566471.2 [2CDs]

Lucia di Lammermoor
with di Stefano, Tito Gobbi, Rafaele Arie
Orchestra and Chorus of the Maggio Musicale Fiorentino, conducted by Serafin
EMI CMS 566483.2 [2CDs] (r. 1953)

Lucia di Lammermoor
with Ferrucio Tagliavini, Bernard Ladysz, Piero Cappuccilli
Philharmonia Orchestra and Chorus, conducted by Serafin
EMI CDS 556284.2 [2CDs] (r. 1959)

Lucia di Lammermoor
with di Stefano, Panerai, Zaccaria
RIAS Orchestra and Chorus of La Scala, conducted by Herbert von Karajan (live 29.09.1955)
EMI CMS 566438.2 [2CDs]

Poliuto
with Corelli, Ettore Bastianini, Zaccaria
Orchestra and Chorus of La Scala, Milan, conducted by Votto (live 07.12.1959)
EMI CMS 565448.2 [2CDs]

GLUCK

Ifigenia in Tauride
with Cossotto, Francesco Albanese, Anselmo Colzani
Orchestra and Chorus of La Scala, Milan, conducted by Nino Sanzogno
(live 01.06.1957)
CMS 565451.2 [2CDs]

LEONCAVALLO

I pagliacci
with di Stefano, Monti, Gobbi, Panerai

MASCAGNI

Cavalleria rusticana
with Anna Maria Canali, di Stefano, Panerai
Orchestra and Chorus of La Scala, Milan, conducted by Serafin
EMI CDS 556287.2 [2CDs]

PONCHIELLI

La gioconda
with Fedora Barbieri, Gianni Poggi, Paolo Silveri, Giulio Neri
RAI Orchestra and Chorus, conducted by Votto
Warner Fonit Cetra 3984-29355.2 [3CDs]

La gioconda
with Cossotto, Ferraro, Cappuccilli, Ivo Vinco
Orchestra and Chorus of La Scala, Milan, conducted by Votto
EMI CDS 556291.2 [3CDs]

PUCCINI

La boheme
with Anna Moffo, di Stefano, Panerai, Zaccaria
Orchestra and Chorus of La Scala, Milan, conducted by Votto
EMI CDS 556295.2 [2CDs]

Madama Butterfly
with Lucia Danieli, Gedda, Mario Boriello
Orchestra and Chorus of La Scala, Milan, conducted by Herbert von Karajan
EMI CDS 556298.2 [2CDs]

Manon Lescaut
with Cossotto, di Stefano, Giulio Fioravanti, Franco Calabrese
Orchestra and Chorus of La Scala, Milan, conducted by Serafin
EMI CDS 556301.2 [2CDs]

Tosca
with di Stefano, Gobbi
Orchestra and Chorus of La Scala, Milan, conducted by Victor de Sabata
EMI CDS 556304.2 [2CDs] (r. 1953)

Tosca
with Carlo Bergonzi, Gobbi
Orchestre de la Societe des Concerts du Conservatoire and Choeurs de l'Opera, conducted by Pretre
EMI CMS 566444.2 [2CDs] (r.1964)

Turandot
with Elisabeth Schwarzkopf, Eugenio Fernandi, Zaccaria
Orchestra and Chorus of La Scala, Milan, conducted by Serafin
EMI CDS 556307.2 [2 CDs]

ROSSINI

Il Barbière di Siviglia
with Luigi Alva, Gobbi, Zaccaria
Philharmonia Orchestra and Chorus, conducted by Alceo Galliera
EMI CDS 556310.2 [2CDs]

Il Turco in Italia
with Gedda, Rossi-Lemeni, Calabrese, Mariano Stabile
Orchestra and Chorus of La Scala, Milan, conducted by Gianandrea Gavazzeni
EMI CDS 556313.2 [2CDs]

VERDI

Aida
with Barbieri, Richard Tucker, Gobbi
Orchestra and Chorus of La Scala, Milan, conducted by Serafin
EMI CDS 556316.2 [2CDs]

Un ballo in maschera
with Ratti, Barbieri, di Stefano, Gobbi
Orchestra and Chorus of La scala, Milan, conducted by Votto
EMI CDS 556320.2 [2CDs]

La Forza del Destino
with Elena Nicolai, Tucker, Carlo Tagliabue, Rossi-Lemeni, Renato Capecchi
Orchestra and Chorus of La Scala, Milan, conducted by Serafin
EMI CDS 556323.2 [3CDs]

Macbeth
with Gino Penno, Enzo Mascherini, Italo Tajo
Orchestra and Chorus of La Scala, Milan, conducted by de Sabata (live 07.12.1952)
EMI CMS 566447.2 [2CDs]

Rigoletto
with Adriana Lazzarino, di Stefano, Gobbi, Zaccaria
Orchestra and Chorus of La Scala, Milan, conducted by Serafin
EMI CDS 556327.2 [2CDs]

La traviata
with Albanese, Ugo Savarese
RAI Chorus and Orchestra, Turin, conducted by Gabriele Santini
Warner Fonit Cetra 3984–29354–2 [2CDs]

La traviata
with di Stefano, Bastianini
Orchestra and Chorus of La Scala, Milan, conducted by Carlo Maria Giulini (live 28.05.1955)
EMI CMS 566450.2 [2CDs]

La traviata
with Alfredo Kraus, Mario Sereni
Orchestra and Chorus of the Teatro Nacional de San Carlo, Lisbon, conducted by Franco Ghione (live 27.03.58)
EMI CDS 556330.2 [2CDs]

Il trovatore
with Barbieri, di Stefano, Panerai
Orchestra and Chorus of La Scala, Milan,conducted by Herbert von Karajan
EMI CDS 556333.2 [2CDs]

RECITALS

EMI CDM 566457.2 CALLAS AT LA SCALA
Cherubini: Medea – Dei tuoi figli (Act I)
Spontini: La vestale – Tu che invoco (Act II)
– O Nume tutelar (Act II)
– Caro oggetto (Act III)
Bellini: La Sonnambula – Compagne, tenere amici ... Come per me sereno (Act I)
– Oh! Se una volta sola ... Ah! non credea mirati ... Ah! Non giunge (Act II)
Orchestra del Teatro alla Scala, conducted by Serafin

EMI CDM 566458.2 LYRIC & COLORATURA ARIAS
TESTAMENT 33CX1231
Cilea: Adriana Lecouvreur – Ecco: respiro appena. Io son l'umile ancella (Act I)
– Poveri fiori (Act IV)
Giordano: Andrea Chenier – La mama morta (Act III)
Catalani: La Wally – Ebben? Ne andro lontano (Act I)
Boito: Mefistofele – L'altra notte in fondo al mare (Act III)
Rossini: Il Barbiere di Siviglia – Una poco voce fa (Act I)
Meyerbeer: Dinorah – Ombra leggiera (Act II)
Delibes: Lakme – Dov'e l'indiana bruna? (Act II)
Verdi: I vespri siciliani – Merce, dilette amiche (ActV)
Philharmonia Orchestra, conducted by Serafin

EMI CDM 566459.2 MAD SCENES
TESTAMENT SAX2320
Donizetti: Anna Bolena – Piangete voi? Al dolce guidami castel natio (Act II)
Thomas: Hamlet – A vos jeux ... Partagez-vous mes fleurs ...
Et maintenant, ecoutez ... ma chanson. (Act IV)
Bellini: Il pirata – Oh! S'io potessi ... Col sorriso d'innocenza (Act II)
Philharmonia Orchestra, conducted by Serafin

EMI CDM 566460.2 VERDI ARIAS Vol. 1
Macbeth – Nel di della vittoria ... Vieni t'affretta (Act I)
– La luce langue (Act II)
– Una macchia e qui tuttora (Act IV)
Nabucco – Ben io t'invenni ... Anch'io dischiuso un giorno (Act II)
Ernani – Surta e la notte ... Ernani, Ernani, involami (Act I)
Don Carlo – Tu che la vanita (Act IV)
Philharmonia Orchestra, conducted by Serafin

EMI CDM 566461.2 VERDI ARIAS Vol. 2

Otello – Mi parea. M'ingiunse ... Mia madre aveva una povera ancella (Act IV)
– Piangea cantando (Act IV)
– Ave Maria piena di grazia (Act IV)
Aroldo – Cile, ch'io respiri ... Salvami, salvami tu gran Dio! (Act I)
– O cielo! Dove son io? (Act II)
Don Carlo – Non pianger, mia compagna (Act II)
– O don fatale (Act III)
Orchestre de la Societe des Concerts du Conservatoire, conducted by Nicola Rescigno

EMI CDM 566462.2 VERDI ARIAS Vol. 3

I Lombardi – O Madre, dal cielo soccorri (ActII)
Attila – Liberamente or piangi ... Oh! nel fuggente nuvol (Act I)
Il corsaro – Egli non riede ancor ... Non so le tetre immagini (Act I)*
– Ne sulla terra ... Vola talor dal carcere ... Verro ... Ah, conforto e sol la speme (Act II)*
Il trovatore – Tacea la notte placida ... Di tale amor (Act I)
I vespri siciliani – Arrigo! Ah, parli a un core (Act IV)
Un ballo in maschera – Ecco l'orrido campo ... Ma dell'arido stelo divulsa (Act II)
– Morro, ma prima in grazia (Act III)
Aida – Ritorna vincitor (Act I)

Orchestre de la Societe des Concerts du Conservatoire
*Orchestre du Theatre National de l'Opera de Paris
conducted by Nicola Rescigno

EMI CDM 566463.2 PUCCINI ARIAS
TESTAMENT 33CX1204

Manon Lescaut – In quelle trine morbide (Act II)
– Sola, perduta, abbandonata (Act IV)
Madama Butterfly – Un bel di vedremo (Act II)
– Con onor muore (Act II)
La boheme – Si, Mi chiamano Mimi (Act I)
– Donde lieta usci (Act III)
Suor Angelica – Sensa mamma
Gianni Schicchi – O mio babbino caro
Turandot – Signore, ascolta (Act I)
– In questa reggia (Act II)
– Tu che di gel sei cinta (Act III)

Philharmonia Orchestra, conducted by Tullio Serafin

EMI CDM 566464.2 ROSSINI & DONIZETTI ARIAS

Rossini: La Cenerentola – Nacqui all'affano ... Non piu mesta (Act II)
Guglielmo Tell – S'allontanano alfine ... Selva opaca (Act II)
Semiramide – Bel raggio lusinghier (ActI)
Donizetti: La filia del reggimento – Convien partir (ActI)
Lucrezia Borgia – Tranquillo ei posa ... Com'e bello (Act I)
L'elisir d'amore – Prendi, prendi, per me sei libero (Act II)

Orchestre de la Societe des Concerts du Conservatoire, conducted by Nicola Rescigno

EMI CDM 566465.2 MOZART, BEETHOVEN & WEBER ARIAS

Beethoven: Scena and Aria – Ah! perfido, Op.65
Weber: Oberon – Ocean! Thou mighty monster (Act II)
Mozart:: Le nozze di Figaro – Porgi, amor (Act II)
Don Giovanni – Or sai chi l'onore (Act I)
– Crudele? Non mi dir (Act II)
– In quail eccessi, o Numi ... Mi tradi quell'alma ingrata (Act II)

Orchestre de la Societe des Concerts du Conservatoire, conducted by Nicola Rescigno

EMI CDM 566466.2 CALLAS À PARIS Vol. 1
TESTAMENT SAX2410

Gluck: Orphee et Eurydice	– J'ai perdu mon Eurydice (Act IV)
Alceste	– Divinites du Styx (Act I)
Bizet: Carmen	– L'amour est un oiseau rebelled (Habanera) (Act I)
	– Pres des ramparts de Seville (Seguedille) (Act I
Saint-Saens: Samson et Dalila	– Printemps qui commence (Act I)
	– Samson, recherchant ma presence ... Amour! Viens aider ma faiblesse! (Act II)
	– Mon Coeur s'ouvre a ta voix (Act II)
Gounod: Romeo et Juliette	– Ah! Je veux vivre dans ce reve (Act I)
Thomas: Mignon	– Ah, pour ce soir ... Je suis Titania (Polonaise) (Act II)
Massenet: Le Cid	– De cet affreux combat ... Pleurez, mes yeux! (Act III)
Charpentier: Louise	– Depuis le jour (Act III)

Orchestre National de la Radiodiffusion Francais, conducted by Georges Pretre

EMI CDM 566467.2 CALLAS À PARIS Vol. 2

Gluck: Iphigenie en Tauride	– O malheureuse Iphigenie (Act II)
Berlioz: La Damnation de Faust	– D'amour l'ardente flame (Part 4)
Bizet: Les Pecheurs de perles	– Me voila seule ... Comme autrefois (Act II)
Massenet: Manon	– Je ne suis faiblesse ... Adieu, notre petite table (Act II)
	– Suis-je gentile ainsi? ... Je marche sur tous les chemins (Act III)
Werther:	– Werther! Qui m'aurait dit ... Des cris joyeux (Act III)
Gounod: Faust	– Je voudrias bien savoir ... Il etaiat un Roi de Thule ... O Dieu! Que de bij oux ... Ah! je ris (Act III)

Orchestre de la Societe des Concerts du Conservatoire, conducted by Georges Pretre

CMS 566468.2 THE EMI RARITIES
Mozart: Don Giovanni – Non mi dir (Take 1)
– Non mi dir (Take 2)
Orchestra del Maggio Musicale Fiorentino, conducted by Tullio Serafin (1953)

Verdi: Macbeth – Una macchia e qui tuttora (Act IV)
Philharmonia Orchestra, conducted by Nicola Rescigno (1958)

Rossini: Semiramide – Bel raggio lusinghier (Act I)
Verdi: I vespri siciliani – Arrigo! Ah, parli a un core (Act IV)
Philharmonia Orchestra, conducted by Antonio Tonini (1960)

Donizetti: Lucrezia Borgia – Tranquillo ei osa ... Com'e bello (Act I)
Rossini: Guglielmo Tell – S'allontanano alfine ... Selva opaca (Act II)
Semiramide – B el raggio lusinghier (Act I)
Bellini: Il pirata – Sorgete ... Lo sognai ferito, esangue (Act I)
with Monica Sinclair (contralto), Alexander Young (tenor)
Philharmonia Orchestra and Chorus, conducted by Antonio Tonini (1961)

Verdi: Don Carlo – O don fatale (Act IV)
Rossini: La Cenerentola – Nacqui all'affanno ... Non piu mesta (Act II)
Weber: Oberon – Ocean! Thou mighty monster (Act II)
Philharmonia Orchestra, conducted by Antonio Tonini (1962)

Verdi: Aida – Pur ti riveggo, mia dolce Aida (Act III)
with Franco Corelli and Orchestre du Theatre National de l'Opera de Paris, conducted by Georges Pretre (1964)

Verdi: I Lombardi – Te, Vergin santa (Act I)
Il trovatore – Vanne ... D'amor sull'ali rosee (Act IV)
Orchestre de la Societe des Concerts du Conservatoire, conducted by Nicola Rescigno (1964/65)

Verdi: I vespri siciliani – Arrigo! Ah, parli a un core (Act IV)
Attila – Liberamente or piangi (Act I)
Orchestre de la Societe des Concerts du Conservatoire, conducted by Nicola Rescigno (1969)

EMI CZS 572030.2 LIVE IN CONCERT

Puccini: Madama Butterfly – Un bel di vedremo

"Nina Foresti", Major Bowes Amateur Hour Broadcast, US [07.04.1935]

Proch: Aria and variations – Deh! Torna mio bene

Orchestra della RAI, Torino, conducted by Manno Wolf-Ferrari [12.03.1951]

Verdi: Macbeth – Vieni t'affretta ... Or tutti sorgete (Act I)

Donizetti: Lucia di Lammermoor – Il dolce suono ... Ardon gli incensi (Act III)

Verdi: Nabucco – Ben io t'invenni ... Anch'io dischiuso un giorno (Act II)

Delibes: Lakme – Dov'e l'indiana bruna (Act II) [Bell Song]

Orchestra delle RAI, Roma, conducted by Olivero de Fabritiis [18.11.1952]

Mozart: Il Seraglio – Tutte le torture (Act II)

Meyerbeer: Dinorah – Ahime! Che notte oscura ... Ombra leggiera (Act II)

Charpentier: Louise – Depuis le jour (Act III)

Rossini: Armida – D'Amore al dolce impero (Act II)

Orchestra della RAI, San Remo, conducted by Alfredo Simonetto [27.12.1954]

Thomas: Hamlet – Ai vostri giochi ... Ed ora a voi (Act IV)

Orchestra della RAI, Milan, conducted by Alfredo Simonetto [27.09.56]

Wagner: Tristan and Isolde – Dolce e calmo (Liebestod) (Act III)

Athens Festival Orchestra, conducted by Antonino Votto [05.08.1957]

Spontini: La vestale – Tu che invoco (Act II)

Verdi: Ernani – Surta e la notte ... Ernani, Ernani, involami (Act I)

Don Carlo – Tu che la vanita (Act IV)

Bellini: Il pirata – Oh, s'io potessi ... Col sorriso d'innocenza (Act II)

Concertebouw Orchestra, conducted by Nicola Rescigno [11.07.1959]o

NIMBUS NI7864 MORE LEGENDARY VOICES

Bellini: I puritani – Qui la voce (r. 1949)

COMPILATIONS

EMI Eminence CD-EMX2123 MARIA CALLAS SINGS OPERATIC ARIAS

Rossini: Il Barbiere di Siviglia – Una voce poco fa (Act I) [r.1957]
Verdi: Macbeth – La luce langue (Act II)
Don Carlo – Tu che la vanita (Act IV)
Puccini: Tosca – Vissi d'arte (Act II) [r. 1964]
Gluck: Alceste – Divinites du Styx (Act I)
Bizet: Carmen – L'amour est un oiseau rebelled [Habanera[(Act I)
– Pres des ramparts de Seville [Seguedille] (Act I)
– Voici l'ordre (Act I)
Saint-Saens: Samson et Dalila – Printemps qui commence (Act I)
Massenet: Manon – Je ne suis que faiblesse … Adieu, notre petite table (Act II)
Charpentier: Louise – Depuis le jour (Act III)

EMI CDM 769543.2 MARIA CALLAS & GIUSEPPE DI STEFANO – DUETS

Bellini: I puritani – Fini! Me lassa! … Nel mirati un sol instante … V ieni, fra questa braccia (Act III)
Verdi: Rigoletto – Signor principe … T'amo! T'amo … E il soldell'anima … Addio, addio (Act I)
Il trovatore – Miserere … ah, che la morta ognora (Act IV)
Un ballo in maschera – Tec io sta … M'ami, m'ami … oh qual soave brivido (Act II)
Puccini: Manon Lescaut – Tu,tu, amore? Tu?..O tentatrice (Act II)
La boheme – Che gelida manina; Si, chiamano Mimi; O soave fanciulla (Act I)
Tosca – E lucevan le stelle; Franchigia a Floria Tosca; O dolci mani; Senti, 'ora a vicina; Amaro sol per te; Trionfal … Di novo spemi, son pronto; Com'e lunga l'attesa! (Act III)

EMI CDM 763182.2 THE INCOMPARABLE MARIA CALLAS

Bellini: Norma	– Casta diva (Act I) [r. 1960]
Donizetti: Lucia di Lammermoor	– Regnava nel silenzio (Act I) [r. 1959]
Verdi: Ernani	– Surta la noote … Ernani, Ernani, involami (Act I)
Aida	– Ritorna vincitor (Act I) [r. 1964]
Ponchielli: La gioconda	– Suicidio (Act IV)
Puccini: Tosca	– Vissi d'arte (Act II) [r. 1964]
Bizet: Carmen	– Les tringles des sisters tintaient; Carreau, pique … la mort! (Act III)
Saint-Saens: Samson et Dalila	– Mon Coeur s'ouvre a ton voix (Act II)
Gluck: Orphee et Eurydice	– J'ai perdu mon Eurydice (Act III)
Gounod: Romeo et Juliette	– Je te vivre dans ce reve (Act I)
Massenet: Le Cid	– Pleurez, mes yeux (Act III)
Thomas: Mignon	– Je suis Titania (Act II)

EMI CMS 763244.2 [4CDs] THE ART OF MARIA CALLAS

Bellini: Norma	– In mia man … Dammi quell ferro … Qual cor tradisti … Norma! Act II) [r. 1960]
Il pirata	– Oh1 s'io potessi … Col sorriso d'innocenza (Act II)
La sonnambula	– Care compagne … Come per me sereno … Sovra il sen (Act I)
I puritani	– O rendetemi la speme … Qui la voce … Vien, diletto (Act II)
Cherubini: Medea	– Dei tuoi figli la madre (Act II) [r. 1955]
Donizetti: Anna Bolena	– Piangete voi? ... Ah, dolce guidami castel natio (Act II)
Lucia di Lammermoor	– O giusto cielo … Il dolce suono … Alfin son tua … Spargi d'amaro pianto (Act III) [r. 1953]
Gluck: Iphigenie en Tauride	– O malheureuse Iphigenie (Act II)
Mascagni: Cavalleria Rusticana	– Voi lo sapete, o mamma … Tu qui, Santuzza

Ponchielli: La gioconda	– Nessun v'ha visto?..O pietos i … Suicidio (Act IV)
Puccini: Madama Butterfly	– Bimba, bimba, non piangere (Act I)
Tosca	– Mario! Mario! ... Non la sospiri (Act I)
Rossini: Il Barbiere di Siviglia	– Una poco voce fa (Act I) [r. 1954]
l turco in Italia	– Il poeta ha regione
Spontini: La vestal	– Tu che invoco (Act II)
Verdi: Un ballo in maschera	– Ecco l'orrido campo … Ma dall'arido stelo … Teco io sto Act II)
Macbeth	– Una macchia e qui tuttora! (Act IV)
La traviata	– Un di felice; Ebben? Che diavol fate; Si ridesta in ciel l'aurora; e strano … Ah fors e lui … Follie! follie! ... Sempre libera (Act I) [r. Lisbon 1958]
Il trovatore	– Timor de me?..D'amor sull'ali rosee … Miserere (Act IV)
I vespri siciliani	– Merce, dilette amiche (Act V)

EMI CDC 754702.2 LA DIVINA
Excerpts from Madama Butterfly, Carmen, La Wally, Il Barbiere di Siviglia, Norma, Samson et Dalila, Rigoletto, La traviata, Romeo et Juliette, La boheme, Don Giovanni, Cavalleria rusticana, La gioconda, Gianni Schicchi, Turandot, Tosca

EMI CDC 555016.2 LA DIVINA 2
Excerpts from Alceste, Carmen, Ernani, Manon Lescaut, Aida, Orphee, I vespri siciliani, Louise, La boheme, Mignon, La traviata, Don Carlo, Samsom et Dalila, La sonnambula, Adriana Lecouvreur, Lucia di Lammermoor

EMI CDC 555216.2 LA DIVINA 3
Excerpts from Andrea Chenier, La vestale, Manon, Carmen, Manon Lescaut, Il Barbiere di Siviglia, Lakme, Aida, La boheme, Turandot, I pagliacci, Il trovatore, Madama Butterfly, Dinorah

EMI CMS 565746.2 LA DIVINA LUXURY SET
EMI CDC 754702.2 La Divina
EMI CDC 555016.2 La Divina 2
EMI CDC 555216.2 La Divina 3
EMI CDM 565822.2 Callas in conversation with Edward Downes 1967/8 New York [Only available as part of this package]

EMI CDC 556411.2 MASTER CLASS
Excerpts from Il Barbiere di Siviglia, La sonnambula, La boheme, Macbeth, Tosca

EMI CDC 749502.2 THE VOICE OF THE CENTURY
Excerpts from Norma, La sonnambula, Il Barbiere di Siviglia, La traviata, Rigoletto, Tosca, Madama Butterfly, La Wally, Turandot, Carmen, Werther

EMI CDCALLAS1 [2 CDs] THE VOICE OF THE CENTURY
Excerpts from Norma, La sonnambula, Il Barbiere di Siviglia, Lucia di Lammermoor, Rigoletto, La traviata, La boheme, Madama Butterfly, Tosca, Turandot, La Wally, Andrea Chenier, Orphee, Alceste, Dinorah, Romeo et Juliette, Faust, Lakme, Samson et Dalila, Les Percheurs des perles, Carmen, Le Cid, Louise, Manon

EMI 520653.2 LEGENDS OF THE 20th CENTURY: (MARIA CALLAS)
Excerpts from Norma, Orfeo, Romeo et Juliette, Samson et Dalila, Carmen, Il Barbiere di Siviglia, Rigoletto, Il trovatore, La traviata, Tosca, Gianni Schicchi, Andrea Chenier, Adriana Lecouvreur, La sonnambula, Lucia di Lammermoor

EMI 7243 557050.2 (1CD)
EMI 7243 567466.2 (2CDs)
EMI 7243 557062.2 (2CDs de luxe)
MARIA CALLAS: POPULAR MUSIC FROM TV, FILMS AND OPERA

HIGHLIGHTS

EMI CDM 566662.2 BELLINI: NORMA (r. 1960)
EMI CDM 566665.2 BELLINI: I PURITANI
EMI CDM 566663.2 BIZET: CARMEN
EMI CDM 566664.2 DONIZETTI: LUCIA DI LAMMERMOOR (r. 1959)
EMI CDM 566670.2 PUCCINI: LA BOHEME
EMI CDM 566666.2 PUCCINI: TOSCA (r. 1964)
EMI CDM 566671.2 ROSSINI: IL BARBIERE DI SIVIGLIA
EMI CDM 566668.2 VERDI: AIDA
EMI CDM 566667.2 VERDI: RIGOLETTO
EMI CDM 566669.2 VERDI: IL TROVATORE

ISSUE DATE

Title	Issue date & no.	LP Re-issue	CD	CD edition 1997
Casta diva [Norma]	12/51 R30041	02/59 LPC50175		
Qui la voce [Puritani]	03/52 R30043	02/59 LPC50175	02/95 NI7864	
Liebestod [Tristan und Isolde]		02/59 LPC50175		
Puritani	11/53 33CX1058-60	11/78 SLS5140	09/87 CDS 747308.8	CDS 556275.2
Tosca (53)	12/53 33CX1094-95	03/73 SLS825	09/85 CDS 747175.8	CDS 556304.2
Lucia (53)	03/54 33CX1131-32	03/77 SLS5056	10/89 CMS 769980.2	CMS 566483.2
Cavalleria rusticana	10/54 33CX1182/83	02/74 SLS 819	10/87 CDS 747981.8	CDS 556287.2
Norma (54)	11/54 33CX1179/81	05/78 SLS5115	03/86 CDS 747304.8	CDS 556271.2
Puccini Arias	12/5433CX1204	10/79 ALP3799	12/87 CDC 747966.2	CDM 566463.2
La Forza del Destino	06/55 33CX1258-60	09/78 SLS5120	10/87 CDS 747581.8	CDS 556323.2
Pagliacci	09/55 33CX1211/12	02/74 SLS 819	10/87 CDS 747981.8	CDS 556287.2
Operatic Arias	10/55 33CX1231	03/80 ALP3824	11/86 CDC 747282.2	CDM 566458.2
Lyric Arias	10/55 33CX1231	01/74 SLS 869		
Coloratura Arias	10/55 33CX1231	03/76 SLS5018		
Turco in Italia	10/55 33CX1289/91	02/79 SLS5148	12/87 CDS 749344.8	CDS 556313.2
Madama Butterfly	12/55 33CX1296-98	05/76 SLS5015	10/87 CDS 747959.8	CDS 556298.2
Aida	01/56 33CX1318-20	02/78 SLS5108	11/87 CDS 749030.8	CDS 556316.2
Rigoletto	02/56 33CX1324-26	03/76 SLS5018	02/87 CDS 747469.8	CDS 556327.2
Sonnambula	10/57 33CX1469-71	12/78 SLS5134	06/86 CDS 747378.8	CDS 556278.2
Ballo in maschera	10/57 33CX1472-74	06/79 RLS736	09/87 CDS 747498.8	CDS 556320.2
Trovatore	11/57 33CX1483-85	01/74 SLS869	12/87 CDS 749347.8	CDS 556333.2
Traviata (53)	01/58 LPC 1241-1/3	12/73 GVC2345	03/00 3984-29354.2	
Barber	02/58 33CX1507/09			
	03/59 SAX2266	12/74SLS853	06/87 CDS 747634.8	CDS 556310.2

Title	Issue date & no.	Re-issue	CD	CD edition 1997
Boheme	03/58 33CX1464/65	08/76 SLS5059	11/87 CDS 747475.8	CDS 556295.2
Callas at La Scala:	03/58 33CX1540			
Puritani (exc) (53)	06/58 33CX1540			
Sonnambula (exc) (57)	06/58 33CX1540			
Sonnambula arias (55)		09/78 ASD3535	12/87 CDC 747966.2	CDM 566457.2
Medea aria (55)	06/58 33CX1540		11/86 CDC 747282.2	CDM 566457.2
Vestale arias (55)	06/58 33CX1540		11/86 CDC 747282.2	CDM 566457.2
Turandot	09/58 33CX1555-57	09/79 RLS741	11/87 CDS 747971.8	CDS 556307.2
Gioconda(52)	12/58 LPC1241-1/3	12/74 GVC 34/6	03/00 3984-29355.2	
Medea	03/59 33CX1618-20			
	12/59 SAX 2290	11/79 OCL16014-6	02/91 CMS 763625.2	CMS 566435.2
Verdi Heroines	03/59 33CX1628			
	03/60 SAX 2293	02/80 ASD 3801	09/87 CDC 747730.2	CDM 66460.2.
Mad Scenes	05/59 33CX1645			
	06/60 SAX 2320	11/79 ASD 3801	06/86 CDC 747283.2	CDM 566459.2
Manon Lescaut	12/59 33CX1583-85	04/80 RLS 737	03/86 CDS 747393.8	CDS 556301.2
Lucia (58)	07/60 SAX 2316-7	10/79 SLS5166	01/87 CDS 747440.8	CDS 556284.2
Gioconda (59)	10/60 33CX1706-8			
	11/60 SAX2359	11/79 SLS5176	02/88 CDS 749518.2	CDS 556291.2
Great Arias from French Opera	10/61 33CX1771			
	10/61 SAX2410	06/83 ASD 4306	02/88 CDC 749059.2	CDM 566466.2
Mon Coeur s'ouvre à ta voix		06/83 ASD 4306	02/88 CDC 749059.2	CDM 566466.2
Norma (60)	10/61 33CX1766-8			
	11/61 SAX2412-14	06/80 SLS5186	07/89 CMS 763000.2	CMS 566428.2
Callas à Paris	09/63 33CX1858			
Ifigena	09/63 SAX2503		02/88 CDC 749059.2	CDM 566467.2
Damnation of Faust	09/63 SAX2503		02/88 CDC 749059.2	CDM 566467.2
Pecheurs des Perles	09/63 SAX2503		02/88 CDC 749059.2	CDM 566467.2

Title	Issue date & no.	Re-issue	CD	CD edition 1997
Manon	09/63 SAX2503		02/88 CDC 749059.2	CDM 566467.2
Werther	09/63 SAX2503		CDC 749005.2	CDM 566457.2
Faust	09/63 SAX2503		CDC 749005.2	CDM 566467.2
Mozart, Beethoven, Weber Arias	08/64 33CX1900			
Beethoven	08/64 SAX2540		02/91 CMS 763625.2	
			03/93 CDC 754437.2	CDM 566465.2
Mozart	08/64 SAX2540		CDC 749005.2	CDM 566465.2
Weber	08/64 SAX2540		CDC 749005.2	CDM 566465.2
Verdi Arias	08/64 33CX1910			
	08/64 SAX2550		06/86 CDC 747943.2	CDM 566461.2
Carmen	12/64 AN140-2			
	12/64 SAN140-2		06/86 CDS 747313.8	
			05/92 CDS 754368.2	CDS 556281.2
Donizetti and Rossini Arias	03/65 33CX1923			
Convien partir [Figlia]	03/65 SAX2564	04/81 ASD3984	06/86 CDC 747283.2	CDM 566464.2
Com'e bello [Lucrezia]	03/65 SAX2564	04/81 ASD3984	06/86 CDC 747283.2	CDM 566464.2
Prendi per me [L'elisir]	03/65 SAX2564	04/81 ASD3984	06/86 CDC 747283.2	CDM 566464.2
Non piu mesta [Cenerentola]	03/65 SAX2564	04/81 ASD3984	CDC 749005.2	CDM 566464.2
Selva opace[Guglielmo Tell]	03/65 SAX2564	04/81 ASD3984	CDC 749005.2	CDM 566464.2
Bel raggio [Semiramide]	03/65 SAX2564	04/81 ASD3984	CDC 749005.2	CDM 566464.2
Tosca (64)	07/65 AN149-50			
	07/65 SAN149-50		08/89 CMS 769974.2	CMS 566275.2
Sorgete [Pirata]	03/72 ASD2791		06/86 CDC 747283.2	CMS 566468.2
Liberamente [Attila]	03/72 ASD2791		09/87 CDC 747943.2	CDM 566462.2
Arrigo [Vespri]	03/72 ASD2791		09/87 CDC 747730.2	CDM 566462.2
O madre [Lombardi]	03/72 ASD2791		09/87 CDC 747730.2	CDM 566462.2
Ecco l'orrido [Ballo]	03/72 ASD2791		09/87 CDC 747730.2	CDM 566462.2
Ritorna vincitor [Aida]	03/72 ASD2791		09/87 CDC 747730.2	CDM 566462.2

Title	Issue date & no.	Re-issue	CD	CD edition 1997
Egli non riede [Corsaro]	09/78 ASD3535		09/87 CDC 747943.2	CDM 566462.2
Ne sulla terra [Corsaro]	09/78 ASD3535		09/87 CDC 747943.2	CDM 566462.2
Di tale amor [Trovatore]	09/78 ASD3535		09/87 CDC 747943.2	CDM 566462.2
Morro, ma prima [Ballo]	09/78 ASD3535		09/87 CDM 747943.2	CDM 566462.2
Liebestod (57) [Tristan und Isolde]			09/87 CDC 749428.2	CZS 572030.2
Tu che la vanita (59) [Don Carlo]			09/87 CDC 749428.2	CZS 572030.2
Sol corrisi (59) [Pirata]			09/87 CDC 749428.2	CZS 572030.2
Non piu mesta [Cenerentola] (62)			09/87 CDC 749428.2	CMS 566468.2
Selva opace [Guglielmo Tell] (61)			09/87 CDC 749428.2	CMS 566468.2
Bel raggio [Semiramide] (60)			09/87 CDC 749428.2	CMS 566468.2
Te santa [Lombardi] (64)			09/87 CDC 749428.2	CMS 566468.2
Arrigo [Vespri] (69)			09/87 CDC 749428.2	CMS 566468.2
Liberamente [Attila] (69)			09/87 CDC 747428.2	CMS 566468.2
Operatic arias			02/88 EMX2123	
Duets with di Stefano			10/88 CDM 769543.2	
The Art of Maria Callas			02/90 CMS 763244.2	
The Incomparable Callas			02/90 CDM 763182.2	

Title	Issue date & no.	Re-issue	CD	CD edition 1997
Non mi dir (Don Giovanni) [take2](53)			11/91 CMS 763750.2	CMS 566468.2
Marten alla Arten [Seraglio			02/93 CDC 754437.2	CZS 572030.2
Ocean [Oberon] (62)			02/93 CDC 754437.2	CMS 566468.2
D'amore al dolce [Armida]			02/93 CDC 754437.2	CZS 572030.2
Com'e bello [Lucrezia] (61)			02/93 CDC 754437.2	CMS 566468.2
O don fatale [Don Carlo] (61)			02/93 CDC 754437.2	CMS 566468.2
Arrigo [Vespri] (60)			02/93 CDC 754437.2	CMS 566468.2
D'amor sull'ali rosee [Trovatore] (64/5)			02/93 CDC 754437.2	CMS 566468.2
Te, Virgin santa [Lombardi] (64/5)			02/93 CDC 754437.2	CMS 566468.2
Pur' ti riveggo [Aida] (64)			02/93 CDC 754437.2	CMS 566468.2
Non mi dir [take1] (53)			02/93 CDC 754437.2	CMS 566468.2
Sleepwalking scene [Macbeth – mono]				CMS 566468.2
Bel raggio [Semiramide] (60)				CMS 566468.2
Un bel di [Madama Butterfly] (1935)				CMS 566468.2
Proch Variations(51)				CZS 572030.2
Vieni, t'afretta [Macbeth – 1952]				CZS 572030.2
Mad scene [Lucia – 1952]				CZS 572030.2
Anch'io dischiuso [Nabucco –1952]				CZS 572030.2
Bell song [Lakme – 1952]				CZS 572030.2
Ombra leggiero [Dinorah –1954]				CZS 572030.2
Depuis le jour [Louise – 1954]				CZS 572030.2
Mad Scene [Hamlet –1956]				CZS 572030.2
Tu che invoco [Don Carlo – 1959]				CZS 572030.2
Ernani, involami [Ernani – 1959]				CZS 572030.2

LIVE PERFORMANCES

Outside the scope of this book, but chronologically listed below, Callas' live performances, variously available on the following CD labels:

Arkadia, Diva, Divina, Gala, Golden Melodram, Hommage, Myto, Palladio, Sakkaris, Standing Room Only, Urania, Virtuoso

20.05.49 Buenos Aires: *Turandot* (exc) with Arizmendi, del Monaco, Zanin c.Serafin

17.05.49 Buenos Aires: *Norma* (exc) with Barbieri, Vela, Rossi-Lemini c.Serafin

22.12.49 Naples: *Nabucco* with Pini, Sinimberghi, Bechi, Nerone c.Gui

23.05.49 Mexico City: *Norma* with Simionato, Baum, Moscona c.Picci

30.05.49 Mexico City: *Aida* with Simionata, Baum, Weede, Moscona c.Picco

08.06.50 Mexico City: *Tosca* with Filippeschi, Weede c.Mugnai

20.06.50 Mexico City: *Il trovatore* with Simionato, Baum, Warren, Moscona c.Picco

02.10.50 Rome: *Aida* (exc) Stignani, Picchi, de Falchi, Neri c. Bellezza

19.10.50 Rome: *Il Turco in Italia* (exc) with Canali, Valletti, Bruscantini, Calabrese, Stabile c. Gavazzeni

20/21.11.50 RAI Rome: *Parsifal* with Pagliughi, Baldelli, Panerai, Modesti, Christoff c.Gui

27.01.51 Naples: *Il trovatore* with Elmo, Lauri-Volpi, Silveri, Tajo c.Serafin

30.05.51 Florence: *I vespri siciliani* with Kokolios, Mascherini, Christoff c.Kleiber

03.07.51 Mexico City: *Aida* with Dominguez, de Monaco, Taddei, Silva c.de Fabritiis

17.07.51 Mexico City: *La traviata* with Valletti, Taddei c.de Fabritiis

24.09.51 Rio de Janeiro: *Tosca* with Poggi, Silveri c.Votto

07.12.51 La Scala: *I vespri siciliani* with Conley, Mascherini, Christoff c.de Sabata

26.04.52 Florence: *Armida* with Albanese, Filippeschi, Raimondi, Salvarezza, Ziliani c. Serafin

29.05.52 Mexico City: *I puritani* with di Stefano, Campolonghi, Silva c.Picco

03.06.52 Mexico City: *La traviata* with di Stefano, Campolonghi c.Mugnai

10.06.52 Mexico City: *Lucia di Lammermoor* with di Stefano, Campolonghi, Silva c.Picco

17.06.52 Mexico City: *Rigoletto* with Garcia, di Stefano, Campolonghi, Ruffino c.Mugnai

01.07.52 Mexico City: *Tosca* with di Stefano, Campolonghi c.Picco

18.11.52 Covent Garden: *Norma* with Stignani, Picchi, Vaghi c.Gui
07.12.52 La Scala: *Macbeth* with Penno, Mascherini, Tajo c.de Sabata*
23.02.53 La Scala: *Il trovatore* with Stignani, Penno, Tagliabue, Modesti c.Votto
07.05.53 Florence: *Medea* with Tucci, Barbieri, Guichandut, Petri, c.Gui
10.06.53 Covent Garden: *Aida* with Simionato, Baum, Walters, Neri, Langdon c.Barbirolli
19.11.53 Trieste: *Norma* with Nicolai, Corelli, Christoff c.Votto
10.12.53 La Scala: *Medea* with Nache, Barbieri, Penno, Modesti c.Bernstein
18.01.54 La Scala: *Lucia* with di Stefano, Panerai, Modesti, c.Karajan
04.04.54 La Scala: *Alceste* with Gavarini, Silveri, Panerai c. Giulini
07.12.54 La Scala: *La vestale* with Stignani, Corelli, Sordello, Rossi-Lemini c.Votto
08.01.55 La Scala: *Andrea Chenier* with de Monaco, Protti c.Votto
05.03.55 La Scala: *La sonnambula* with Ratti, Carturan, Valletti, Modesti c. Bernstein
28.05.55 La Scala: *La traviata* with di Stefano, Bastianini c. Giulini*
29.06.55 RAI Rome: *Norma* with Stignani, del Monaco, Modesti c.Serafin
29.09.55 Berlin: *Lucia* with di Stefano, Panerai, Zaccaria c.Karajan*
07.12.55 La Scala: *Norma* with Simionato, del Monaco, Zaccaria c.Votto
19.01.56 La Scala: *La traviata* with Raimondi, Bastianini c.Giulini
16.02.56 La Scala: *Il Barbiere di Siviglia* with Alva, Gobbi, Rossi-Lemini, Luise c. Giulini
22.03.56 Naples: *Lucia* with Raimondi, Panerai, Zerbibi c.Molinari-Pradelli
25.11.56 CBS New York: *Tosca* Act II (abr.) with London c.Mitropoulos
08.12.56 New York Met: *Lucia* with Campora, Sordello, Moscona c.Cleva
17.04.57 La Scala: *Anna Bolena* with Simionato, Carturan, Raimondi, Rossi-Lemini, Clabassi c.Gavazzeni*
01.06.57 La Scala: *Ifigenia in Tauride* with Cossotto, Albanese, Colzani, Dondi, c.Sanzogno*
26.06.57 RAI Rome: *Lucia* with Fernandi, Panerai, Modesti c.Serafin
04.07.57 Cologne: *La sonnambula* with Angioletti, Cossotto, Monti, Zaccaria c.Votto
21/26.08.57 Edinburgh: *La sonnambula* with Martelli, Cossotto, Monti, Zaccaria c.Votto
07.12.57 La Scala: *Un ballo in maschera* with Ratti, Simionato, di Stefano, Bastianini, Stefanoni, Cassinelli, c.Gavazzeni
02.01.58 Rome: *Norma* [Act I] with Pirazzini, Corelli, Neri, c.Santini
27.03.58 Lisbon: *La traviata* with Kraus, Sereni c.Ghione*

20.06.58 Covent Garden: *La traviata* with Valletti, Zanasi c.Rescigno
06.11.58 Dallas: *Medea* with Carron, Berganza, Vickers, Zaccaria c.Rescigno
19.12.58 Paris: *Tosca* [Act II] with Lance, Gobbi c. Sebastian
27.01.59 Carnegie Hall: *Il pirata* with Sarfaty, Ferraro, Ego c.Rescigno*
30.06.59 Covent Garden: *Medea* with Carlyle, Cossotto, Vickers, Zaccaria c. Rescigno
07.12.60 La Scala: *Poliuto* with Corelli, Bastianini, Zaccaria c.Votto*
11/14.12.61 La Scala: *Medea* with Tosini, Simionato, Vickers, Ghiaurov c. Schippers
21/24/30.01.64 Covent Garden: *Tosca* with Cioni, Gobbi c.Cillario
19.03.65 New York Met: *Tosca* with Corelli, Gobbi c.Cleva
25.03.65 New York Met: *Tosca* with Tucker, Gobbi c.Cleve
14.05.65 Paris: *Norma* with Simionato, Cecchele, Vinco c.Pretre
21/29.05.65 Paris: *Norma* with Cossotto, Cecchele, Vinco c.Pretre
05.07.65 Covent Garden: *Tosca* with Cioni, Gobbi c. Pretre
1973/74 Recitals with di Stefano, accompanied by Ivor Newton and Robert Sutherland
*Issued by EMI

NOTES

Chapter One

1. Opera Vol.3 No.4 April 1952 p.238
2. Gramophone Vol.29 No.346 March 1952 p.231
3. Ibid. Vol.30 No.253 October 1952 p.100
4. Ibid. Vol.36 No.429 February 1959 p.417
5. Ibid. Vol.31 No.366 November 1953 p.198
6. Opera Vol.5 No.1 January 1954 p.38
7. Musical America January 1954
8. Gramophone Vol.31 No.371 April 1954 p.419
9. Musical Times Vol.95 No.1333 March 1954 p.132
10. Gramophone Vol.56 No.666 November 1978 p.956
11. Ibid. Vol.65 No.772 September 1987 p.486
12. Ibid. Vol.31 No.367 December 1953 p.244
13. Ibid. Vol 30 No.355 December 1952 p.172
14. Musical Times Vol.95 No.1334 April 1954 p.193
15. Opera Vol.5 No.3 March 1954 p.173
16. Gramophone Vol.31 No.371 April 1954 p.419
17. Opera Vol.24 No.5 May 1973 p.438
18. Gramophone Vol. 50 No.598 March 1973 p.1729
19. Ibid. Vol.63 No.748 September 1985 p.400
20. Classic CD No.85 May 1997 p.40
21. Gramophone Vol.74 No.887 April 1997 p.36
22. Gramophone Classical Good CD Guide 2000 p.737
23. Opera Vol.16 No.9 September 1965 p.670
24. Gramophone Vol.43 No.506 July 1965 p.69
25. Ibid. Vol.67 No.795 August 1989 p.366
26. Opera Vol.40 No.12 December 1989 p.1508
27. Gramophone Vol.35 No.416 January 1958 p.305
28. Ibid. Vol.31 No.370 March 1954 p.399
29. Opera Vol.5 No.5 May 1954 p.301
30. Musical Times Vol.95 No.1336 June 1954 p.315
31. Gramophone Vol.38 No.446 July 1960 p.77
32. Opera Vol.11 No.9 September 1960 p.636
33. Ibid. Vol.28 No.8 August 1977 p.766
34. Gramophone Vol.54 No.646 March 1977 p.1444
35. Opera Vol.30 No.10 October 1979 p.974
36. Gramophone Vol.57 No.677 October 1979 p.703
37. Ibid. Vol.67 No.797 October 1989 p.738
38. Gramophone Classical Good CD Guide 2000 p.317
39. Gramophone Vol.31 No.370 March 1954 p.400

Chapter Two

1. Gramophone Vol.32 No.377 October 1954 p.212
2. Opera Vol. 5 No.12 December 1954 p.758
3. Gramophone Vol.51 No.610 February 1974 p.1605
4. Opera Vol.25 No.5 May 1974 p.421

5. Gramophone Vol.65 No.773 October 1987 p.618
6. Opera Vol.39 No.6 June 1988 p.759
7. Classic CD No.85 May 1997 p.40
8. Gramophone Vol.74 No.887 April 1997 p.37
9. Gramophone Classical Good CD Guide 2000 p.525
10. Opera Vol.3 No.3 March 1952 p.177
11. Gramophone Vol.29 No.343 December 1951 p.156
12. Ibid. Vol.32 No.378 November 1954 p.265
13. Opera Vol.5 No.12 December 1954 p.758
14. Gramophone Vol.32 No.380 January 1955 p.339
15. Musical Times Vol.95 No.1341 November 1954 p.604
16. Gramophone Vol.39,No.462 November 1961 p.263
17. Ibid. Vol.39 No.464 January 1962 p.342
18. Opera Vol.13 No.1 January 1962 p.51
19. Gramophone Vol.55 No.660 May 1978 p.1925
20. Opera Vol.31 No.9 September 1980 p.910
21. Gramophone Vol.58 No.685 June 1980 p.65
22. Ibid. Vol.63 No.754 March 1986 p.1195
23. Opera Vol.40 No.12 December 1989 p.1508
24. Classic CD No.85 May 1997 p.40
25. Gramophone Vol.32 No.379 December 54 p.315
26. Opera Vol.6 No.3 March 1955 p.183
27. Gramophone Vol.32 No.380 January 1955 p.
28. Opera Vol.31 No.7 July 1980 p.687
29. Gramophone Vol.57 No.677 October 1979 p.709
30. Ibid. Vol.65 No.775 December 1987 p.995

Chapter Three

1. Gramophone Vol.33 No.385 June 1955 p.26
2. Musical Times Vol.96 No.1350 August 1955 p.424
3. Opera Vol.6 No.9 September 1955 p.592
4. Gramophone Vol.33 No.388 September 1955 p. 126
5. Ibid. Vol.33 No.391 December 1955 p.283
6. Ibid. Vol.38 No.451 December 1960 p.347
7. Ibid. Vol.56 No.664 September 1978 p.549
8. Opera Vol.29
9. Gramophone Vol.65 No.773 October 1987 p.814
10. Ibid. Vol.33 No.388 September 1955 p.146
11. Opera Vol.6 No.11 November 1955 p.718
12. Gramophone Vol.51 No.610 February 1974 p.1605
13. Opera Vol.25 No.5 May 1974 p.421
14. Gramophone Vol.65 No.773 October 1987 p.61
15. Opera Vol.39 No.6 June 1988 p.759
16. Gramophone Classical Good CD Guide 2000 p. 525
17. Gramophone Vol.33 No.388 September 1955 p.151
18. Opera Vol.6 No.12 December 1955 p.790
19. Gramophone Vol.51 No.609 January 1974 p.1423
20. Ibid. Vol.51 No.611 March 1974 p.1507

21. Opera Vol.27
22. Ibid. Vol.31 No.7 July 1980 p.687
23. Gramophone Vol.57 No.682 March 1980 p.1445
24. Ibid. Vol.64 No.762 November 1986 p.751
25. Musical Times Vol.96 No.1354 December 1955 p.640
26. Gramophone Vol.33 No.389 October 1955 p.190
27. Opera Vol.6 No.12 December 1955 p.787
28. Opera Vol.30 No.4 April 1979 p.357
29. Gramophone Vol.78 No.669 February 1979 p.1465
30. Ibid. Vol.66 No.775 December 87 p.1001
31. Ibid. Vol.74 No.887 April 1997 p.37
32. Classic CD No.85 May 1997 p.40
33. Gramophone Vol.33 No.391 p.280
34. Musical Times Vol. 97 No.1357 March 1956 p.140
35. Opera Vol.7 No.3 March 1956 p.176
36. Ibid. Vol.27
37. Gramophone Vol.53.NO.636 May 1976 p.1796
38. Ibid. Vol.65 No.773 October 1987 p.626
39. Opera Vol.38 No.12 December 1987 p.1415

Chapter Four

1. Gramophone Vol.34 No.402 November 1956 p.221
2. Opera Vol.7 No.12 December 1956 p758
3. Ibid. Vol.7 No.3 March 1956 p.176
4. Gramophone Vol.33 No.392 January 1956 p.322
5. Musical Times Vol.97 No.1357 March 1956 p.140
6. Gramophone Vol.55 No.657 February 1978 p.1465
7. Classic CD No.85 May 1997 p.40
8. Gramophone Classical Good CD Guide 2000 p.1032
9. Gramophone Vol.33 No.393 February 1956 p.361
10. Opera Vol.7 No.4 April 1956 p.251
11. Musical Times Vol. 97 No.1357 March 1956 p.140
12. Gramophone Vol.53 No.634 March 1976 p.1507
13. Ibid. Vol.64 No.765 February 1987 p.1181
14. Opera Vol.38 No.12 December 1987 p.1415
15. Gramophone Vol.74 No.887 April 1997 p.36
16. Gramophone Classical Good CD Guide 2000 p.1040
17. Musical Times Vol.97 No.1365 November 1956 p.586
18. Gramophone Vol.34 No.407 April 1957 p.402
19. Ibid. Vol.33 NO.386 July 1955 p.47
20. Ibid. Vol.35 No.416 January 1968 p.328
21. Opera Vol.9 No.1 January 1958 p.53
22. Gramophone Vol.51 No.607 December 1973 p.1252
23. Ibid. Vol.77 No.925 March 2000 p.116

Chapter Five

1. Gramophone Vol.35 No.413 October 1957 p.188
2. Musical Times Vol.98 No.1368 February 1958 p.87

3 Opera Vol.8 No.11 November 1957 p.718
4. Opera Vol.30 No.2 February 1979 p.147
5. Gramophone Vol. No.56 Bo.667 December 1978 p.1164
6. Ibid.Vol.64 No.760 September 1986 p.437
7. Gramophone Classical Good CD Guide 2000 p.142
8. Gramophone Vol.35 No.416 January 1958 p.305
9. Ibid.Vol.35 No.413 October 1957 p.190
10. Opera Vol.8 No.11 November 1957 p.718
11. Musical Times Vol.98 No.1368 February 1958 p.87
12. Gramophone Vol.35 No.416 January 1958 p.305
13. Opera Vol.30 No.9 September 79 p.880
14. Gramophone Vol.57 No.673 June 1979 p.103
15. Ibid.Vol.65 No.772 September 1987 p.481
16. Classic CD No.85 May 1987 p.40
17. Gramophone Classical Good CD Guide 2000 p.1033
18. Gramophone Vol.35 No.414 November 1957 p.233
19. Opera Vol.9 No.1 January 1958 p.53
20. Gramophone Vol.35 No.416 January 1958 p.305
21. Opera Vol.25 No.3 March 1974 p.224
22. Gramophone Vol.51 No.609 January 1974 p.1423
23. Ibid.Vol. 65 No.775 December 1987 p.1007
24. Gramophone Classical Good CD Guide 2000 p.1043

Chapter Six

1. Gramophone Vol.35 No.417 February 1958 p.370
2. Ibid.Vol.36 No.430 March 1959 p.470
3. Opera Vol.9 NO.4 April 1958 p.260
4. Ibid.Vol.26 No.2 February 1975 p.165
5. Gramophone Vol.52 No.619 December 1974 p.1211
6. Opera Vol.38 No.12 December 1987 p.1415
7. Gramophone Vol.65 No.769 June 1987 p.102
8. Ibid.Vol.74 No.887 April 1997 p. 33
9. Opera Vol.9 No.4 April 1958 p.261
10. Gramophone Vol.35 No.418 March 1958 p.417
11. Ibid.Vol.54 No.639 August 1976 p.332
12. Opera Vol.27
13. Gramophone Vol.65 No.774 November 1987 p.814
14. Opera Vol.39 No.1 January 1988 p.72
15. 'Gramophone Vol.74 no.887 April 1997 p.36
16. Ibid.Vol.36 No.421 June 1958 p.21
17. Opera Vol.9 No.9 September 1958 p.602
18. Gramophone Vol.64 No.762 November 1986 p.751
19. Ibid.Vol.56 No.664 September 1978 p.551
20. Opera Vol. 29 No.11 November 1978 p.1092
21. Gramophone Vol.65 No.775 December 1987 p.995
22. Opera Vol.9 No.12 December 1958 p.800
23. Gramophone Vol.36 No.424 September 1958 p.158
24. Opera Vol.30 No.11 November 1979 p.1071

25. Gramophone Vol.57 No.676 September 1979 p.517
26. Ibid. Vol.65 No.774 November 1987 p.817
27. Opera Vol.39 No.1 January 1988 p.72
28. Radio 3 Building a Library May 1998
29. Gramophone Vol.74 No.887 April 1997 p.36
30. Gramophone Classical Good CD Guide 2000 p.738
31. Opera Vol.10 No.1 January 1959 p.53
32. Gramophone Vol.31 No.368 January 1954 p.274
33. Ibid. Vol.36 No.427 December 1958 p.314
34. Ibid. Vol.38 No.449 October 1960 p.227
35. Ibid. Vol.38 No.449 November 1960 p.287
36. Opera Vol.11 No.11 November 1960 p.772
37. Gramophone Vol.52 No.619 December 1974 p.1211
38. Gramophone Vol.77 No.925 March 2000 p.116
39. Ibid. Vol.57 No.678 November 1979 p.908
40. Opera Vol.31 No.2 February 1980 p.166
41. Ibid. Vol.64 No.765 February 1988 p.1240
42. Opera Vol.39 No.6 June 1988 p.759
43. Gramophone Vol.74 No.887 April 1997 p.37
44. Classic CD No.85 May 1997 p.40
45. Gramophone Classical Good CD Guide 2000 p.704

Chapter Seven

1. Gramophone Vol.36 No.430 March 1959 p.468
2. Opera Vol.10 No.4 April 1959 p.253
3. Musical Times Vol.100 No.1384 June 1959 p.331
4. Gramophone Vol.37.No.434 July 1959 p.49
5. Ibid. Vol.37 No.439 December 1959 p.299
6. Ibid. Vol.57 No.678 November 1979 p.903
7. Ibid. Vol.68 No.813 February 1991 p.1553
8. Ibid. Vol.74 887 April 1997 p.37
9. Ibid. Vol.36 No.430 March 1959 p.474
10. Ibid. Vol.37 No.442 March 1960 p.475
11. Ibid. Vol.37 No.434 July 1959 p.49
12. Musical Times Vol.100 No.1384 June 1959 p.
13. Opera Vol.10 No.5 May 1959 p.327
14. Gramophone Vol.57 No.681 February 1980 p.1301
15. Opera Vol.31 No.7 July 1980 p.687
16. Gramophone Vol.65 No.772 September 1987 p.
17. Ibid. Vol.36 No.432 May 1959 p.49
18. Opera Vol.10 No.7 July 1959 p.467
19. Gramophone Vol.37 No.434 July 1959 p.49
20. Ibid. Vol.57 No.678 November 1979 p.912
21. Opera Vol.31 No.3 March 1980 p.271
22. Gramophone Vol.37 No.439 December 1959 p.301
23. Opera Vol.11 No.1 January 1960 p.53
24. Gramophone Vol.57 No.683 April 1980 1593
25. Opera Vol.31 No.12 December 1980 p.1215

26. Gramophone Vol.63 No.754 March 1986 p.1196
27. Ibid. Vol.64 No.760 September 1986 p.438
28. Ibid. Vol.74 No.887 April 1997 p.36
29. Gramophone Classical Good CD Guide 2000 p.733
30. Gramophone Vol.77 No.927 April 2000 p.120

Chapter Eight

1. Gramophone Vol.39 No.461 October 1961 p.221
2. Ibid. Vol.39 No.464 January 1962 p.342
3. Opera Vol.13 No.1 January 1962 p.52
4. Gramophone Vol.61 no.721 June 1983 p.79
5. Ibid. Vol.65 No.777 February 1988 p.1244
6. Ibid. Vol.41 No.484 September 1963 p.150
7. Opera Vol.14 No.11 November 1963 p.761
8. Gramophone Vol.65 No.777 February 1988 p.1244
9. Ibid. Vol.42 No.495 August 1964 p.97
10. Opera Vol.15 No.12 December 1964 p.824
11 Gramophone Vol.68 No.813 February 1991 p.1553
12. Ibid. Vol.70 No.837 February 1993 p.78
13. Ibid. Vol.42 No.495 August 1964 p.97
14. Opera Vol.15 No.12 December 1964 p.824
15. Gramophone Vol.42 No.495 October 1964 p.175
16. Ibid. Vol.65 No.772 Septembet 1987 p.485
17. Ibid. Vol.42 No.499 December 1964 p.291
18. Opera Vol.16 No.4 April 1965 p.291
19. Gramophone Vol.42 No.499 December 1964 p.317
20. Ibid. Vol.64 No.757 June 1986 p.86
21. Ibid. Vol.69 No.828 May 1992 p.105
22. Ibid. Vol.74 No.887 April 1997 p.37
23. Classic CD No. 85 May 1997 p.40
24. Gramophone Vol.42 No.502 p.441
25. Opera Vol.16 No.8 August 1965 p.594
26. Gramophone Vol.58 No.695 April 1981 p.1361
27. Ibid. Vol.64 No.757 June 1986 p.86

Chapter Nine

1. Gramophone Vol.49 No.586 March 1972 p.1577
2. Ibid. Vol.65 No.772 September 1987 p.486
3. Ibid. Vol.64 No.757 June 1986 p.86
4. Ibid. Vol.56 No.664 September 1978 p.551
5. Opera Vol.29 No.11 November 1978 p.1092
6. Gramophone Vol.65 No.772 September 1987 p.485
7. Opera Vol.38 No.11 November 1987 p.1467
8. Gramophone Vol.70 No.837 February 1993 p.78

Chapter Ten

1. Gramophone Vol.58 No.869 October 1980 p.541
2. Ibid. Vol.65 No.774 November 1987 p.818

3. Ibid. Vol.65 No.777 February 1988 p.1244
4. Ibid. Vol.67 No.801 February 1990 p.1529
5. Ibid. Vol.66 No.785 October 1988 p.569
6. Ibid. Vol.65 No.772 September 1987 p.486
7. Ibid. Vol.67 No.801 February 1990 p.1529
8. Ibid. Vol.56 No.664 September 1978 p.534
9. Ibid. Vol.68 No.813 February 1991 p.1554
10. Opera Vol.42 No.4 April 1991 p.476
11. Gramophone Vol.74 No.887 April 1997 p.35
12. Ibid. Vol.56 No.662 July 1978 p.244
13. Ibid. Vol.68 No.813 February 1991 p1558
14. Opera Vol.42 No.4 April 1991 p.476
15. Gramophone Vol.74 No.887 April 1997 p.35
16. Classic CD No.85 May 1997 p.40
17. Gramophone Vol.56 No.662 July 1978 p.244
18. Ibid. Vol.71 No.848 January 1994 p.98
19. Opera Vol.45 No.1 January 1994 p.122
20. Gramophone71 No.848 January 1994 p.91
21. Opera Vol.45 No.1 January 1994 p.121
22. Gramophone Vol.56 No.666 November 1978 p.91
23. Ibid. Vol.71 No.848 January 1994 p.91
24 Gramophone Classical Good CD Guide 2000 p.315
25. Gramophone Vol.75 No.894 November 1997 p132
26 Gramophone Classical Good CD Guide 2000 p.319
27. Gramophone Vol.56 No.662 July 1978 p.
28. Opera Vol.49 No1 January 1998 p.69

Epilogue

1. Gramophone Vol.65 No.772 September 1987 p. 486
2. Ibid. Vol.65 No.772 September 1987 p.369
3. The Opera Quarterly Vol.16 No.2 Spring 2000

BIBLIOGRAPHY

James Anderson: Dictionary of Opera and Operetta [Bloomsbury 1989]
Stelios Galatopoulos: Maria Callas Sacred Monster [Fourth Estate 1998]
Michael Scott: Maria Meneghini Callas [Simon and Schuster 1991]
ed. Máire Taylor: Gramophone Classical Good CD Guide 2000
[Gramophone Publications Limited]

INDEX

NOTES: 1. Operas/works are listed under composers.
2. Theatres/concert halls are listed under cities.
3. No attempt has been made to distinguish between different recordings of the same work. All relevant details will be found in the tables between pages 175 and 195

PHOTOGRAPH CREDITS

Agip
18

Luxurdo
54

Ben Martin
156

Luis Mendes
139

Erio Piccagliani
Cover, frontispiece, 14, 34, 42, 46, 51, 59, 63, 69, 74, 77, 84, 89, 94, 110, 150, 154, 158, 160, 162

Publifoto
10, 20, 31, 99

O. Savio
67

Brian Seed
23

Jerry Tiffany
136

Sabine Weiss
123

Unknown
71, 80, 91, 146